One for Sorrow

By

Ann Nobbs

Published by New Generation Publishing in 2015

Copyright © Ann Nobbs 2015

First Edition

The author asserts the moral right under the Copyright, Designs and Patents Act 1988 to be identified as the author of this work.

All Rights reserved. No part of this publication may be reproduced, stored in a retrieval system or transmitted, in any form or by any means without the prior consent of the author, nor be otherwise circulated in any form of binding or cover other than that which it is published and without a similar condition being imposed on the subsequent purchaser.

www.newgeneration-publishing.com

 New Generation Publishing

This book is dedicated to my parents, Richard and Lillian Hoskings. My Dad introduced me to the love of books with Enid Blyton when I was a small child and that began my joy of writing which has continued all my life.

Chapter 1

Basra Iraq April 2003

Mark was tired desperately tired. Totally exhausted and weary, inside and out. The dust and heat seemed to permeate his whole body and soul. The sound of gun fire and random explosions filled his ears and mind whether waking or sleeping.

He thought achingly of the peace and quiet of Wiltshire and he longed for the feel of soft English rain on his face. All his demons had returned as soon as he had arrived in Iraq .Being a soldier was never easy, and he had long since realised the futility of fighting against his instincts and feelings that he shouldn't, and did not want to be here. The nightmares from Bosnia recurred and rolled into the original nightmare of war, once more ensuring sleep was not a blessed release from his pain.

War was everywhere, inside his head, invading his ears eyes and even his taste. He wanted to be able to spit it out. It was never that easy. The picture of his mum came suddenly into his head and he heard again her words, when he had first told her that he would be amongst the first soldiers to leave for the war with Iraq. I know it's your life Mark, but I sometimes wish you had been a farmer like your dad and Miles. At least I'd know where you were and that you'd be safe. I'm so against this war, and everyone I speak to feels the same.

Now sitting in the centre of Basra, seeing again the bodies of civilians, women and children included, Mark wondered not for the first time, what was he doing here in the middle of this Holy, historic, once beautiful country.

He watched as a solitary bird flew out of a skeletal tree and marvelled at the incongruous strength of nature. It was his last conscious thought before the earth and air around him exploded with a deafening roar.

Stratford St. Peter Wiltshire May 2003

In a country churchyard Celia raised her face to the soft rain of an English shower. She knelt in the spongy wetness of the turf and placed a small posy of spring flowers on the grave in front of her. The dampness sent a chill through her slim body as it clung to her knees and she shivered, as shaking her head, drops of clear spring rain dripped inside her upturned collar. She pushed herself to her feet and began walking briskly towards the gate and the warmth of her waiting car.

Stratford St. Peter March 2002

In the soft early summer afternoon, the air was heavy with the sound of bees droning as they darted in and out of the pale purple wisteria that climbed lazily over the old walls of Stratford House. A dark red butterfly settled its wings a banner of scarlet against the pale leaves of buddleia. The sounds and smells of a lazy English June day vibrated and hung in the air like a static radio channel. Somewhere nearby the thud of leather on willow and a distant faint clapping of hands conjured up the village team that was playing out over the tops of the trees. A flock wild of geese honked their presence, hardly looking down on the tree tops in their speedy journey home. The sun was high in the sky, casting long shadows onto the old mellow bricks that had stood in the quiet Wiltshire countryside for hundreds of years. To anyone watching it appeared a perfect early summer's day in rural Wiltshire.

Not for Celia. Inside the two feet thick walls, she was sitting in the kitchen, sipping a cup of scalding tea. Her hands were clasped around the pale china cup and her body was hunched as though against the cold. She shivered despite the rays of yellow that streamed in through the glass putting her in a pool of warmth that still seemed not to permeate her stooping body, and tried to rationalise her feelings.

Staring deep into the cup, she looked at the pattern of tea leaves dark against the white porcelain and realised she must have finished the drink. What could she see in the wet brown leaves, her future? She shrugged her hunched shoulders and tried to reason what had changed in the three years she had been living in this cold unforgiving old house since her marriage to Seb. It sometimes seemed to her that the noise of his voice had always been echoing around inside her head, but in her saner unquestioning moments, she knew this was not the case. His anger, and there was a never ending supply of it, was always exploding out of him and attacking her. She often felt like putting up her arms to ward off the barrage of bullet like harsh words and imagined one day exploding and parts of her spreading out into the far corners of the dark, dank building. She tried without success to shut it out. It was bad enough when they were alone, but when he bawled her out in front of their friends she was so humiliated. Thank heavens for friends. Placing the cup down, it clattered noisily onto the china saucer echoing around the stillness in the high ceilinged kitchen as she tried to reason what had gone wrong. Standing slowly, she stretched her arms high and tried to ease the tension that was knotting her shoulders, and then absentmindedly walked to the large old sink and rinsed the cup under running water, the silvery drops showered out onto the cream and beige tiles reminding Celia of tears that always seemed to be splashing from her eyes. She was aware of the sound her high heeled shoes made on the tiled floor, and the antiseptic smell of cleanliness that was an obsession with the housekeeper. Her thoughts went immediately to the homely smells she associated with her friend Gilly's kitchen and she sighed.

"For God's sake Cee why ever do you stand for it"

Her good friend Gilly said the next afternoon over lunch. They were sitting in Gilly's kitchen. Celia loved Gilly's kitchen. It was warm from the heat of the Aga and really cosy. The early spring sun was streaming in through the window and a bowl of daffodils were sitting in a pool of golden light on the large refractory table that was the centre piece of Gilly's farmhouse kitchen. The aroma of baking made her feel hungry.

Celia was thinking just how would she have coped if she had never met Gilly, who would she have been able to confide in and pour out all her problems. She thanked God that her dog Skip had run into Parsonage Farm that day three years before when she had first come to live at Stratford House after her marriage to Seb. Or

"The Honourable Sebastian Stratford", to give him his full title.

She had taken an age to get used to being Lady Stratford. It had been very lonely at first. Celia had missed all her friends that she had left behind in London and found that many of the local people were put off by her being married to Sebastian. He in turn seemed to think that she shouldn't need anyone except him. He had forgotten that she was used to having people around her. Running her catering company had always kept her busy and brought her into contact with lots of people. She had also found it difficult to be idle. He frowned on her actually going into the kitchen and cooking. That's why they had a housekeeper wasn't it? She recalled how wary Gilly had been at first, but Skip had soon broken the ice when she became entangled with Gilly's own dogs. She had somehow managed to wriggle through a tiny gap under the gate and had bounded excitedly up to the two dogs, yelping and barking in an effort to make friends. Celia had come to love Parsonage farm. She remembered as if it was yesterday, looking up at the honey coloured brickwork and the sun glinting off the windows. The front door of the old farmhouse had been painted white and clematis trailed around the porch, the flowers like blue pointed stars. It always gave Celia a feeling of peace.

She dragged her thoughts back to the present and looked at her friend standing at the Aga with a fresh pot of coffee in her hand. She thought how different they were. Whoever said opposites attract had been right Gilly was plumpish and dressed more for comfort than style in faded blue jeans and a tee shirt that had seen better days. Her red hair was cut short with a natural curl and her fair skin was freckled and rosy from helping out on the farm. Her hands also reflected how hard it was being a farmer's wife, even one who was doing reasonably well, like Ralph.
In contrast, Celia was tall with dark, almost black shoulder length hair which curled provocatively onto her slim shoulders.

"The thing is Gilly, it wasn't always like this. When we were first married he used to be so gentle and caring, it's my fault for not giving him the son and heir he wants so badly."

"You don't know that it's your fault, it could just as easily be him, Cee"

Said Gilly placing her hand over her friend's which was resting on the kitchen table. She gave Celia's hand an empathetic squeeze and smiled warmly into her troubled face. She tried to think back to when she and Ralph were first married. Alice had been conceived almost immediately and their Son Jake two years later. She had not been through the trauma that was facing her friend. She thought about Sebastian. She had never liked him, even before she had met Celia. He was well known in the area and had a reputation for being a ladies' man. He was always showing off some beautiful woman or other at the hunt ball long before Celia came on the scene. Gilly had been surprised when first meeting Celia that she really liked her. Their friendship had gone from strength to strength in the three years since that first chance meeting.

"Oh Gilly what would I do without you, you're such a good friend to me, I'm so pleased we met all those years ago. By the way, are you able to come for a ride tomorrow morning? Seb's going up to town for an all-day meeting."

Gilly was shaking her head

"Sorry I've got to take Alice to the dentist and then take her back to school, so no can do."

"OK don't worry I'll go alone, if the weather is like today it'll be glorious."

On her way back from Gilly's farmhouse, Celia reflected again on what she had said to her friend about being happy with Seb in the beginning. The first year of her marriage had been such an idyllic year. They had been so happy and so in love. She recalled how they took every opportunity to make love, even outside, the thrill of possibly being seen only adding to the excitement. Who could have foreseen that their happiness would dwindle away to what she now felt. Moving from London to Stratford St. Peter she had been filled with such a feeling of excitement and anticipation for her new life. As happy as she had been in Chiswick, if she was honest, she had sometimes been lonely. She had been happy to be sharing the rest of her life with a man she loved and respected. She also welcomed the wild remote countryside of Wiltshire, the thrill of having her own horse, Amber, a wedding present from Seb and the spaciousness of her new home. She had been full of ideas to renovate and modernise the old house. When had it all started to go from the perfect union and companionship they had shared to the shambles of hate and terror she felt now? A picture came into her mind of them making love in the meadow at the rear of the old House. She could almost hear the sweet sounds of summer birdsong, and hear the gentle lapping of the silvery waters on the edge of the lake. It had always been one of their favourite places. She felt again Seb's warm lips exploring her body and the thrill of being out in the open and the thought that they just might be seen from the windows of the stately old grey walls, their cries of passion mingling with the sounds of the mallards and swans. She also recalled Seb saying that they would be like the swans, which always mated for life. How wrong he had been. Her life had been so great then. Was it only two short years ago?

As she drove in through the gates and up the drive of her home, the sun caught the many windows of the beautiful old building. She thought if only it was as beautiful on the inside; she was suddenly reminded of the old pastor in Bristol where she grew up and his sermon about "whited sepulchres", dragging her thoughts back to the present she realised with relief that Seb's Porche was not in the garage. As she approached the house her boots crunching on the gravel, a sudden noise, caused her to look up into the dark greenness of the tangled branches of the large old oak. There was a rustling, which seemed to add to the tension already causing her neck and shoulders to stiffen. Suddenly, she ducked her head as a large blackbird swooped down with a loud flapping of wings and a loud cry. Startled she took a step backward and almost fell. Celia watched it flying away, high into the grey sky and wished that she was able to fly away from here as easily and freely as the bird. Struggling to recover, she pushed the heavy door open and entered the dark hallway. As always it took a minute for her eyes to adjust from daylight to the darkness within. She called out to Mrs Popple the housekeeper that she was going to have a bath before dinner and walked up the stairs to the master bedroom and began to undress; she stood naked in front of the mirror looking at her reflection. She splayed out her fingers over her slim hips and flat tummy noticing the deep contrast between her pale translucent skin and the soft curly tangle of hair between her long slim legs. Breathing a deep sigh she turned and walked into the adjoining bathroom. Lying in the bath as the beautiful voice of Maria Callas soared to the high ceiling she massaged her body and languorously and slowly began to relax. She felt the cold Chablis slip down her throat and immediately begin to release the knots of tension in her neck and shoulders. She wondered if being so tense all the time was a contributory factor in her nor having conceived .She remembered again how Seb had been an energetic and enthusiastic lover but lately he seemed to want her less and less. It made her feel that he had only ever wanted her to produce a son. How she longed for tenderness and loving words of their early years together.

Later, when dressing in a soft cream silk shirt and black velvet trousers, she was fastening the diamond and pearl studs in her ears when Seb walked into the room. She looked at the man she had married and thought how much he had changed in the three years since their wedding. He was still tall but no longer slim. He had a paunch and his stomach spilled over his trousers. His dark hair no longer thick was receding and thinning and had lost the glossiness she had loved so much. All that drinking was taking its toll she thought. He never used to drink.

"Where have you been all day?"

His words rudely interrupted her thoughts,

"I suppose you think it's funny to switch off your mobile when you know I need to speak to you, I wanted to tell you I have to go out again this evening and wouldn't be in for dinner. Mrs Popple said she didn't even know where you were or when you'd be back home"

"Since when have I had to keep the housekeeper informed about my whereabouts" she answered softly, "and my mobile was not switched off but must have been out of range."

She was determined not to let him get to her. Already the knots were back in her neck and shoulders and all the soothing effects of the bath and wine were already unravelling as her body tensed under the barrage of his angry words.

Later that evening, sitting at the table eating a solitary dinner, she played with the lasagne on her plate unable to work up an appetite and thought enviously of Gilly surrounded by her family and the warmth and colour of her farmhouse kitchen.

When Seb arrived home she had been asleep for a couple of hours and was dreaming. She was swimming in a beautiful warm, tranquil pool. All around was sunlight and the sound of exotic birds, their wings bright and gaudy catching the light. Suddenly she realised that the water was no longer tranquil but was becoming wild and frothy and that she was about to fall over the edge of a steep rushing waterfall. Just as she began to fall she was woken by someone shaking her hard. For a moment she couldn't think where she was or even who she was. As she realised it was Seb she felt the weight of his body heavy on top of her and the terror of the water turned into the terror of suffocation. She struggled in the dark but her struggles only seemed to arouse him more and she felt his hands pushing roughly up her thighs prising her legs apart. He was hard and as he pushed himself into her she felt him breathing against her face and she felt sick as the hot, sour stench of whisky hit her.

"Don't pretend you don't like it rough you bitch, I know you can't get enough".

The dark of the room and the weight of his body were unbearable. She couldn't breathe and felt the panic rise as she fought to stay in control. Suddenly she felt him shudder and groan as he came and immediately rolled off her and began snoring loudly. Thankful it was over Celia lay for a moment in the dark before rising from the bed she walked into the bathroom and sat on the toilet seat catching her breath before turning on the tap she began tearing at her skin in an attempt to wash off the smell and touch of him.

Chapter 2

It was the next morning and as Celia rode through the beautiful Wiltshire countryside the events of the previous night went round and around in her head. Had it really happened, or was it just a bad dream? Seb had been all charm and courtesy at breakfast, and kissed her lightly on the cheek before setting off for his meeting in London. She had the whole day to herself and it stretched gloriously in front of her.

How she loved Wiltshire. When she had first arrived here she had been fascinated by Stonehenge. The mystery of the stones held a strong fascination for her and it was now a favourite haunt of hers. The spring sun shone down and she breathed in the scent of early primroses and daffodils as Amber, her beloved mare shook her mane and snorted.

"You love it too my beauty, don't you" she said to her horse as she leaned forward and spoke softly into Amber's silky ear. Together, as one they rode on over Salisbury plain. She raised her head eagerly to feel the sun and spring air on her face in an effort to forget the awful feeling of suffocation and terror that had invaded her mind and body the previous night. The thoughts went round and round in her head and she wondered why she had such a fear of being pinned down. She remembered somewhere reading that the things that terrified us in this life were often a hang up from some terror experienced in a previous life. Was there any truth in that?

Up ahead she became aware of an Army land rover stopped at the side of the track. A man was leaning against the bonnet. In his hands there was a large map which he seemed to be having difficulty holding down as a sudden gust of wind almost tore it from his grasp. Engrossed in the concentration of keeping it from blowing away and examining it closely he was oblivious to her approach. She was able to watch him for a few moments, unobserved. He was tall and slim dressed in Army Captains uniform of combat trousers and shirt. Celia couldn't help notice how attractive he looked with his blonde hair catching the spring sunlight under his blue beret that picked up the colour of his eyes. Celia brought Amber to a halt and he looked up, momentarily startled as the horse snorted. He raised a hand to brush away a feather that had suddenly appeared and was floating slowly down towards him.

They both spoke at the same time,

"Good morning,"

He laughed and said

"After you"

Celia said again.

"Good morning, and isn't it a beautiful one, do you need any help?"

"No thank you I'm fine,"

He answered,

"I've just taken over here and we have an exercise planned for this afternoon, I'm sure you know to stay off the places marked with the danger sign."

"Oh yes, we're used to that round here."

It was a sore point with Celia. She and a lot of the locals resented the Army being on their beautiful countryside. She and Gilly were always talking about it, and Ralph,

Gilly's husband said he was sure his cattle were affected by the noise of the guns. He was sure that was the reason the milk yield was down. He stepped nearer to Celia and Amber and reached up his hand.

"Captain Mark Riordan"

He smiled up at Celia. She took his hand in her gloved one feeling the warmth of his hand even through the thin leather, and said,

"Celia Stratford"

"Well, I mustn't keep you" he said.

And turning, on his heel got back into his Land Rover.

Later, as Celia was returning home she tried to push out the sickening image of last night. It seemed hard to imagine the terror of the previous night here with the wind blowing grey and white clouds fast across the expanse of pale sky. The sun was in turn appearing and dipping out of sight causing the shadow of her and Amber to be thrown onto the pale springy turf. Despite this the horror of last night pushed itself back into her unconscious mind and the awful fear and claustrophobic terror made her feel hot and she ran her finger around the inside collar of her riding jacket in an effort to cool down. She was dreading his return later today, and then she remembered it was Wednesday and her ladies group were meeting at their local The Nags' Head this evening. It would be good to see Gilly and the thought lifted her heart. Her mind went back to the man she had seen earlier and the image of him so tall and slim with the sun catching his blonde hair under the blue of his beret caused her heart to skip a beat. Would she tell Gilly about the encounter? Don't be silly she said to herself, there really was nothing to tell.

As Mark climbed back into the army jeep he felt the warmth of the early spring sunshine through his combat trousers, and his fingers on the steering wheel. He inhaled deeply relishing in the clear spring air. He filled his lungs and slowly breathed out through his mouth letting his body relax. His thoughts went to the evening ahead He had been in the Army for the last fourteen years. He had been an officer since leaving Camberley College and had travelled all over the world. He had always wanted to be a soldier since he had been a little boy. It was all he had ever wanted to do. He was happy at first, and loved the life making friends easily. It had all changed when he went to Bosnia. It was worse than anything he had seen before, or could imagine. Even Northern Ireland hadn't affected him this way, so when this posting was offered, he had jumped at it.

Mark had thrown himself into his new posting with energy and vigour, pushing himself to the limit of his physical endurance his nightmares waking him constantly. They had receded and become less frequent. He had made new friends and life was OK. Tonight one of his fellow officers was celebrating his birthday and a small group were meeting at the Nags' Head. He hadn't been that keen, but it was becoming increasingly difficult to keep turning down invitations. Will had said

"This time we're not taking no for an answer, Mark. You need to get out there and enjoy life. All work and no play, you know what they say"

He had placed a hand on Mark's shoulder,

"look mate, I know how you feel, I saw what effect Bosnia had on my friend Stewart. He was completely fucked up when he got back, and he had the love of a good woman to help him pull through".

Mark had winced at this. He had never opened up and told anyone about his private life, and he didn't intend to start now.

****

Later, he and Will and a small group were seated in the bar of the Nag's head. They all seemed to be in good spirits and Mark was thinking he was glad he had made the effort. There was a coal fire against the chilly evening. Mark looked into the flames his mind on the stories his Mum had told him about seeing fairies in the fire when she was a little girl. He looked deep into the glowing heat and jumped as a log fell into the hearth with a crackle as the sparks flew out and landed in the old grate. The light from the flames flickered and danced on the walls of the old Inn casting shadows. Suddenly he was back in Bosnia he could see the flames shooting up and roaring out of the houses and he once again heard the screams of people trapped inside. He remembered the charred bodies of whole families, even small children. He had to get out of the pub. Clumsily he got up and almost fell as he staggered against the table. There was a crash as his drink toppled and fell in a shower of broken glass and liquid. He felt a hand reach out and Will's voice coming from the bottom of a long dark tunnel, but he kept going his only thought to get outside. He bumped into someone as he reached the passageway of the pub, but not stopping pushed open the main door and felt the cold air on his face. He leaned against the outside wall taking deep breaths in an attempt to calm himself and stop his heart racing. Gradually he began to feel the colour return to his face and his body stop trembling. There was a movement behind him and someone spoke.

"Hello again, are you alright?"

Looking at the woman he realised it was the person he had almost knocked over in his haste to get outside. She was slim with shoulder length dark hair curling onto her shoulders .She was dressed casually in jeans and a cream roll neck cashmere sweater, but although her face and voice was vaguely familiar, Mark, in his confused state, couldn't place her.

"Wait",

She said and turning she disappeared back into the pub, returning almost immediately, it seemed to Mark, with a small glass.

"Here, drink this"

She said, handing him the glass.

"It's brandy it will make you feel better."

He gulped it down coughing as the burning liquid hit the back of his throat. As it went down he felt his body begin to relax and gradually stop trembling.

He looked at her, embarrassed now that he was beginning to feel more normal.

"Thank you; I don't know what came over me?"

"You don't recognise me, do you?"

She said,

"We met this morning when I was out riding"

Of course, he thought, the beautiful Celia

"You look different in those clothes."

He noticed the tiny emeralds in her ears that matched her eyes.

"I'm sorry I bumped into you just now, did I hurt you, I was in a bit of a hurry"

"No, I'm Fine, but are you sure you're OK you looked ghastly if you don't mind me saying so."

"Thanks very much."

He tried to laugh but it didn't quite come off.

"Can I buy you a drink to say thank you?"

Her reply was quick

"I'm sorry, I'm here with a group, and I really must get back, they'll be wondering where I've got to."

Before Mark could respond she had turned and walked quickly back inside. He watched her slim figure disappear into the dark of the pub and suddenly felt a palpable emptiness.

He returned to Will and his friends his eyes searching the other people in the bar, but he could not see Celia or the group she had said she was with. He realised suddenly that he felt disappointed. It was many months since he had felt anything, or been in the least attracted to anyone. It had been the last year in Bosnia that had been his undoing. Sickened by the horrors he had seen and heard. He had continued having nightmares when he got home. At first Lucy had been kind and full of sympathy. When he woke sweating and in a panic, she had been loving and supportive but when his nightmares had continued she had told Mark that she would sleep in the spare room as she needed to get a good night's sleep as her job as a high flyer in the city was very demanding. For Mark, that had been the beginning of the end. Their relationship limped along until he had told her he was moving out to Old Sarum to take up a new challenge. She had tried to hide her relief but Mark had seen it in her eyes, and they said goodbye and moved on.

Chapter 3

Celia and Gilly were driving along the M4 towards London. It was the following Monday and they were on their way to Harley Street.

"I really don't want to do this, Gilly, I'm absolutely terrified. I hate being poked around"

"Well, when you've had a couple of kids you get used to it".

Breaking off embarrassed, she realised what she had just said.

"Oh Cee I'm so sorry, can you forgive me? It just slipped out, me and my big mouth."

"Oh don't be silly, I don't want you to have to go tippy toeing around. Forget it, I have already"

"You know Cee; I still think it should be Sebastian who should be tested. They always do the sperm count thing first".

"Huh, try telling him that, he simply won't have it that there could be anything wrong with him. He comes from a long line of Stratford's and says it *has* to be my fault, like everything else that's wrong in his life, or in the World for that matter."

Gilly sat in the waiting room of Professor Hart's practice. She looked around not able concentrate on the magazine in her hand. Well, she thought to herself, I certainly imagined there would be a better waiting room than this. The room was largish with high ceiling typical of the Victorian houses in Harley Street. The décor was drab and could have done with a makeover like those programmes on T.V. she thought. The traffic noise was loud in her ears from the street outside and she wished she could have taken the place of her friend. When I think what this must be costing she thought to herself, but that was the least of their worries Money was certainly not a problem to The Honourable Sebastian. Poor Cee, I hope she won't be long.

Fifteen minutes later Celia emerged from the consulting room and smiled weakly at Gilly.

"Come on, let's get out of here."

She said.

"We can go to John Lewis at the bottom of the street and get a cup of coffee, I don't know about you but I certainly need one."

After a short walk in the cool spring sunshine they were sitting at a table in the noisy environment of the coffee shop sipping their cups of steaming latte, Celia opened a packet of brown sugar and watched the golden granules falling in a stream into her cup. Stirring thoughtfully, she looked up as her friend spoke.

"So how did it go, have you got the result?"

"No I have to wait a week, after all that, I still have to wait a week. It was strange having the ultra sound scan, not painful but uncomfortable, I can think of better ways to spend a morning."

Gilly nodded to her friend thinking of the scan's she had had when Alice and Jake had been born. That was so different though. Ralph had always been with her to give his love and support, and of course they had the pictures of the baby to look and marvel at. How they had loved trying to work out where the head and tiny limbs were.

"Do you have to come back for the result, Cee?"

"No it'll be posted on next week, probably just as well as Seb would probably not take anything from me, without seeing it in black and white".

On the drive back, Gilly mentioned the Woman's group this coming week. Celia's mind went back to last Wednesday and she immediately thought of Mark. She saw him in her mind. He had looked different out of uniform, even more attractive, she thought, in cream slacks and a mid-blue shirt that was the exact colour of his eyes. His ash blonde hair cut short suited him well. Celia wasn't sure whether to mention Mark to Gilly but she decided as Gilly was a good friend why not. After all it was only a brief meeting. Not a brief encounter she smiled to herself and immediately could hear Rachmaninoff's 2nd piano concerto playing in her head. She described to Gilly the two brief meetings with Mark the week before, but she said little about how distressed he had been as she thought it would be disloyal to him. Strange, to feel she owed him that, even though she hardly knew him. She didn't want to explain even to her good friend, just what an impact he had had on her. Gilly had surprised her by saying she had seen Celia talking to a strange man last Wednesday, when she had been going to the ladies. She explained to Celia that she had been curious but as Celia hadn't mentioned it, she decided to wait for her friend to explain. How typical of her. She realised once again just what a good friend Gilly was.

Mark had hardly been out of her mind since last week and she had taken Amber out on Friday in the hope of bumping into him but had been disappointed. There was no sign of his Land Rover on Salisbury plain, only the sound of distant gun fire reminded her that the army presence was in evidence as usual.

Over dinner on Saturday evening, Seb brought up the subject of the fertility test she had undergone a few days before. They were seated in the large dark ornate dining room. Celia had wanted to change the style when they were first married but Seb was a traditionalist and disliked change. Celia found the décor suffocating and formal and longed for the pale white walls and sea blues and greens that she had had in her flat in Chiswick before meeting Seb.

"So when will we get the result, Celia?"

His voice interrupted her thoughts,

"Not that it isn't a foregone conclusion, the Stratford's have always been prolific when it comes to multiplying. Never had any problem in that direction, quite the opposite."

He had a knowing smile that made Celia feel sick and she wondered how he could have changed so much from the loving man she thought she had married. She shivered imagining the weight of his body on top of her and the feeling of his hands bruising her pale skin. His voice cut into her thoughts and she started as she realised he was staring at her waiting for her to answer

"We should get a letter from Professor Hart on Monday or Tuesday, so we should know one way or another soon"

She thought how her surroundings matched her mood. The dark walls and the rust coloured sofas doing nothing to lift her spirits .How ridiculous they must look seated at one end of the vast dining table. Celia was dreading the letter. She had gone over and over it in her mind. If the result was that there was no problem with her being able to conceive, she dreaded the thoughts of Seb making love to her. She thought to herself "making love" was not what they did anymore. Sex had become a nightmare. He always seemed to be drunk and showed little concern for her. She had begun to dread going to bed and feigned sleep as often as she could. This didn't seem to put him off and the less responsive she was, the more it seemed to inflame his desire. On the other hand, if the test result showed that she was not able to have a child, where would that leave her? Would he take it out on her? Either way, it seemed to Celia that she was in a no win situation.

Monday morning was dark and gloomy. The sky was heavy and rain was threatening. Celia had been planning to ride out to Stonehenge. She was still hoping she might run into Mark again, but before breakfast was over, the heavens opened and the noise of rain bounced off the windows. Seb left the table and walked to the hall where the mail was always placed on the consul. She heard his steps echo on the parquet floor and stop. She made a huge effort to stop thinking what he was going to do next, and tried to relax. She knew the letter would be addressed to her, but that had never stopped him. He came back into the dining room almost at a run.

"For God's sake, what does that man think he's doing? I thought he was an expert in his field, well he must have made a mistake this time".

He threw the letter at Celia and stood over her waving a long silver paper knife, his face contorted with anger and blood red. She looked at the typed words that told her the result of the scan and blood tests she had undergone last week. There was no medical reason why she should not conceive. It wasn't her that was responsible for them not having a child. She looked up at Seb but he was already gone. She was relieved to hear the door of his study slam behind him and she sat at the dining table wondering what to do next. She went to pick up the phone to call Gilly and dropped it quickly when she heard Seb bellowing at someone on the extension in his study. The few words she overheard made her realise he was speaking to Professor Hart's office and she felt sorry for the secretary who was bearing the brunt of his anger. When he returned, he barked at her

"Idiot, he says I should make arrangements to have myself tested, me!! I said we need to get a second opinion on your result and he said that's up to me but he thought we'd be wasting time and money, bloody idiot."

He turned quickly and was gone. Celia realised she was holding her breath and let it out slowly and tried to gather her thoughts, pleased that for the moment at least it was quiet.

Chapter 4

Mark realised he was looking forward to something for the first time since...... he couldn't remember. Last Wednesday, before leaving the Nags Head he had had a quiet word with the landlord and mentioned he had seen Celia earlier. John told him about the ladies group who met every Wednesday in one of the upstairs rooms and Mark was determined to be there again tonight on the chance he might bump into her. He pulled his land Rover into the car park at 7.00pm and sat listening to Classic FM.

Celia always called for Gilly and they drove together the short distance from Parsonage Farm to the village. Tonight she had been disappointed to learn that Jake was unwell and Gilly, being reluctant to leave him had told Celia to go without her. Celia reassured her friend that she understood.

"Of course you must stay with Jake, I'll phone you in the morning to see how he is, don't worry about me", and leaning forward, she gave Gilly a kiss on the cheek and walked out to her car, she drove off towards the village listening to a C.D. whilst driving.

The thoughts of Puccini brought the image of her father clearly into her mind, and she felt the sharp pricking of tears behind her eyes as she realised how much she missed him. She could see his smiling face and imagined him sitting in his surgery. The love and respect she had for him was as strong now as it had ever been and she wished he was here now to confide in, but whether she would be able to tell him about Seb's drunken attacks was another matter. Hugh Manning was a G.P and he and Celia's mum lived in Bristol in the house she and her brother had grown up in. She spoke to them every week and missed their closeness. Her mum had been a domestic science teacher at the girls Grammar school until she had taken early retirement last year. They were, and always had been, so happy together and she was used to seeing the affection that was so apparent in a happy, stable relationship. She swallowed away her threatened tears and smiled to herself as she remembered the tender way they looked at each other that seemed to exclude everyone else. After all these years to have such a close bond, that's exactly what I always wanted for myself, and look where that's got me she thought bitterly.

She looked like her Mum. Her Grandparents had come to Cardiff from Cork just before her mum was born, and her Mum and Celia had the same Celtic looks of dark hair and pale porcelain skin. The only difference was Celia's eyes were the colour of emeralds, and her Mum's were more aquamarine.

The chain of thoughts took her from her Mum to her old life in Chiswick .It had been her Mum's love of cooking that had made Celia first interested, and they had pottered about in the kitchen together since she had had to stand on a chair to reach. She had however, never wanted to teach. Her Mum had been keen for her to follow in her own footsteps; instead, she had set up a catering company in London after graduating from college there.

She had specialised in corporate functions and private dinner parties and it had grown into a small yet successful company. She had revelled in doing all the cooking herself and only employed Anna to help with serving and general dog's body stuff. It had taken off quite slowly and she had put all her energies into developing an imaginative and successful enterprise. She had loved the smallness of it and seen this as a plus allowing her to keep control and not have to take on too much, or lots of staff, thus giving the pleasure of being paid for doing something she enjoyed. Cooking had always been her main passion, and she loved both the therapy of it combined with the sheer pleasure of other people's enjoyment of good food simply cooked. When her clients told her how much they had enjoyed the meals it always gave Celia a buzz of satisfaction.

She worked from her tiny flat in Chiswick and had loved being so near to the river. Another Cancerian trait, being near to water, too near, sometimes as the river often came to the bottom step when it was high tide. She had been on the top floor, so it hadn't really affected her, except that she had to keep an eye on the tides as her small van had to be moved to prevent it being flooded, when the tide was high.

Celia thought that was a small price to pay in exchange for the sheer pleasure that the water gave her. She spent many happy minutes staring out of the window looking at the changing face of the river Thames as it moved slowly along. On dark wintry days the swooping of the gulls and the sun going down casting its incandescent light over the stillness of the water appealed to her romantic spirit. She was never happier than when she was living near water.

She had loved that flat *so* much. She had decorated it herself. The walls were all white, and the colours of the sea, rich blues and soft greens, were brought in with carpets and curtains. There were soft restful water colour paintings on the white walls, and her collection of china and glassware made the place seem special and restful. Celia often wondered why she had ever left such a beautiful place. She had never been able to recapture the feeling of sheer contentment.

She had met Sebastian through one of her corporate clients. Miles had asked her to cater for a small dinner party he was giving for five of his friends, and Seb had been one of his guests. They had been at Marlborough College together. He had been *so* persistent, calling her frequently and begging her to go out with him. Finally when all else failed, he had booked her to cater for a dinner party for two people and when she had arrived at his London Pied a Terre, she discovered that she was his guest and that the menu she had so carefully prepared had been for herself. She had had to smile at his ingenuity and originality, and had finally given in and agreed to go out with him. Her thoughts went back to that night and she pictured in her mind, his flat. It was near to Tower Bridge and looking out at the lights of London had given her a buzz of excitement. She remembered that she had been flattered that he had gone to so much trouble just for her. She pictured herself again walking in to the smart foyer balancing all her boxes and catering equipment she had struggled to push the buzzer and his voice coming suddenly from the intercom had caused her to jump and almost drop a glass dish. He had been so charming and attentive, even helping her to carry everything into the lift, himself. She couldn't help smiling now as she recalled the way he had allowed her to set the table beautifully, with the deep cornflower blue serviettes and the marching hyacinths to compliment the simple white porcelain dishes. She could almost smell their deep heady scent. He had wanted everything to be perfect for a very important guest. He had only finally let her into the secret when everything was ready and she was dishevelled and her face pink and shiny from her exertions in the kitchen. He had smiled at her obvious discomfort and insisted that she go and freshen up in his bathroom before pulling out a chair for her to sit at his table and eat the delicious meal, she herself had prepared. Afterwards, sitting in one of his large leather armchair, sipping a coffee she had looked at the good looking sophisticated man opposite her and wondered what he could possibly see in her. She wondered when it all had changed. Where was the handsome tender man she had married? Was it her fault that things were now so difficult and strained between them?

Dragging her thoughts back to the present Celia realised suddenly that she was almost at the Nags Head and she thought about the evening stretching out in front of her with pleasure.

She pulled into the familiar car park and switched off the engine. As she began to alight, she realised that there was someone in the car next to hers. The man inside had his head turned away from her and as she began to lock the car he looked up and smiled at Celia and she realised it was Mark.

"Hello again" he said. She looked up into his eyes and felt her heart beating so loudly she thought he must have heard it.

"Oh hello, are you feeling better?"

He looked embarrassed and she didn't know what to say next as she could feel his discomfort. He said,

"I was hoping to bump into you to apologise for last week. I really don't know what came over me. I'm not usually such a wimp."

They looked at one another both wondering what the other was thinking, and finally Mark said,

"Please let me buy you a drink to say thank you for your kindness, it's the least I can do."

Celia hesitated; she looked at her watch and said

''I really have to go, our meeting starts at 7.30 and I'm five minutes late already".

''Well how about later, when your meeting finishes, please"

His eyes looked directly into Celia's and she said,

"Well it'll have to be quick, but OK I'll see you in the bar at 9.30"
And with that she was gone.

Mark stood at the bar and ordered an orange juice. He could allow himself one drink, as he was driving, and he wanted to save it for when Celia joined him. He had been so pleased to see her and then stupidly tongue tied, like a teenager, he thought to himself. He was usually relaxed and confident with women, but it had been a long time since Lucy had left him and he was out of practice. Anyway, why get so worked up. She was beautiful and he had noticed the Gold band on her left hand so knew the score. He tried to relax and sipped his drink whist he eagerly waited for 9.30.

Upstairs in the meeting, Celia was in the chair. The group were discussing guest speakers for the coming month and one of the local ladies had mentioned the army. They all seemed to resent the military presence in the beautiful Wiltshire countryside and Celia suggested they invite someone to put the army's side. They all seemed to think that was a good idea, and said they would leave it to Celia to make the approach. They also thought that who she was married to would carry more weight. The meeting finished at 9.30pm and people began leaving. Celia called out her goodbyes until she was the only one left. She wondered if she had been right to agree to meet Mark, and was thinking about changing her mind when he suddenly appeared in the door way.

"Hi there, I hope you don't mind my coming up, I saw your ladies leaving and …."

He broke off and looked embarrassed. Celia couldn't help feeling a little sorry for him and smilingly replied.

"Oh that's OK I need to talk to you anyway, why don't we go downstairs and you can buy that drink you promised me."

When they were seated in the comfortable bar sipping their drinks, Celia told Mark about her idea for the army to defend its right to be in the area, and asked if he would be interested in speaking to *"the ladies of this parish"* she laughed, and was relieved when he began to join in, and suddenly the ice was broken and she sensed him relax. They were chuckling together like old friends and she was surprised to realise she felt completely relaxed with Mark. After all the tension she had been feeling with Seb it was so good. She leaned back in the high backed chair and took a deep breath. Looking around the room she realised how much she liked the old Inn. It was very old, fourteenth century and there were many pictures of the area as it used to be, decorating the walls. The ceilings were very low and a lot of people had to duck to come in through the doorways .She noticed many familiar faces but everyone seemed engrossed in what they were doing and seemed not to be watching her and Mark. This thought made her realise that everyone in the room would be expecting her to talk to a potential new speaker, in her role as Chairwoman. The feelings of guilt were purely in her mind because of the way she had begun to feel about him.

The time seemed to pass very quickly, and Celia was surprised to hear John call

"Time gentlemen please, and ladies" he added smiling in Celia's direction.

"Gosh, is that the time?"

She looked at her watch and was amazed to see that it was twenty minutes to eleven.

"I must be going, my husband will be wondering where I am"

Mark saw her tense and the change of mood, and wondered not for the first time, about her husband. Was he the reason she seemed so uptight? Or was it his imagination.

They walked together out to the car park. It was a beautiful starry night and the full moon seemed to hang above the trees. Celia was always drawn to the moon, she always felt as though there was an invisible thread connecting it to her. She could see Mark looking at her in the bright moonlight and she felt a blush spread up into her face. She wanted to reach out to him, and then said to herself, don't be so stupid and romantic he's not interested in me, anyway, I'm a happily married woman, aren't I? She realised Mark was speaking to her.

"Oh by the way, I have the chance of a horse this weekend, and thought I would ride out towards Stonehenge, I don't suppose you would care to join me? We could finalise the details about the talk I'm going to give to your ladies".

They had reached Celia's car and she pressed the key to unlock the door and turned to answer Mark

"Oh, so you will do it, thanks Mark"

She smiled and Mark thought how beautiful she looked. Her hair was blue black in the moonlight and her eyes were shining. He wanted so badly to reach out and touch her but he held back and pushed his hands deep into his pockets to resist the urge.

"Well, I'll consider it if you'll agree to come riding with me this weekend"

Before Celia could answer, her mobile phone rang and she said

"Sorry, I really must go, perhaps Sunday morning, I can't promise"

And she moved swiftly into the driving seat of her BMW and Mark heard her say into her phone

"I'm on my way, I'll see you in ten minutes, No I'll explain when I see you"

And she drove away with a screech of car tyres. Mark stood in the moonlight and watched the tail lights of her car disappear up the lane and he realised he didn't even know where she lived. He suddenly felt empty and getting into the driving seat of his car, sat for a long moment lost in thought .The scent of her was still strong in his head. His hands were on the steering wheel and the sudden hooting of an owl brought him back to the present and where he was. With a loud sigh he turned the key in the ignition and the car roared into life as he manoeuvred out through the gate and headed back towards the barracks wishing she was still beside him.

When Celia pulled into the drive her heart fell at the thoughts of what she was about to face. Seb had been angry. She could tell that he had been drinking. He was slurring his words and swearing at her. With any luck he would have fallen asleep in the fifteen minutes it had taken her to drive home.

As she put her key in the lock, the door was pulled open from inside and he stood in front of her. He was swaying and unsteady on his feet. She could feel her heart pounding in her chest and hammering in her ears. She was aware of the strong smell of whisky on his breath and he reached out and tried to pull her toward him. His hand caught hold of her left shoulder and he moved his other hand under her chin and brought it to his mouth. She recoiled as his wet mouth closed over hers and she tried not to struggle as she knew that would only make things worse. His mouth was bruising hers and he forced his tongue into her mouth exploring the inside and grazing her teeth. His hand moved and tore at the blouse she was wearing, pulling it from her trousers and up underneath until he felt the bear flesh of her breast. Her nipples were hard and erect under his fingers despite herself. She recoiled from his touch and tried to speak but it was impossible with his tongue in her mouth. He pulled at her trousers and she felt the button fly off and heard it roll on the parquet tiles of the hall. She wished she could roll away as easily as that. He was trying to force her hand onto the bulge in his trousers. They were unzipped and she felt him hard against her. He was pushing her head down and guiding him into her mouth. She gagged as he thrust deep and caught the back of her throat.

"I suppose you think it's funny staying out this late when you knew I'd be waiting for you, you must think I'm some sort of idiot to not know what you've been up to going out dressed so provocatively." She fell onto the wooden tiles as he pushed her down and onto her back and dragging her trousers down to her feet he pulled at her panties and pushing them aside entered her. Celia felt the wood digging into her back and her tears hot and salty running down her face and into her mouth.

"I'm going to make sure you give me the son and heir I deserve. If that Doctor says there is nothing wrong, we'll see if he's right."

Celia felt as though the nightmare was never going to end, but suddenly it was all over and she felt the weight of his body move as he rolled off her and lay on his back staring up at the high ornate ceiling. He was red in the face and sweating.

As Celia got to her knees and began to stand, he rolled over and vomited onto the wooden floor. The sour smell hit her and made her want to gag, and she pulled off her trousers and walked quickly up the wide staircase. She wanted to run, but forced herself to walk until she got to the bedroom. She sank onto the bed and sat there scalding tears running unchecked down her pale cheeks.

After a while she went into her bathroom and stood under the shower. She turned it to maximum and let the hot water rain against her skin. As she let the needles of water wash every trace of the touch and smell of Seb away, she began to feel calmer.

Stepping out of the shower cubicle, she wrapped herself in a large fluffy white towel and went back into the bedroom, relieved to see that it was still empty, but unsure exactly what to do next. Mrs Popple didn't live in anymore, but Arthurs the butler would take care of Seb and the mess. She felt humiliated and embarrassed just thinking about what he would have to deal with.

Chapter 5

Later, Celia was lying awake trying to put the horror of the last few hours out of her mind. She heard the old Grandfather clock in the hall strike 3.am and she tossed and turned her thoughts in turmoil. The moon shone brightly through the curtains that she had forgotten to close in her distressed state earlier. She knew she couldn't go on like this, but just what to do about it? She couldn't think straight and her mind was heavy with sleep. She must have eventually dropped off, because she was woken by the telephone ringing and she struggled to think where she was. She realised it was her mobile and she was relieved to see Gilly's name on the screen. Her friend sounded concerned.

"What's the matter Cee? You sound awful"

"It's nothing; I'm fine" Celia answered

"Well you certainly don't sound fine, why don't you come over for coffee, Jake is still home from school, or I'd come over to you. Please Cee, you sound upset and I'm concerned about you. Say you'll come."

She could hear the reluctance in her friend's voice but she breathed a sigh of relief when she heard her say slowly

"OK I'll see you about 11.00am"

Celia was relieved that there was no evidence of Seb or any mess in the Hall. Arthurs must have done a good job. She felt sorry for him. She went into the kitchen to make herself a cup of tea, another thing Seb chastised her for.

"What do you think we have servants for".

He was always saying. Staring into the white porcelain cup she was deep in thought when the spell was broken by, Arthurs coming in to the kitchen.

"Good morning."

He smiled at Celia. She and Arthurs had become firm friends ever since she had first come to live here three years ago and she never treated him like a servant. She always picked up on his moods and was always kind and considerate to him. He in turn, was a tower of strength to her and she relied on him heavily when she needed to. He had never abused her trust in him. She gave him a conspiratorial look, and said

"Have you seen him this morning?"

"The master is asleep in his study, I think it would be best not to disturb him"

They smiled wryly at each other and he stepped forward to pour the boiling water into the china teapot.

Driving to Parsonage Farm, Celia's heart was heavy. The weather seemed to match her mood as heavy rain sent a river of water which her windscreen wipers were loudly trying to cope with. The swishing of them seemed to have a hypnotic effect and Celia was pleased when she saw the gates of Gilly's farmhouse ahead in the misty dampness. She was so pleased to be away from her bleak home and couldn't wait to get into the peace and tranquillity of Parsonage Farm. She was determined to put on a brave face in front of Gilly, but as soon as she walked in to the bright warm kitchen, to her dismay she was unable to stop the tears pouring down her pale cheeks and her shoulders shook with quiet sobs. She was soon enveloped in Gilly's warm comforting arms. And all her pain and unhappiness flowed out as freely as her tears.

Back at the House, Sebastian was waking. He was confused and couldn't think where he was. He struggled to sit up and realised he was in his study. His head was aching and the pain had settled over his right eye. He put his hand up as if to rub it away but it did little good to the pounding in his temple. His body was stiff and sore from lying in the cramped confines of the too small sofa. He could remember very little about the night before and how he had come to end up here.

There was a light knock on the door and Arthurs appeared carrying a small tray with a cafetiere of steaming coffee and a glass which was fizzing loudly. Too loudly, but the aroma of strong black coffee was too hard to resist.

"Good morning Sir, I trust you slept well"

He said with tongue in cheek. He held Sebastian in contempt and would have moved on long ago if it hadn't been for his fondness for Celia. He looked at Sebastian and saw an overweight overbearing bully. His sparse hair was standing up on end, his eyes bloodshot and his unshaven face added to the total look of despair and slovenliness. Arthurs hated slovenliness and had always prided himself on his own immaculate appearance.

"I've brought you coffee and Alka-Seltzer, I thought you might need. Would you like some breakfast"?

The mere mention of food almost brought Sebastian's stomach into his mouth and he fought not to gag. He felt the contempt his butler had for him. It was almost tangible.

"Just leave the tray" he said not meeting the man's eyes. Left alone he began to remember the events of the night before. To his credit he felt really guilty as the savage attack on Celia unfolded slowly in his fuddled brain. What was happening to him? What had turned him into the monster he had become? He of all people should know the awful effect of being on the receiving end of bullying treatment. It was something that seemed to have always been a part of his life starting when he had been sent away to boarding school when he was only seven. He often wondered what he had ever done to deserve such harsh treatment. Now his Father seemed to take great delight in humiliating him in front of everyone. The only people that had ever shown him love and affection were his Mother and Celia. His Mother had died some years ago and now he was systematically killing off any love Celia had ever had for him He seemed set on a path of self-destruction.

When they had first married, their love making had been wonderful, hadn't it? He had had plenty of women but Celia seemed to bring out the best in him. She was so beautiful. She had been almost shy at first, and had told Sebastian that she hadn't been as experienced as he and didn't want to let him down. The very fact that she was so shy and inexperienced inflamed him even more and she had been an eager and willing learner. He remembered their honeymoon in Barbados. It had been idyllic. Sex had gone from strength to strength and he had taken great delight in her willingness to learn and become responsive and to begin to take the initiative in bed.

He tried to remember when it had all begun to change. Why had it all gone so wrong?
He got up from the sofa and stumbled into the small table at the side. There was a crash and a photograph toppled and fell at his feet. He bent to retrieve it and looked into the unsmiling, stern eyes of his Father.

The face of the Honourable George Stratford looked out of the photograph and Sebastian thought how much he hated his Father. All his life he had been bullied by him. Why couldn't he be more like his brother, Charles? Charles had been four when Sebastian was born in 1960, and was everything Sebastian was not. He had already been riding for two years and as he got older, became an accomplished rider who had gone on to be Captain of the Polo team at Marlborough College. Charles was good at everything Sebastian was not. Skiing, shooting and his academic record had also brilliant. It had been whilst he was skiing in Switzerland a year ago, that he had been killed in an avalanche. His Father had never got over the death of his beloved elder son.

Sebastian had always been made to feel second best. He was not a great sportsman and was not keen on horses. If the truth was known he was a little afraid of them ever since he had fallen off when he'd been six years old. His Father seemed to take great delight in humiliating him in front of other people. He would shout and call him names until Sebastian wanted to crawl away into a corner and die. When Charles had been killed, it had escalated. His Mother had died in 1997 and Sebastian knew that she had also been intimidated by the bullying overbearing man she had married.

Charles had been married to Penny and they had three children all girls, whom his Father idolised, but he needed a grandson to carry on the title that had passed to Sebastian when Charles had been killed. He was forever taunting Sebastian.

"What in God's name is the matter with you? You're really letting the side down you know. Aren't you even man enough to even get your wife pregnant? Can't you even get that right? You're not a man like Charles was, you'll never be as good as him. When are you and Celia going to give me a grandson to carry on the title?"

He didn't care who he spoke in front of, and Sebastian had felt part of him die many times as he suffered embarrassment and humiliation in front of his friends, staff and even Celia. He found it hard to talk to Celia about it as it only served to make his humiliation worse.

He had begun to lose himself and all his worries in Whisky. It dulled the pain and he could just about bear it if he saw everything through the fog it gave him the pain was still there but it seemed less of a problem. The alcohol was also responsible for the savage attacks on Celia. He knew it was wrong, but he couldn't seem to stop himself, and her struggles only seemed to inflame his desire for her. He desperately wanted her to get pregnant so that he could look his Father in the face. He dreaded facing the fact that it could possibly be his fault. That would be the final blow and one he knew that would fuel his Father's wrath and make the situation even more unbearable. He simply could not face the final indignation of being told he was infertile, so he avoided the issue and pretended it would go away, or right itself. When he was sober, he vowed to change, but alcohol turned him into someone he even hated himself. It was a slippery slope and he felt out of control. Unsteadily, for he still felt hung over, he went upstairs to shower and dress for the day ahead. He was determined that he would stop drinking and try to make it up to Celia. He would go into Salisbury and buy her a present. That would win her round, he was sure.

Chapter 6

In Parsonage farm, Gilly was appalled at the state her friend was in. She had known for some time that things between her and Sebastian had not been good but this!! It was hard to take in, and she had the impression that she had only heard a fraction of the story

"You really don't have to put up with this Cee, you know that don't you. You are welcome to come and stay with us. Ralph and I would love to have you."

Her friend shook her head and a curtain of silky hair fell across her face. Gilly couldn't help noticing that her friend still managed to look beautiful even though there was obviously so much pain beneath the outwardly composed exterior. It was her eyes that gave her away. The usually clear bright emerald colour was dulled, and her long lashes still had traces of tears making them cling to her pale cheeks. Gilly's heart went out to her.

"Thanks Gilly. Once again I really don't know what I would do without you, staying with you and Ralph, however tempting would only be putting things off and I'd feel as though I was running away, no, I'll go home and try and sort out this mess, now how about another cup of coffee."

When Celia arrived back home she breathed a sigh of relief to discover Seb was out and she had the place to herself. Skip came bounding up to her and she reached down and ruffled the warm soft fur behind his neck, taking comfort from the welcome he always gave her. She decided that she would go into the kitchen to indulge in the therapy of cooking. It always relaxed her and she missed it since leaving her catering company. She checked the fridge and found cream and eggs. She knew she had vanilla pods in her store cupboard and planned crème Brule for dessert. She had recently bought herself a new gas blow torch and was eager to try it out.

The main course was more difficult. There were chicken breasts and some salad stuff, and after a little thought she had an idea. Thai green curry, it was a favourite of hers and she knew Seb liked spicy food. Why on earth she should consider his likes and dislikes after the way he behaved, she thought to herself but she was doing this for herself, not Seb but old habits die hard. Before things had started to deteriorate she had loved to do things to please him. It was simply part of her nature, after all when you really love someone you want to care for their every need. She could never understand women who let their men fend for themselves. She knew that it was the modern way and she remembered Anna, who had helped her with her catering business talking about her boyfriend.

"He expects me to wait on him hand and foot, I've told him I'm not his slave, I'm also earning a living so he should pull his weight"

Celia thought again about her parents. They both had busy lives and always worked together on everything. She remembered with a smile how her Mum would lovingly iron her Dad's shirts taking great pride in making them look nice for him. Of course, her Mum had always done the cooking. Celia often thought that a lot of her contemporaries missed out on the loving feeling one had from really doing things simply to please someone you love. That's how she had always felt and had taken pride in doing as much for Seb as was possible when he employed servants.

What a pity then, that Seb had begun to kill her feelings for him by his brutal and uncaring treatment of her lately.

She would pop down to the village to pick up some fresh garlic, green chillies and coriander. She knew she had lemon grass and the rest of the spices she would need, besides the walk would help to clear her head and sort out her thoughts. She quickly went to her bedroom and changed into jeans and a warm sweater, and donning a comfortable pair of soft tan leather loafers, she set out with Skip running ahead and barking excitedly.

The big old house was quickly left behind as she walked briskly towards the village.

It was a beautiful March day and the wisps of white clouds blew fast across the blue sky. She thought she heard a cuckoo in the distance. Her steps were light on the springy turf and the air was full of the promise of summer. She breathed in the spring air and tried to put the events of last night out of her mind. Easier said than done, she thought to herself. She could still feel her face flush with humiliation when she remembered the indignities Seb had subjected her to. It crossed her mind how very odd it was that the sex act between two people could be both wonderful and horrific. Their honeymoon in Barbados came to her mind. It had been so romantic and memorable and Seb had been gentle and considerate and a fantastic lover. She closed her eyes and could hear the Caribbean Sea, its waves crashing onto the shore, as she and Seb lay in a tangle of pale sheets in the air-conditioned luxury of their honeymoon hotel. She stumbled, and was instantly back in the cool spring afternoon of the English countryside. She pushed her hands deeper into the pocket of her sweater and realised there was a dipped flake hiding there. She had a real weakness for this chocolate bar, and tearing aside the wrapper, bit hungrily into the wonderful smooth creamy flake.

The sensation of chocolate, melting in her mouth distracted her thoughts for a moment. She thought again of their honeymoon was it really only three short years ago? How had he changed from such a gentle man into the savage brute she now felt married to? She knew that alcohol had a lot to answer for, but what was making him drink so heavily. Her thoughts turned to Seb's father George. She knew he had always treated Seb badly and had frequently humiliated him in front of other people. He seemed to delight in making Seb look small in front of his friends, family and even her, his own wife. She also knew that Seb found it difficult to talk about it, especially to her. It was as though he wanted to ignore it and shut it out, as if by doing so he could pretend it wasn't happening.

What to do now was the burning question in her mind. Did she still love him? Walking away from someone you no longer love is relatively easy. If she did still love him why did she find herself so attracted to Mark? She remembered something her Mum had said to her once when they had been talking about an old school friend of Celia's who had divorced her husband because she had discovered he had been unfaithful. Deirdre had said

"It's the easiest thing in the world to sleep with someone else, if you don't love your man, and the easiest thing in the world to stay faithful, if you love him."

Celia had not really thought about her mum's words before, but now they seemed to be particularly significant.

Shopping completed, she tucked her basket under her arm and set out briskly for home, passing the sign for their village Stratford St. Peter, with Skip now on a long lead running ahead. The weather had changed and there were a few black clouds replacing the wispy white ones. Celia quickened her step, wishing she had brought the car when she saw Seb's silver Porche approaching around the bend in the road. He stopped and leaning across opened the passenger door.

"Darling, looks as though we're going to have rain, hop in. Good thing I came along"

For a moment Celia hesitated and then, picking Skip up, she slid into the seat taking care not to let any part of her body touch her husband. He seemed not to notice and leaned across to kiss her cold cheek. She recoiled and pulled herself even further away pressing her body against the passenger door.

"Don't touch me"

She said, raising her hands as if to protect herself. He had the grace to look uncomfortable, and said softly,

"Look Cee, I'm really sorry about last night, I don't know what got into me, please forgive me, I promise nothing like that will ever happen again."

Celia knew he only ever called her Cee when he was trying to get on her good side. Her eyes flicked sideways at him and she tried to sort out her emotions. Her head was in turmoil.

"If it does ever happen again, I'm leaving you. End of story. I can't live in fear of you treating me that way. What's happening to us Seb? It used to be so good between us".

"I know, and it will be again, I promise." He answered.

When they arrived home they both made a dash for the door as the rain was now coming down in torrents. Arthurs appeared to take care of a very wet Skip and Celia went upstairs to change and try to think straight. Her emotions were all mixed up. Did she still love him? Should she give him one more chance? She walked down to the lounge where Seb was sitting. Arthurs appeared with a tray of coffee and she smiled at him, as he placed the tray in front of her and walked out through the double doors, closing them quietly behind him. Left alone with her husband Celia realised that she was nervous, and she knew he had picked up on it. The room was dark and gloomy and the small windows never seemed to let in enough light. Celia thought again longingly of the bright light in her old Chiswick flat. It had had large windows and the close proximity of the Thames always gave the light in the rooms an ethereal quality, which she had loved.

Her Husband now stood up and held out a slim velvet box.

"This is for you, to say sorry"

Celia didn't move

"Do you really think that buying me a present will make up for the way you keep treating me, you can't buy me off that easily. I simply want you to be the kind and gentle man I married"

Please Celia, at least take a look at it, I really am trying to make it up to you."

Celia reached out her hand for the box. She slowly opened it. Inside was a diamond and white gold cross. The stones sparkled and shone with colours and fire shooting off at tangents. Celia reached out to touch it, gently holding it up with her fingers. He took it and made as if to fasten it around her neck

"No Seb, just leave it, I'll try it later." She got up from her seat and began to walk out.

"I'm going to cook, *I want to!!"*

She said as she caught the look on his face,

"I need to"

She walked out and across to the kitchen relieved to note that he wasn't following her.

She set about preparing the meal she had planned and felt her body begin to relax as the therapy of loosing herself in the concentration it demanded began to work on her mind and body. She dropped the knife she was using to chop the lemon grass stalks, and it fell with a clatter onto the pale tiled floor. Stooping to retrieve it, she rinsed it under the tap and carried on with chopping the tough stalks of lemon grass. It wasn't long before the enticing aroma of lemon grass and coriander permeated her brain and she felt her shoulders relax as the cooking eased the tensions.

Chapter 7

The next few days passed uneventfully, and Celia was pleased that he seemed to have turned over a new leaf. He was not drinking and had not attempted to touch her. She thought ironically it seemed to be all or nothing.

Sunday dawned bright and clear. Seb had mentioned at dinner last night that he was playing golf and even asked Celia if she minded. She had assured him that she would be fine and she thought about Mark and his invitation to join him for a ride. She wasn't sure it was a good idea. She was beginning to admit to herself that she was attracted to Mark, and with the vulnerability of her feelings toward Seb it probably wouldn't be a good idea to see him. She felt torn. She knew she really did want to see him, but surely that was enough reason to stay away. She realised she was arguing with herself when her thoughts were interrupted by the ringing of her mobile.

She saw Gilly's name on the screen and spoke to her friend.

"Hi Gilly, how are you?"

"We're all fine, more to the point how are you? I've been worried about you. How are things between you and Seb?"

She suddenly felt irritated by her friend's concern and realised her voice sounded sharp as she said

"Oh, please don't worry about me; you just caught me at a bad moment the other day. He's been much better since then."

She could hear the relief in her friend's voice and felt guilty about unburdening herself last Thursday morning.

"Are you and Ralph still OK for dinner this evening? I'm looking forward to seeing you."

"Yes, we're looking forward to it too, see you at 7.30pm."

Gilly ended the call and felt Ralph's arms around her waist. She turned her head and looked up into his brown smiling eyes.

"Are you really looking forward to this evening? He said, I know I'm not, I can think of better ways to spend time rather than listening to Sebastian being nasty to Celia. I don't know how or why she puts up with him."

He hugged Gilly closer to him and she felt warm and secure in his arms.

"We are so lucky Ralph; whatever would I do without you? I'm pleased to be going for Celia's sake. She needs good friends around her. I'm sure she'll be glad of our support although she says he's been much better since last week".

"Well I certainly hope so; if he start's on her tonight I'll be giving him a piece of my mind".

"That will just make things more difficult for her; he always takes it out on her after we've gone."

They both looked at each other. Their own life certainly wasn't all plain sailing and there had been times when they had to really work at their marriage, but through it all they had become even closer. Gilly realised even more, just how difficult her friend's life must be.

Celia rode across the fields. She felt Amber's warmth beneath her and began to relax into the sheer pleasure that riding always gave her. The air rushed passed her face and overhead somewhere a bird was singing. She thought it might be a sky lark, but nature had never been her strong point, so it could have been anything. It was a beautiful day and she felt exhilarated by the combination of feelings inside her head, freedom, the most important being the strongest. Free to fly across Salisbury plain with only Amber for company. She was reluctant to admit; even to herself that part of the excitement was the anticipation of seeing Mark. She saw Stonehenge in the distance and rode faster, digging her heels into Amber's side to spur him on. The ancient stones stood majestically, as if to attention, and there were a few people walking around with their heads leaning back and looking high to the tips of the stones and the bright sky beyond. Celia tipped her own head back and marvelled at the way the sun, hiding behind a cloud, had seemingly iced the edges with silver. As she watched, it appeared and a bright beam caused her to raise her hand to shade her eyes from the sudden dazzle. Steering a course around the ancient monument, a flapping of wings overhead caused her to turn and look as a large blackbird flew past and settled on the pinnacle of the nearest stone. Subconsciously, she thought how unusual to see a solitary bird they were usually in large flocks. She continued riding hard with Stonehenge forming a backdrop that got smaller as she rode further away. Her heart was beating loudly in her ears, and she knew it wasn't only from the exertion and exhilaration of the ride.

Mark was also riding fast. He had been thinking about Celia almost constantly since last Wednesday. His head told him he was mad. She was a married woman, but his heart told him a different story. He had the typical fiery passion of an Arian male and he pictured the slim body and imagined her naked, in his arms with a cloud of dark curls brushing against his face. The smell of her filled his nostrils. It had been so long since Lucy had left and he had to admit the thoughts of the beautiful Celia were really turning him on. Mark had always been a passionate man, and longed for the tenderness that came from the intimacies of a loving relationship. He had felt a lot better these last few weeks. Even his nightmares seemed to have abated, and he had tried hard to put the horrors he had seen in Bosnia out of his conscious and unconscious thoughts.

Will had tried to get him interested in one of their female co officer's but so far he had resisted his efforts. Julie was quite attractive if you liked the blonde, voluptuous type. Mark did not. He was more interested in the slim dark quiet type that was Celia. Funny how all his thoughts seemed to bring him straight back to Celia. He thought with anticipation of seeing her. Would it be today? She hadn't promised, but that didn't prevent him looking forward to the possibility.

He rode on and felt the relaxed contentment that riding always gave him. He had grown up on a farm, and had been riding almost as long as he could walk. His parents still had the farm in Yorkshire but it was now run by Mark's eldest brother and his wife. Suzie and Giles lived there with their twin sons Jack and Patrick, and Mark's parents had the small cottage nearby. The farm was near Runswick bay on the Yorkshire coast and Mark suddenly was filled with longing to see the sea, hear the gulls and to walk down the steep winding path, onto the lonely beach passing the tiny houses that had been there for centuries. He loved the fact that the beach was never busy, even at the height of the summer season, unlike nearby Whitby and felt a sudden longing to go home.

His horse gave a snort, which brought Mark back to the present and he realised there was another horse and rider just ahead of him. She sat there smiling at him and he felt the blood hot in his veins and he slowed to a trot and came alongside Celia. Before he had time to do anything except smile, there was a loud roaring of wings and a large bird flew out of the nearby trees and passed close to the head of Celia's horse. Amber, taken by surprise reared up and Celia slipped off the horses back onto the ground. Mark was off his horse and in an instant by her side. Celia was trying to sit up and looked pale and confused. He reached out his hand to help her and was appalled when she moved away as if to fend off a blow. Mark realised with horror that she was terrified.

"Celia it's OK it's me Mark."

She still looked terrified and pulled away from him. Mark felt a sense of des ja vous but in his confused state couldn't remember what exactly had triggered it off in his mind. Suddenly, with a great weight of sadness he realised why the look was so familiar. The faces of Serbian Women who had been raped by the Croatian soldiers came into his mind. He had seen dozens of these women and Mark would never be able to get their look of terror out of his mind. A tear trickled down his cheek and he reached up a hand to brush it away. Celia suddenly seemed to compose herself and looked up at Mark as realisation of her whereabouts flooded back into her confused brain. She got to her feet, almost fell and reached out her hand to Mark to steady herself. She saw that his cheeks were wet and putting her hands on his shoulders looked up into his face.

"What is it Mark? I'm OK you just startled me".

She took a step nearer and suddenly the tears ran from her own eyes and she sobbed until she thought her heart would break. They clung together and gradually she began to feel calmer. Mark had his arms tightly around her and her head was on his chest. She felt the roughness of the tweed of his jacket on her soft skin and suddenly, lifting her face, they were kissing. Gently at first and then her mouth opened and Mark's tongue was in her mouth, exploring and probing. They both felt their passion mount and just as suddenly they broke apart and stood panting for breath. They looked into each other's eyes, and both saw sadness mixed with the passion that had suddenly over taken them both.

Celia spoke first "Mark I'm so sorry, that shouldn't have happened".

As she spoke she put her foot into the stirrup and was mounting her horse. Mark put out his hand saying.

"Celia, please wait, we have to talk, don't go like this"

"I'm sorry Mark, I must, please don't try and stop me"

She began to move away and Mark quickly took a pen from his jacket pocket and scribbled something onto a scrap of paper. He ran alongside and held it up.

"Please Celia, at least take my mobile number, please."

She reached out and took it from his outstretched hand and digging her heels into Amber's side, galloped off.

Mark stood looking at horse and rider disappearing into the distance. He felt frustration and disappointment. He desperately needed to talk to her and there were so many unanswered questions whirling around inside his head. Please God let her contact him, soon.

Celia rode Amber at a gallop, faster and faster as if trying to push all thoughts out of her mind. What had happened back there? Her heart was still beating loudly in her ears, and it wasn't just from the exertion of riding. Kissing

Mark had been a mistake. It should never have happened, so why had it felt so incredibly good. She had thought that after Seb's rough attacks and complete lack of tenderness she would never feel such longing and passion again, and the fact that Mark had aroused her so much, both excited and scared her.

Chapter 8

Pulling up outside the wide double doors of Celia and Sebastian's home, Gilly thought with some irony that the saying "An Englishman's home is his Castle" was certainly right in this case. The sun was just going down and the sky was a breathtaking silvery pink that made the trees in front look like lace, as it shone through the bare branches. It was also reflected in the many windows of the beautiful old house making it look inviting and romantic. Gilly knew, however that inside was not at all romantic with the strained relationship between her friend and the man she had married. She was looking forward to seeing Celia but the prospect of the evening ahead filled both her and Ralph with apprehension.

"If he starts talking down to Celia again this evening I'll have difficulty keeping my temper"

Ralph said as they approached the entrance.

"Yes I know, I understand. I was talking to Celia about the whole situation yesterday and I got the feeling she didn't want us to provoke things as it would probably only make things worse for her after we've left, although she didn't actually say that in so many words. I've known her too long not to read between the lines."

"Why ever does she put up with it?"

Ralph said and they shot each other a conspiratorial glance as the heavy old door creaked open to reveal the smiling face of Arthurs.

They were ushered into the large old hall that was heavy with the overpowering heady perfume from a large crystal vase of white lilies, which Gilly always associated with Celia. Taking their coats he walked to the double doors of the lounge and pushing them open, announced them. Celia was on her feet immediately and came toward Gilly giving her friend a hug and kissing her with affection, on both cheeks. She then turned and offered her cheek to Ralph.

"How lovely to see you both"

She smiled and Gilly thought not for the first time, how stunning she was. Celia was wearing caramel coloured suede trousers with a clinging low cut cream top which flattered her slim waist and accentuated the swell of her breasts. Around her neck, nestling in her cleavage was a beautiful diamond cross that shot fire as it was caught by the last rays of the sun. Gilly noticed that she was fiddling with it as though it was uncomfortable; also her friend looked tense so in an effort to ease the situation she said

"Wow, Cee you look beautiful, I feel quite dowdy beside you."

Before Celia had time to protest, the loud voice of Sebastian cut in

"yes, she certainly *is* beautiful, isn't she, *my wife.*"

He placed his hands on Celia's shoulders and pulled her back toward him in a gesture that said she's mine hands off. Gilly noticed the look on Celia's face as she shrugged him off and took a seat on the sofa beside the fire. Gilly sat next to her friend and Ralph and Sebastian stood together near the Adam fireplace. The scent of lilies was also heavy in the air in this room and Gilly noticed the large arrangement of her friend's favourite white flowers on the side table

"What would you like to drink?"

Sebastian asked and they noticed that he already had a large tumbler of whisky in his hand the amber liquid catching the light of the fire.

They sat together chatting until Arthurs announced that dinner was served and they walked into the dining room.

Mrs Popple had done them proud as usual and the white porcelain plates were set off beautifully with heavy sapphire blue glass retainers underneath. The lamb was succulent and slightly pink and the smell of fresh rosemary wafted up and set the juices flowing. The whole effect was a tempting and mouth-watering banquet. The meal progressed somewhat uncomfortably and Gilly noticed that although Sebastian seemed to be drinking heavily Celia had hardly touched her glass of wine and seemed to be pushing her food around her plate without really noticing how beautifully presented and tempting it was. Sebastian, on the other hand seemed to be eating and drinking with noisy enthusiasm. He raised his wine glass and swallowed greedily.

"We seem to have finished that bottle. Arthurs,"

He raised his voice

"where the devil is that man; he's never here when you need him."

The door opened and the slight figure of the butler appeared at the door.

"Didn't you hear me calling? Get us another bottle of the Fleurie, no on second thoughts, better make it two, and be quick for God's sake, a man could die of thirst waiting for you."

The meal struggled along. Celia noticed with disgust that Sebastian had a smear of food on his chin and seemed to be totally oblivious of it. She tried to catch his eye but as this seemed to fail she reached out her hand and attempted to wipe his chin with her napkin. He caught her hand and putting it to his mouth said with a grin,

"can't wait to touch me, eh my darling. I think I'm on a promise here Ralphie." Celia pulled her hand away as if she'd been burned.

The evening wore on. Ralph was doing his best to keep the conversation going and attempted to interest Sebastian in Parsonage farm.

"I leave all that to my estate manager, he keeps me up dated on what my tenants are up to. I must say, they don't seem to be pulling their weight, they don't know how lucky they are to have such a good estate to work on, and lazy buggers some of them."

Ralph was about to protest and speak up for the tenant farmers, most of whom he had known all his life, when he caught his wife's eye and changed the subject.

"I hope Jake takes after me and wants to run Parsonage farm when he's older, the way I took in over from my Dad"

Gilly was watching Celia's face and could see the colour creeping up from her neck. She sensed that Ralph's innocently meant words had triggered of the pain of not being pregnant in her friend's mind and she put out a hand and squeezed Celia's which was resting on the white linen table cloth. Sebastian cleared his throat noisily and seemed to be about to say something, when Gilly said quickly,

"Talking of Jake, we mustn't be too late as he's been unwell and I want to make sure he's fully recovered."

She looked at her watch and was relieved when Ralph backed her up

'Yes, we promised Jane that we would be home before 11.00pm.'

"Please stay for coffee"

Celia said,

"I'll ask Arthurs to bring it into the lounge."

"No Cee thank you but we really must get off."

She and Ralph stood up and Celia walked with them to the door. Sebastian was still sitting at the dining table with a large glass of brandy clutched in his hand. He raised it to them and said,

"Goodnight, sweet dreams"

And Celia noticed with dread that his words were slurred. She and Gilly stood in the hall and Gilly gave her a hug, whispering in her ear

"Are you alright Cee?"

"Yes, I'll be fine, don't worry about me"

She said, wishing she believed it herself. She was so envious seeing the tenderness and obvious affection between them. She watched the lights of Ralph's car disappear down the long driveway and her heart sank at the prospect of facing Seb. She took a deep breath and walked back into the dining room. He was still seated at the table and was pouring himself yet another brandy, Celia suddenly felt brave and facing him said

"I'm going to bed, and I'm sleeping in one of the guest bedrooms, don't try to follow me or I'll leave and go and stay with Gilly."

She saw with relief the look of resignation on her husband's face and she walked out of the dining room and up the wide staircase. She entered the bedroom she shared with Seb and took a pair of silk pyjamas from the drawer, and walked across the landing into the guest bedroom. Celia breathed a sigh as she began to relax for the first time that evening. She lit the small candle under the oil burner and breathed in the relaxing scent of lavender. It always helped her to sleep.

Lying in the bed she tried to sort out her feelings. She knew that she couldn't go on like this. The love she had once had for Seb seemed to have gone. She asked herself if he changed and stopped drinking would everything be alright again, and she knew deep in her heart that she would never feel the same way about him. He had killed her love and the sooner she admitted that to herself the better. She had the beginning of an idea, and turning onto her side, settled down to sleep which to her surprise came quickly.

She awoke next morning and for a moment couldn't think where she was. She automatically stretched her arm to feel the bed beside her and realised with relief that she was alone and not in the bed that she shared with Seb. The clock on the bedside table showed 8.00am and she knew that her husband would be out of the house as he always left at 7.30am. She got out of bed and walked across the landing to their room and standing under the shower she let hot water wash over her clearing her mind as she planned what she was going to do.

****

Mark was in the officer's mess eating breakfast with his thoughts in turmoil. Since Sunday morning he hadn't been able to get Celia out of his head. He wished she hadn't run away There was so much he wanted to say to her and he felt frustrated as he realised that he had absolutely no way of contacting her. He didn't know where she lived or really anything about her. The only chance he had of bumping into her again was on Wednesday evenings at the pub and today was only Monday. He couldn't wait another two whole days. He felt as though he was going mad. He remembered what kissing her had been like. She had responded with passion initially, and kissed him back. Mark knew that it hadn't been one sided. What had made her run away? He wanted so desperately to talk to her and sort things out. If only she would call him. He had given her his mobile number, but he would just have to wait, and the waiting was driving him mad. He suddenly had an idea and looking at his watch rose from the table and left the mess.

Driving along the A4 away from Salisbury towards the M4.Celia was trying to sort out her thoughts. Skip was sitting on a rug on the back seat as she drove steadily through the Wiltshire countryside. She pushed the buttons on her mobile phone and listened to the ringing tone which came through the speakers. She heard with relief her mum's voice.

"Hi mum, it's me Celia"

She could hear the pleasure in her Mother's voice.

"Darling, how lovely to hear from you, where are you?"

"I'm on the way to you; can I stay for a few days?"

As if you have to ask, you know we'd love to have you, are you alone, is Sebastian with you?"

"No, Mum, it's just me and Skip, I'll explain when I see you, I should be with you around lunch time"

"Great, drive carefully, see you soon."

The journey passed quite quickly and Celia realised how happy she was at the thought of seeing her parents. The prospect was marred only by the situation between herself and Sebastian and she wondered if she should tell them or just think of some excuse. She knew that wouldn't work as her Father always picked up on her moods. He had always been able to tell what she was thinking even when she was a child. She had never been able to hide things from him. She knew that that was why he was such a good GP. All his patients loved him. He was a very warm compassionate man. She and her Father had always had a lot in common, and she remembered how she had picked up on his dislike of Sebastian. He had never actually said much but Celia knew that he thought he wasn't right for her. Well he had been right but he would never say *"I told you so"* and she knew she could rely on him to be supportive, whatever she decided to do. If only she knew herself!

Mark walked quickly to Will's room and knocked on the door. He knew that his friend had been surprised when he had asked him earlier to come out for a drink this evening.

"Hey Mark of course I'll come, I'd love to. It's about time you came out of yourself; I was beginning to wonder about you."

His friend opened the door and smiled

"Good timing, I was just coming to look for you, let's go"

They arrived at the Nag's head and walked into the lounge. It was quite busy, and they stood at the bar and ordered two pints of lager. John, the landlord smiled as he placed the two glasses in front of them. He knew there was some resentment locally to the army but he also knew it was good for his business. He remembered the two officers and they were always polite and well mannered. The dark one was often in here but the fair one was not such a regular.

Mark was waiting for an opportunity to have a word with John about Celia. He had been the one who had told Mark about the Women's group meeting's and he was hoping to be able to get more information about Celia without making it look as though he was especially interested. His opportunity came when Will went to the Gents and Mark said he'd get another drink. He stood at the bar and waited until John had finished serving.

"John, I need to get hold of the women's group as they have asked me to speak at one of their meetings. Do you have a telephone number for Celia?"

"Yes I have the number of Stratford House but beware of her husband The Honourable Sebastian is the jealous type, don't get on the wrong side of him, he has a reputation for losing his temper and is extremely jealous. Don't know what she sees in him, beautiful gentle woman like that, still he wasn't always so bad tempered, takes after his Father, the Honourable George. He's another one you don't want to get on the wrong side of."

Mark was back at the table when Will entered the door talking animatedly to two women. As they all came across the bar to where Mark was sitting, he realised with sinking heart that they were two fellow officers from the camp and one of them Julie, was dressed in skin tight jeans and a top that clung to her breasts accentuating her curvaceous figure. Mark was aware of the drooling stares of some of the local men in the bar and realised that he'd been set up by his friend Will.

"Look who I've just bumped into, he said, what a surprise, what would you two ladies like to drink?"

And he walked to the bar leaving Mark alone with Julie and her friend Caitlin officers from the camp.

Julie spoke first

"It's so good to see you Mark, Will said you'd both be here so we thought you'd like some female company."

Mark was angry with Will for setting him up this way and he vowed he's sort him out later. The evening dragged on and all he could think about was getting out of the pub and back to his room. He urgently needed to sort out his thoughts about Celia. Not only was she married, but she was obviously way out of his league. What chance did he have against such odds? If that was the case, why could he still feel her body against his when she had clung to him the other day. Why had she kissed him back matching his passion and perhaps, more importantly what had she been so terrified of. He couldn't forget the fear he had seen in her eyes that had immediately transported him back to Bosnia and his own demons.

At a nearby table Gilly and Ralph were sitting discussing the events of last night.

"I'm really concerned about her Ralph, She seems so afraid of him, I don't know what to do for the best. I was so relieved when she phoned me today from the car. A trip home to see her Mum and Dad will do her good. I wish I knew how to advise her".

Ralph was about to reply when John appeared at their table.

"Gilly, that guy over there was asking about Celia earlier, something to do with your Women's group meetings, he's a Captain in the army here and says Celia has asked him to speak at one of your meetings"

Gilly followed his gaze and saw a group of two men and two women at the nearby table. They were laughing and the blonde woman had a hand on the arm of the fair haired man sitting next to her. She was looking up expectantly into his eyes and Gilly thought what her friend had told her about Mark. Looked as though he was already spoken for, still just as well, Celia certainly didn't need any more complications in her life at the moment.

"Thanks John, I'll try and speak to him before I go"

Later, as Ralph drove them home through the dark lanes, they neared the familiar gates to Parsonage farm, and he turned his head slightly and spoke to his wife.

"You're very quiet, are you thinking about what John said about the army captain"?

"No not really, she lied, I was wondering how Jake is."
She wasn't in the habit of keeping secrets from her husband, but she didn't want to betray her friend by talking about the Mark situation. She had intended to have a quick word with Mark before they left the pub but she hadn't seen an opportunity as he seemed to be very involved with his friends. The girl he was with was all over him and it was obvious to Gilly that they were an item. How to deal with it? That was the question. She didn't want Celia to be disappointed, but then why should she be? Gilly realised she was probably over reacting. After all it wasn't as though there was really anything

going on between him and her friend. She decided she would drop it into the conversation when they were next speaking. She immediately felt better and turning to her husband said,

"I hope Jake is better, he's been on my mind all evening, let's get inside and find out."

Chapter 9

Celia drove off the M4 and followed the familiar route to her parent's home. They lived in a quiet Bristol suburb near the downs and Celia felt her depression lift at the prospect of seeing her parents again. They had spent time with her and Sebastian at Christmas, but it hadn't been a great success, and she knew her Dad was disapproving of Seb's drinking habits. His drinking hadn't even been that heavy then, goodness knows what her Dad would think if he saw how much worse things were now. She didn't want him to find out as she felt so ashamed.

She pulled the car into the driveway of the house and felt the pleasure that she always felt on seeing the familiar red bricks.

The house had been extended to include a surgery for her Dad. Celia knew he had always nursed the hope that she would follow him and train to be a doctor, but to his credit, he had never pushed her when she had decided to follow her Mum into catering instead. Her brother Alistair had followed their Dad and was now a successful surgeon in a leading London hospital. Celia thought she must call him soon as it had been an age since they had seen each other.

The front garden was a mass of grape hyacinth and daffodils and Celia noticed their heads bending and dancing in the breeze as she climbed out of the driving seat and stretched her aching back. The drive was a mass of pale petals of blossom that had fallen from the large old cherry tree that dominated the drive ay of her parents house. It lay deeply and reminded Celia of confetti, which in turn reminded her of her own Wedding. She swallowed a lump in her throat and was just letting Skip out of the car, when the front door was opened and her Mother stood there smiling. Celia though how great her Mother looked. She never seemed to age. Her face only had a few lines around her eyes and her dark hair was still thick and glossy with only a few stray grey hairs at the sides.

The two women hugged and Deirdre pulled away and looked with concern at her daughter's face.

"What's up Celia, you are so pale, and I'm sure you've lost weight since Christmas, is everything ok?"

"Mum, I'm fine don't fuss; let's get inside"

She said taking her small weekend case from the car, she knew her voice sounded harsh and immediately regretted the way she had snapped. Making an effort to soften her tone she said.

"How's Dad, I can't wait to see him".

"He's out on call so you'll have to wait until later, let's get you inside. I've made a sandwich for now and I'll cook us something special this evening."

****

Mark was glad to be back in his room. He was angry with Will and had told him so on the way back.

"Don't try and set me up with Julie, I'm not interested"

"Come on Mark, loosen up, you need to relax and let yourself go now and then. I'm sure Julie would love to help to take your mind off Bosnia. She's really interested. Did you see the way she was looking at you in the pub, most guys would envy you, she's very popular, you know?"

Mark had lost his temper.

"Just leave it Will. If I want female company I'm quite able to take care of it for myself, and I'd really appreciate you staying out of my life."

He knew his friend had been upset and felt a bit guilty when Will had flushed slightly. He suddenly made a decision and settled down to sleep with an idea whirling around inside his head.

He woke suddenly in a panic with clammy hands and his body shivering with cold although he felt hot. He had been having one of his nightmares. He was back in Bosnia and his patrol had come across a house where the body of a man had been nailed to the outside wall. One of his men had retched and been violently sick. Mark had walked cautiously into the house with his rifle raised, and had found the bloodied bodies of three women one old and two younger, with their dresses pushed up around their waists and their faces showing the terror they had endured before being shot through the head. When Mark had gone closer, he realised they all had Celia's face and he woke in a blind panic struggling for breath. He fought to control the spasms in his body and gradually they began to fade. He had thought his nightmares were receding and was glad that he had made a decision before going to sleep. He knew now that it was the right one.

Sebastian poured himself another large whisky. He knew he was getting drunk and he was pleased, he wanted to shut out all the pain and frustration. He had spent the day with his estate manager Michael going over the March figures and he had not been pleased. To make matters worse his father had shown up unexpectedly and interfered as usual. He had made Sebastian feel stupid by bawling him out in front of his estate manager and compounded it by referring to the lack of an heir to take over. Sebastian had noticed the pity on Michael's face and had lashed out with abuse, which had just made matters worse. On his return home he had got the note Celia had left for him informing him that she was spending a few days in Bristol with her parents, a perfect end to a perfectly shitty day. He made up his mind to get advice. He would keep it to himself, not tell anyone. He would prove to his Father that he was a real man and not the impotent wimp he saw him as.

Celia was sitting in her father's surgery. It was early morning and she had always, since her childhood loved the quiet time spent with him before the rush of patients. She thought how much she loved this quiet gentle man who now sat across the desk from her. He was still young looking with a full head of sandy hair which had just a touch of white at his temples. Celia thought this only added to his attractiveness. No wonder all his female patients were a little bit in love with him.

She realised with a start that he'd been speaking to her

"Sorry dad, I was miles away, what did you say?"

"I said you're not looking like your old self, at all, no colour in your cheeks and no sparkle in your eyes, I noticed it as soon as I saw you yesterday evening, now come on Celia, tell your old Dad what's troubling you, maybe I can help?"

He smiled warmly at Celia and she fought with her emotions. She wanted so much to unburden herself but was reluctant as she knew she would be disloyal to Seb and he was her husband after all. The words she had spoken three years ago came into her head.

"For better for worse."

Well it certainly did seem to be for worse at the moment. She fought to control her emotions and failed as a tear escaped silently from her eye and ran a lonely course down her pale cheek. She reached up and brushed it away and took a deep breath. Her dad was looking at her with such concern, and taking a step in her direction he reached out and putting his hand to Celia's cheek, touched it softly with the pad of his thumb wiping away the tear, just as he used to when she had been a little girl and had fallen off her bicycle. She looked at him with sad eyes and with a miserable attempt at a smile she began to talk.

"We've been trying for a baby ever since the wedding and I'm still not pregnant. Seb wants a son and heir desperately and I'm letting him down"

"Nonsense, it takes two you know, and the harder you try sometimes the more up tight you are. I sometimes feel that half of my female patients are trying to have a baby and the other half are trying not to."

She smiled in spite of herself.

"But Dad, I've been to see a specialist and he says there's nothing wrong so…."

She broke off and wasn't sure how her father would react if he knew how savage and brutal Seb had become. Well that wasn't quite true, she knew he would be very angry if he ever found out how Seb had been behaving toward her recently, but it was difficult to talk to her father about something so intimate and personal, although he was a doctor, he was still her father.

She was relieved when Mrs Ellis, her Dad's receptionist gave a brief knock and put her head around the surgery door,

"Hugh, I've got the notes for your first patient and we've got a full surgery."

Turning she smiled at Celia and said

"Hello my dear how nice to see you"

And turning on her heel she disappeared through the open door.

The sound of rain against the window of her room woke Celia, the next morning. She felt like a little girl again safe and warm in the bed she had slept in until leaving to study in London. She looked around at the familiar room with pale walls and deep blue carpet. There was still an old shabby teddy sitting on the chest of drawers that she had had since childhood. It all felt so familiar and comfortable. She realised how good it was to feel safe and how much she had missed the secure warm feeling lately, as she snuggled down luxuriating in the comfortable feeling of her childhood.

There was a light tap on the door and the sound of her Mum's voice

"Can I come in?"

"Of course" she answered levering herself into a sitting position.

"Oh Mum, you're spoiling me."

She spoke as her mother placed a tray on the bedside table. There was freshly squeezed orange juice, a pot of tea and toast with her Mum's homemade marmalade.

"Well, I don't often get the chance, so indulge me there's a good girl"

Deirdre Manning sat on the end of the bed and watched her daughter, something definitely wasn't right. She had never seen Celia look so peaky and there was a far away almost hunted look in her eyes. She also knew from experience that it wasn't a good idea to keep pressing her. She was sure she would tell her in her own time.

"Don't forget we're driving over the bridge to see your Nan today, do you still want to come with me?"

"Yes of course Mum, I'm really looking forward to it, it's been ages since I saw Nan, I'll finish this and get ready".

Chapter 10

Alone again, she took her mobile phone and punched in the short code for Gilly's number. Her friend answered after a couple of rings.

"Hi Cee, it's good to hear your voice, you must be psychic, I was about to call you."

"Well, I've saved you a call what were you going to say?"

"Ralph and I were at the Nag's head the other night and John said that army captain had been asking about you"

Celia felt the blood rush to her face and she felt excited as the image of Mark's tall slim body was conjured up in her mind. She recalled the heat of his body against hers and his warm mouth against her lips. Despite herself, she felt her body respond.

"He mentioned the talk you asked him to give to our group and said he needs to speak to you. I didn't get a chance to talk to him as he was with some friends and looked very involved."

"Male or female friends?"

Celia couldn't stop herself and felt herself go cold when Gilly said

"Both, it looked like a foursome, and the girl he was with was all over him. He mentioned that you had asked him to give a talk at one of our meetings and needs to talk to you about it"

Celia realised that it had gone right out of her mind with all the other things going on.

"I've got his mobile number, would you be an absolute angel and call him for me; I really can't face it at the moment".

"Of course I will, I'll tell him we will be in touch soon about him speaking; I still think it's a good idea, don't you?"

"I guess so but I can't think about it at the moment, I'll leave it to you, if that's ok Gilly?"

After her lazy breakfast in bed, Celia wandered around the warm comfortable kitchen. She picked up a wooden box containing a set of shiny Sheffield steel knives that had been a present from her parents when she had first started her catering business.

"Do you mind if I take this home with me?"

"Of course not, it's yours anyway sweetheart, are you cooking again, then?"

Deirdre hoped this was a good sign, she knew Celia had missed the therapy of her favourite hobby. She watched as her daughter slid the largest knife out of the case and held it up. The sun caught the blade and reflected a dancing pool of bright light onto the ceiling. She ran her finger carefully along the edge with a faraway look until Deirdre spoke.

"Penny for them? You seem miles away."

Celia started, and slid the knife silently back into the box with a half-smile on her face that didn't quite reach her eyes.

As the car pulled up at the Severn Bridge to pay the toll, Celia always felt as though she was coming home. Seeing the sign

"Croeso I Cymru" Welcome to Wales"

In both languages always had that effect on her and she was proud of her Welsh roots. Celia and her Mum drove along the side of the lake. Celia loved this part of Cardiff. She looked at the familiar sight of the lighthouse that had been built to commemorate Scott of the Antarctic.

The sky was still grey but the wind was blowing the clouds away to reveal patches of blue and white it was almost lunch time and they were going to take her Nan down to Penarth for a treat. The old lady was waiting dressed in her Sunday best next to the window in the front lounge. Celia knew that her Mum and Dad had been reluctant to arrange for her Nan to go into this place after her Gramps had died a year ago, but it really was ideal, with private rooms plus warden assistance. Johanna was still able to have all her personal things around her and her independence. Celia had once overheard her parents arguing about it. She recalled again how surprised she had been to hear her father's raised voice. They had been in the kitchen and Celia had been coming down the stairs when her father shouting had made her stop. She remembered her own feeling of guilt at eavesdropping and had crept back upstairs, but not before hearing her dad saying that it would be the best solution, and her mum's voice, quiet and with a catch, say,

"Yes Hugh, but better for who?"

After Johanna had settled in, they had all relaxed and felt happier seeing that the old lady did seem to be happy with the environment, and Deirdre was able to relax in the knowledge that help was at hand should her Mum need it. They had also liked the location, overlooking the lake and Roath Park near where Deirdre had lived as a child with her mum and dad.

Johanna Beattie was a strong and upright eighty year old. Her once auburn hair was pale and peppery and her skin although lined still bore traces of the freckles that had blighted her life as a young girl. She had hated them and could never understand people who had admired them. Always the ones who didn't have them she had noticed. Her eyes were still bright with a twinkle that belied her years.

They settled the old lady into the back of the car and Celia tucked a warm tartan rug around her Nan's knees for the drive to Penarth. She breathed in the old fashioned heady smell of lavender that always seemed to permeate her Nan's skin and clothes.

Some forty minutes later Celia and her Nan were seated in the restaurant on the sea front. They looked at the menu whilst Deirdre went off to park the car. They were seated opposite each other looking out onto Penarth front with the Pier to the left and the sun which had come out at last shining and sparkling its watery patterns onto the choppy sea. The white frothy edges reminiscent of the lace edged handkerchief that her Nan always had tucked into her left sleeve. The sound of the gulls wheeling in the sky and the salty tang in the air reminded them that they were on the coast. Celia remembered coming here when she and Alistair had been children and looking across the wide stretch of water to see if they could make out the outline of Weston Super Mare, which on a clear day was just about visible.

The old lady looked at her granddaughter and reached her hand out to cover Celia's. The contrast was marked.

Celia's pale slim hand with square nails beautifully manicured only revealed the sharp contrast with the old gnarled and wrinkled hand of her Grandmother.

Johanna began to talk, her voice wavering a little as she looked into Celia's emerald eyes.

"When I saw you today, I was thinking about myself at your age. I had been married for ten years, and we were struggling to make ends meet. I've never told you this before but I nearly left your Granddad. Oh he was a good man but he was never the love of my life. I was in love with someone else."

The old lady suddenly stopped talking and her face took on a dreamy far away expression. Celia waited, her hand resting on the hard arthritic knobs of the bony old fingers.

"Nan"

She spoke softly and the old hand under hers suddenly twitched and she began talking again as if there had been no lapse in concentration.

"We were soul mates but because I was married we decided it was best to deny our love and for me to stay with Christy. We talked endlessly but things were different in those days. People took their marriage vows more seriously.

I have often wondered what my life would have been like if I'd had the courage to follow my heart, and if I'm totally honest I've regretted it. If you're lucky enough to find your true soul mate in this life, you should never ignore your heart. Sometimes you only get one chance."

Celia looked into the pale watery eyes of the old lady in front of her and felt her own eyes getting moist.

"There, there my dear, don't look so sad, your Granddad was a good man and I don't think he ever knew. I had your Mum to think about so I made the best of it."

They both looked up as Deirdre came into the restaurant and they began to examine the menu to decide on their lunch. Johanna Beattie handed a small, gift wrapped parcel to her daughter.

"Happy Birthday for the 24th"

She said,

"I know I'm a bit early but I won't see you on the day so you'd better have it now. I never know what to get you, you seem to have everything."

"Celia and her Mum exchanged conspiratorial smiles. Johanna always said the same thing whenever she gave presents.

"Open it now; I want to see if you like it."

Deirdre tore at the paper and Celia thought how different that was from herself. She always was so careful not to spoil the wrapping on gifts even wrapping it back up afterwards. This always seemed to infuriate Seb. Who quite clearly found this yet another annoying habit? The thought of Seb brought a troubled look to her face and she tried to smile before it was noticed by her mum and Nan. Deirdre looked at the moonstone brooch in the box.

"Oh Mum, thank you so much, you know I've always loved this, it's really beautiful."

"Well you'd probably get it when I've gone anyway but I thought you'd like to have it now"

Deirdre leaned across and kissed her Mum on the cheek and felt the soft papery skin beneath her lips.

Chapter 11

Four hundred miles away Mark was also looking at a menu. He and his brother were sitting in a pub in Runswick bay. He had driven up the night before and had managed to persuade his brother to leave the farm for an hour. Giles had been very reluctant to be away from the farm, even for a short time, but had eventually been persuaded.

"Come on Giles, how often do I see you? It's been almost a year since I was in Yorkshire last, we needn't be long"

Eventually Giles had agreed and Mark and he had driven the short route, past the old potash mine and along the coast where Captain Cook had set sail all those years ago.

Mark thought yet again how spectacular the view was. The old houses fell steeply away below them and the sweep of the bay beyond. It was peaceful and deserted except for one or two walkers on the lonely beach. How he loved it, and how he had missed it. Often when he had been in Bosnia the longing for the peace and tranquillity of this remote and beautiful stretch of Yorkshire coast had made him long to get back. It was such a sane place in all the insanity of the horror of war. The peace and quiet broken only by the roar of the waves breaking on the beach far below and the lonely cries of the gulls. They were suddenly startled as a seagull crashed into the bay window and disappeared from view, only to fly weakly away.

"Must be drunk"

Giles said, with a chuckle.

"So what brings you home? He asked, we certainly don't see much of you these days, how's Lucy?"

Mark looked into the face of his brother. They were very different and had never really been close. Giles was stocky and his hair was receding. His complexion was ruddy and weather beaten from working outside for so many years. Mark couldn't help compare the way he was dressed compared to his brother. Giles was wearing old cord trousers that had certainly seen better days and a worn garish sweater. Mark was immaculate as ever in a camel cashmere crew neck over a blue shirt and beige chinos. Giles had only ever wanted to be a farmer, which Mark thought often was good for him as he'd never wanted to follow in his father's shoes, and someone had had to take over the farm when it had got too much for his Dad.

"Lucy and I split up months ago, I thought you knew"

"Sorry to hear that bro must have been hard for you, but to be perfectly honest I never really liked her. She was too much of a townie for me. She was never seemed to be happy here in the country, didn't want to get her shoes muddy, Suzie and I were never comfortable when she was around, what happened?"

Mark shrugged his shoulders, he didn't want to go into details about the real reason why he and Lucy had gone their separate ways, he had not told any of his family about the atrocities of Bosnia or his recurring nightmares, and he didn't want to get into that now.

"We simply grew apart, I'm not really sorry, the last I heard she was engaged to a stockbroker and I'm sure she'll be happier with him."

"What about you Mark, is there anyone in your life?"

the image of Celia immediately came into Mark's mind. He felt a stirring and longed to reach out and touch her and feel her slim body warm against his with her dark hair brushing his face. His heart had skipped a beat yesterday when his mobile had rung and he recognised the Salisbury code. He had been disappointed when the call turned out to be from Gilly Parsonage. She had said that Celia was away for a few days and had asked her to call to explain to Mark. They would still like him to speak at their woman's group and Celia would call him soon to arrange a meeting. At least that had given him hope but he also realised that he stood absolutely no chance. Not only was Celia married, but she was married to an Honourable!! What chance did a Captain in the army have against such odds? No, the sooner he put all thoughts of Celia out of his head, the better.

He dragged his thoughts back to the present and what Giles was saying.

"Hey Mark, where are you? You were miles away."

"Sorry, what did you say?"

"I asked you if you had a woman in your life"

"No I'm single and happy"

He smiled at his brother and asked him a question about the farm to change the subject.

The fresh local crab wrapped temptingly in locally made wholemeal bread, was brought to their table and they were silent for a moment as they both attacked the food hungrily.

"I've really missed being here,"

Mark said to his brother,"

Although Wiltshire is a beautiful county, I often long for this wonderful coastline and the smell of the sea"

"Well you're here now, so relax and enjoy, how long before you have to go back?"

"I must be back by the weekend so I'll be driving back on Friday, I've got another two days to enjoy being here, and I intend to make the most of it"

"Yes, mum will want to make a fuss of you, I know she really misses you and worries about all the dangerous places the Army keeps sending you, so let her spoil you for a few days."

****

Hundreds of miles away Hugh and Deirdre Manning were waving goodbye to their daughter. It was Friday morning and the wind was blowing a flurry of petals from the cherry blossom tree overhead and a swirl of leaves around their legs as they stood together, their feet scrunching on the gravel drive of their house. The sky was an ominous grey and it seemed dark even though it was still only mid-morning. Deirdre shivered and Hugh put his arm around his wife's shoulder, thinking how she could still excite him after all these years, she would be fifty five in a couple of weeks but seemed not to have changed since the day they were married thirty years ago. Looking up, she smiled into his eyes.

"I'm really worried about her Hugh, something is definitely not right, I just wish she had talked to us about it. It's not like her not to confide in you, she always has since she was a little girl, she usually talks to you about any problems."

"Yes, what worries me is the fact that she was so snappy, so unlike her, she's always been so placid. Something is definitely not right, I only wish I could get to the bottom of it, but I'm not giving up yet".

Yesterday evening, when their daughter had gone to bed early, looking pale and fatigued, with dark circles under her deep green eyes, they had discussed the brief conversation Hugh had had with her about not getting pregnant. They had both come to the same conclusion; there was a lot she was not saying.

Hugh had offered to speak to Sebastian but Celia had been quite short with him and put up such resistance that he had dropped it quickly as it was obviously causing her distress, and that was the last thing he had wanted to do.

Chapter 12

Pushing his finger onto the buzzer, Sebastian was nervous. So nervous he had difficulty keeping his hand steady. A thin metallic voice sprung suddenly out of the panel in the wall and moving his face closer he noticed his face reflected in the shiny metal panel. Bending his tall frame so that his mouth was on a level with the metal grille he said loudly

"The Honourable Sebastian Stratford to see professor Januschevski".

He realised he was shouting. There was a loud buzzing noise in his ear, and he put his hand out and pushing the door he entered the hallway.

It was brightly lit and in front of him, he saw a wide staircase with a red and grey faded patterned carpet. To his left was a door standing ajar, to reveal a middle aged woman in a white uniform, seated at a large dark wood desk. Sebastian noticed an inappropriate, cloying, heavy smell of perfume and it immediately conjured up a picture of his beautiful wife spraying herself with the wonderfully sexy perfume she always wore. The woman looked up and smiled at Sebastian and said

"Please come in, take a seat, I'll be with you in a moment".

"I do have an appointment you know; "

She replied with an effort to keep the ice out of her voice.

"The Professor will be with you soon, he does know you are waiting, please take a seat. Can I get you a cup of coffee?"

"No thank you, he said sitting reluctantly on the dark red sofa. The receptionist noticed that he was perched uncomfortably on the edge and she thought to herself.

"What a pompous, rude man, just because he's an Honourable he thinks he can throw his weight around everywhere he goes, well this certainly isn't the place for that. The professor would soon bring him down a peg or two. She was used to the men who came here being nervous and she could sympathise. It must be humiliating, and a bit of an ordeal, but that was no excuse for rudeness.

Sebastian watched as she picked up the ringing phone on her desk, she smiled at him and said

"the professor will see you now, please go up, it's the door on the left at the top of the stairs."

Thank God she watched the man disappear up the stairs and chuckled to herself, I bet he won't be so pompous when he comes down; this experience is a great leveller.

Sitting on a cold leather chair in front of Professor Januschevski Sebastian could hear his heart beating loudly in his ears and his hands felt cold and clammy. The man in front of him was late fifties with a shock of steel grey hair and rimless glasses and looked kind, if a bit stern.

He was looking down at the notes in front of him and spoke to Sebastian in a slightly accented voice.

"I see that you and your wife have been trying for a baby for about three years, and she hasn't conceived, is that correct?"

"Yes, and she has been to see Professor Hart in Harley Street and I have her results with me"

He reached out his hand and placed an envelope on the desk watching as the man in front of him opened it and scanned through the paper in his hand."

"I see, that seems to be in order."

He wondered why the wife had gone ahead with this rigorous test before her husband had had a simple sperm count, and why wasn't she here supporting him, very strange. Oh well you could never tell with people, he knew that after all these years. This man in particular seemed to be very arrogant; he'd seen his type before.

"Is there any family history that I should know about?"

He went on,

"The test here is a very simple procedure and I will be able to send you the result in a couple of days."

"Oh no, I don't want you to send it, I'll come and pick it up myself, just let me know when".

The professor gave a sigh, but forced a smile as he nodded his head in agreement.

As Sebastian, walked into the room next door, he thought yet again, how ridiculous this whole thing was. The female nurse had explained to him that it was a very simple procedure.

"Try and relax, everyone feels the same, I assure you"

Just to add to Sebastian's humiliation she had left him with a pile of magazines of a certain type and left him to the job in hand. He looked around the room. At least it was comfortable and tastefully decorated. With a deep sigh he unzipped his trousers and picked up the magazine on the top of the pile.

****

Celia decided she would stop off at Parsonage farm on the way home. It seemed ages since she had seen Gilly and she had missed the closeness of confidences shared. She had spoken to her last night and been told that she had phoned Mark and explained that Celia would be in touch. They hadn't talked for long and so had some catching up to do. She was apprehensive about seeing Seb. She knew that her parents were worried about her and had wanted to ask more questions, but she was afraid that they would only make things worse for her if they interfered. They had spoken on the phone once since she had arrived in Bristol and he had told her how much he was missing her. She had tried to detect in his voice if he had been drinking and was relieved when his voice had sounded sober and not slurred with whisky. She had decided to talk to him when she got home, and give him an ultimatum. Either he stopped drinking and being abusive toward her or she would leave him. Surely it was worth one last chance to try and salvage her marriage. The vows she had made in church three years ago came back to her "for better, for worse" well it was about time the "for better" came into play.

She had decided she would speak to Mark and ask him to speak at the Women's group meeting but that was all. She knew that what she had felt for him was probably in her imagination. Gilly had seen him with a woman and said they seemed to be a couple, besides, if she was going to work at her marriage she would need to give it all her attention without any distractions. She began to feel calmer. Once she had made up her mind, there was no going back. After all she had loved Seb once hadn't she? It had been great between them, hadn't it? She had to make it work!

The journey was hard. Heavy rain lashed against the windscreen and the wipers seemed to have difficulty clearing it which made concentration difficult. Added to that there were many large lorries and trucks which threw up spray adding to the poor visibility, their headlights dazzling her as she struggled to stay in control of her car on the slippery roads. The journey dragged on and Celia was tense with fatigue when she eventually pulled in through the gate of Parsonage farm. She had phoned ahead and Gilly was waiting for her and they hugged warmly as she walked into the bright warm kitchen that was so familiar and comfortable. She noticed absent mindedly, that there were a few feathers in the hallway. Gilly kept chickens for their eggs and they must have blown in when she had opened the door. She stooped and absentmindedly picked one up and ran her finger along the thin spine, watching as the pale feather parted.

"Well Cee, I was expecting to see you looking relaxed after this time with your parents but you look exhausted"

"Oh, don't worry, it was the journey, I hate driving in this weather"

Gilly was putting down a bowl of water for skip that was rubbing up against her legs, and yelping in excitement. Gilly's dogs had joined it and there was a skirmish of fur and tails as they all jostled for the bowls Gilly had placed on the tiled Kitchen floor. Celia noticed how at home Skip seemed and was sure he felt the same affection for parsonage farm and its inhabitants as she did.

She leaned back in the comfortable arm chair and rested her aching neck, looking around the familiar kitchen that was so inviting even though the sun was not in evidence today. The rain was lashing against the window and she could hear it dancing on the roof of the old farmhouse. She unconsciously reached up and massaged her shoulders and felt the knots. She hadn't been completely honest with her friend. The tension wasn't only from the driving. She was apprehensive about meeting up with her husband and actually felt nervous about seeing him.

"How were things at your mum and dad's?"

Gilly's voice broke in to her thoughts. Celia gave her friend a brief resume of the last week and glossed over the concern her parents had shown at her state of mind.

"We went over to see my Nan; she looks great and never seems to get any older."

Celia remembered that Gilly's own Gran had died just before Christmas and that they had been particularly close. She saw the wetness in her friend eyes as she blinked her tears away and reached out to give her a hug. They stood together, close and Celia could feel the warmth of her friend's body and the beat of her own heart. They broke apart and smiled into each other's faces.

"Sorry Gilly, I know it still makes you sad to think about your own Gran" she looked into her friend's sad eyes.

"Well at least she had a long and happy life with no regrets so that at least gives me a feeling of peace, but I still miss her"

Celia thought back to Johanna's words about her regret at not following her heart.

"My Nan told me something that surprised me"

She told Gilly how her Gran had wished she had been brave enough to leave her husband all those years ago and asked Gilly what she thought.

"I've always believed you should follow your heart. You only get one chance in this life; you're a long time dead. It's easy for me to say as I can't imagine my life without Ralph, He is my soul mate, but living with someone who doesn't make you happy must be like living in hell. Sorry Cee, I've touched a nerve, haven't I?"

She reached out and hugged her friend again and tried to imagine what it must feel like to be with someone who doesn't make you happy. She couldn't imagine anything worse or lonelier and made her realise once again just how lucky she and Ralph were.

"How about that cup of coffee you promised me I'm parched after that long drive"

Gilly walked to the Aga and busied herself. Within minutes they were seated at the old refractory table and Gilly was handing her home made quiche and banana and walnut loaf as the wonderful aroma reached her nose, she realised just how hungry she was, but the quiche did look a bit dark and crumbly around the edges. She noticed a dark red blistered area on her friend's hand.

"What have you done Gilly?"

"Oh, it's nothing; I just caught it on the Aga as I was taking the quiche out."

Celia thought how unlike her friend, she was always so careful and meticulous. What was on her mind to distract her so?

Later, feeling more comfortable she began to relax and mentioned Mark and the telephone conversation they had had about the talk he had agreed to give at their meeting

"I must call him to discuss it"

"How do you feel about him, now?" Gilly asked.

"I've been thinking it was probably all in my imagination, I was romanticising the whole thing and getting everything out of proportion because I was feeling so low about Seb and me. I've decided to try and make things work, after all for better for worse you know"

Chapter 13

Driving the short journey between Parsonage farm and her home Celia was lost in thought. She had been quite a shy person when growing up in Cardiff and Bristol and not being very sexually experienced when she had married Seb she had thought she might have had problems but he seemed to be happy and encouraged her to be more adventurous. She had always dreamed about her future with the certainty that often comes from inexperience, and only ever saw herself loving one man and giving everything to him and the relationship. She knew that she was not fashionable in her views and thought she had probably been born in the wrong era as most of her friends had completely different ideas. They often used to tease Celia and say that she should play the field first. That wasn't to say that she hadn't had boyfriends; there had been a few in London but nothing serious until meeting Seb. She knew quite early on that she was in love with him, and he seemed to feel the same.

She was busy trying to analyse just when things had started to change when she realised that she was driving in through the gates of her home. Seb's car was in the open garage, and she saw to her dismay that his Father's car was also parked in the driveway. Skip was barking excitedly as she got out of the car and a smiling Arthurs took her small overnight bag and walked back into the house in front of Celia.

Glancing into the hallway she called out to him

"I'm just popping over to the stables, I want to see Amber, I've really missed her, I won't be long, please tell my husband."

Arthurs thought to himself, just how telling it was that Celia's first thought was for the one true love of her life. Her horse, not her husband!

Walking into the stable block she took a deep breath and smelt the familiar smell of horses combined with saddle soap and leather, which had its usual calming effect that she always felt when near to her beloved horse. Anyone watching would have realised the obvious warmth and affection between horse and owner. She was engrossed in nuzzling the soft silky head and tickling Amber's ears when she was startled to feel a hand on her bottom. Swinging around Celia came face to face with her father in law who was grinning into her face, his hand still caressing her bottom. She took a step back and gave him contemptuous stare.

"Please don't do that"

She moved away from him as she spoke.

"Well my dear, how nice to see you, you're looking lovely as usual; I hope that son of mine is looking after you properly, beautiful young filly like yourself."

Celia noticed that her words had had absolutely no impression on him and he was still looking at her as if she was completely naked. He always made her feel uncomfortable.

"Why don't you get lost"

She was walking away as she spoke and she kept her pace slow making a huge effort not to run. She was angry at him for being such a letch, and she was angry with herself for letting him get to her. She had always been uncomfortable in Seb's father's presence but it had only been lately that he had actually been so tactile and it repulsed her. She was in two minds whether or not to talk to Seb about it, but the gulf between them seemed to be so wide that it would probably only make things worse.

When she neared the house, she saw her husband framed in the doorway. The rain had cleared and there was a rainbow bright against the dark sky. It appeared to Celia that the end was embedded in the lake at the rear of the House and she contemplated searching for the crock of gold. The edges of the dark clouds appeared to have been lined with silver, reflecting the hidden sun. She couldn't help notice just how miserable he looked, and when she reached him he held out his arms and Celia walked in and allowed his embrace to warm her. He kissed her lightly on the mouth and said

"I'm so pleased to see you my dear, welcome home"

It was much later, after dinner that they were together in the bedroom they had shared since their marriage. Celia was seated at the dressing table, carefully wiping her face to remove her makeup. She had spoken at length during the meal about how she was feeling and had really tried to make him understand that she would leave if things didn't improve. She had begun to dread being alone with him and realised how ridiculous that was. How could you not want to be alone with the man you were married to? The thoughts of his drunken groping and savage attacks caused her to shiver with pain and revulsion, but she wondered if she was brave nought to walk away and start all over again.

"I can't go on living this way Seb, if you hurt me again, I will leave you, and I really mean it."

He had assured Celia that things were definitely going to change for the better and he was going to give up drinking heavily.

"I can't live my life without you, it would have no meaning, I promise things will get better."

She had wanted to believe him, after all their love had once been so strong and passionate, even trusting. She would make the effort and give him a chance to prove things could go back to what they once were.

Now lying in bed next to him she wondered if it really was possible to salvage anything from the wreckage. He reached out his hand and lightly stroked her breast as he brought his head down to hers and kissed her gently. She tried to relax and respond but flashes of his previous brutal attacks kept appearing in her head. His kiss became more urgent and his hand was slowly circling, moving down and down until his fingers slipped easily through the dark curls between her legs, and into her arousing a spark of passion. She opened herself to him and felt him move inside her; slowly at first until his passion aroused he was fully on top with all his weight pressing down the full length of her pale slim body. She felt trapped as her hair caught behind her prevented her from moving her head. She tried to close her mind to what was happening and to give herself up to her own body and allow the feelings of the initial arousal to take over. She felt that if she struggled or appeared not to be enjoying it he would react badly so closing off her mind she put her arms around him and just let the flow carry her along. It seemed to last a long time but she realised that this was her imagination. He rolled off and immediately disappeared into the sleep of the satisfied lover.

Celia lay in the darkness listening to the deep nasal breaths of her husband. She touched her cheek and realised it was wet with salty tears that were slowly coursing down her pale cheeks. Is this how it's going to be? She asked herself, allowing him to make love to me, then the awful feeling of regret and self-loathing. It had been good, even great, so surely it could be again. She must just be patient.

The weekend passed uneventfully. They were polite with each other and at least he was not drinking. She was also pleased that the subject of her not getting pregnant seemed to have been forgotten. She spent the next few days riding and generally relaxing and was pleased when Gilly joined her on Sunday as Ralph was home with the children. They rode out together on Salisbury plain and chatted with the ease and familiarity that good friendship brings. They had stopped in a clearing and tethered their horses to a low branch. Celia took off her riding hat and shook her dark cloud of hair out as she ran her fingers through the shiny mass of waves. As they lay under the old oak, Celia looked up through the branches and watched the clouds rushing across the blue sky. Their horses were tethered loosely, their heads together as they nuzzled each other Amber's pale gold head in sharp contrast to Snowy's white one. The air was heavy with the sounds and smells of the countryside in spring. There were beams of sunlight filtering through the branches and nearby a spiders web shimmered and danced fraily its silken strands like diamonds caught in a net. Somewhere, high up in the branches of the tree a bird flew away with a rustle of leaves and she watched it as it flew high into the blue sky until it was out of sight and squinting her eyes against a shaft of sunlight dancing with tiny specs of dust that appeared through the sprawling old branches Celia looked across to her friend lying beside her.

Celia propped herself up onto her elbows and spoke, noticing that her voice seemed to sail up into the rustling leaves.

"Oh Gilly, I'm so mixed up, I feel like I'm being torn in half. On the one side is my marriage to Seb. It used to be good, perhaps it will be again. Surely it's worth another try; otherwise I'll feel as though I'm throwing away three years of my life. On the other side is how Mark makes me feel and what my Nan told me. I have such tenderness with Mark, that's something I see between you and Ralph, and my brother Allie and his partner Enzo, and being totally honest, I've never had that with Seb and I might never have this again if I let Mark walk out of my life. My Nan gave me the impression that she regretted the decision to stay with my Granddad and not follow her heart."

Gilly pushed herself up and looked across at her friend.

"If you want my opinion, I think your Nan was trying to tell you to be true to yourself, and to follow your instincts and go with your gut feeling, if your not happy, and you're not are you Cee.?"

"Oh, Gilly, enough of this we're not getting anywhere let's change the subject. What about a speaker for our meeting, do you think Mark is a good choice?"

"Well yes I do but can you cope with that?"

"I really don't mind doing it if you like"

Gilly said.

"No it's ok I really must speak to him as it was me who first approached him, besides, It's time to get over those silly romantic thoughts, I'm determined to make my marriage work."

She hadn't told her friend how she felt about sex with Seb as she was sure in her mind that it would soon improve and get back to how it used to be.

Chapter 14

Mark had been back for a couple of days and felt better for the rest in Yorkshire. His mum had really spoiled him and he had let her fuss and lavish attention on him, which he knew she loved to do. His brother had been almost emotional when they had said goodbye. He had put a hand on Mark's shoulder and said,

"Don't stay alone Mark, having the love and sharing that comes from a good relationship is priceless, believe me"

Then as if he felt he had said too much for a straight talking, unsentimental Yorkshire man, he laughed and banged Mark hard on the back and said,

"Give em hell down there in the south, Mark."

The next few days were busy as he threw himself into work. On Monday evening in the officer's mess he had seen Will. The first time they had met up since the few words they had had before he went home, they had seemed a bit awkward with each other, but when Will had held out his hand in a gesture of friendship, Mark had taken it and putting his hand on his friend's shoulder said

"No hard feelings eh Will, life's too short, let's have a drink and you can bring me up to date with what's been happening around here whilst I've been away."

They had chatted about the events of the past week but the subject of Julie was not mentioned and Mark was pleased as he didn't want to start all that again. When he was alone he pushed away all thoughts of Celia and the longing he felt for her He had made up his mind that she was unattainable. During the day it was easy to keep busy and not think about her, but alone in his room at night it was much more difficult. He imagined her lying next to him and could almost smell the perfume she always wore combined with the inexplicable scent of a desirable woman. He wanted her so badly, it had been so long since he had had a woman and he felt the stirring in his groin as he closed his eyes and thought about her in his arms responding and opening up to his touch like the petals of a beautiful flower. Perhaps Will was right, he did need a woman, and Julie was available and seemed more than willing. Maybe he ought to give in and let her get closer to him. With that thought running through his head he turned over and settled down to sleep.

For once his dreams were not full of horror. He dreamed he was walking through a beautiful meadow the sun was hot on his head and there was the sound of a nearby stream. He was holding someone's hand and she was looking up into his eyes, but try as he might, he couldn't make out her face. It seemed to be obliterated by the dazzle of sun in his eyes. On the edge of the meadow, shrouded in shadow a figure was standing looking in his direction. She too was far away but he could just make out her cloud of long dark hair and pale skin.

The next morning the dream was only a distant memory. At lunchtime, he saw Julie in the officer's mess and he walked over to where she was sitting and said

"Hi, mind if I join you?"

She looked up startled and her face broke into a grin as she said

"Sure, help yourself"

He reluctantly had to admit that in her uniform, she looked less tarty. Her voluptuous figure disguised by the severe cut of the shirt and her bright hair hidden under her beret. They chatted for a while as they ate their lunch and Mark was surprised when he heard himself asking if she would like to go out with him one evening. She agreed eagerly and he suggested they should go into Salisbury to see a film. They decided on Wednesday evening and he left her at the table, smiling up at him as he left the mess.

As he did so, the ringing of his mobile phone interrupted his thoughts; answering it he felt a rush of adrenaline as he recognised Celia's voice.

"Mark, hello it's Celia, can you talk?"

"Yes, go ahead"

His voice sounding a lot calmer than he felt.

"I'm calling about the talk you agreed to give at our Woman's group meeting, are you still O.K with it?"

He pictured her, and wondered what she was wearing, his mind playing tricks as her slim body swam before his eyes, pulling his thoughts together and tried to concentrate.

"Yes of course, I promised you I would, when are you thinking of?"

At the other end of the phone, Celia was also struggling to concentrate, She was imagining Mark standing tall and proud in his captain's uniform, and the beautiful blue of his eyes. Perhaps it had been a mistake to call him, but she had asked him to speak and the group were looking forward to it so she didn't want to let them down, at least that was what she was telling herself.

"Can you meet me to talk it through?"

He heard her say,

"How about Wednesday evening before my meeting, about 7.0pm?"

He thought about the arrangement he had only just made with Julie. He was undecided as to what to do when he suddenly made up his mind and heard himself say,

"Yes, that's fine I'll meet you at the Nag's head at 7.pm."

He would have to change his date with Julie, she would understand. He couldn't wait to see Celia again. They had had no contact since the fateful meeting when she had run away a couple of weeks ago, but he knew there could be no future for them, there were far too many things against it.

Before she had time to think about the possibility of seeing Mark her phone rang again, Hello mum she said with the phone against her ear, but it was her Dad's voice she heard.

"It's your Dad love, can you talk?"

"Yes Dad, It's good to hear your voice is everything ok?"

"Yes we're both fine, more to the point, how are you, we've been worried about you, are you sure there's not something you're hiding. You never were good at keeping secrets even as a little girl. Anything on your mind always has come pouring out, good thing too, much healthier than keeping things bottled up."

"Dad, I told you everything that was on my mind."

She hated keeping things from her dad but she knew she couldn't say anything about the brutal streak that seemed to have developed lately in her husband.

"I'm ringing with a bit of good news; at least I hope you'll think so. We've got tickets for La Boehme at the E.N.O and thought we'd stop off at your place on the way, if that's ok with you and Sebastian of course."

Celia ended the call having assured her father that they would both be welcome and thought ahead to the coming weekend with a mixture of emotions. Pleasure at seeing her parents again, mixed with apprehension at her husband's behaviour.

Chapter 15

Wednesday evening, Celia drove the short distance from home to Parsonage farm to collect Gilly. She had spent an age in front of the full length mirror in her bedroom trying to decide what to wear. The third outfit she had settled on was a plain slim black skirt and a simple cashmere sweater in soft emerald that really picked up the colour of her eyes. She rejected the diamond cross that Seb had bought her; she couldn't even look at it without remembering that painful night and the horrors he had put her through, instead she left her neck bare choosing only the simple emerald studs for her ears. Black high heeled court shoes completed her outfit and she was pleased at the woman who looked back at her in the mirror. Driving through the silvery evening she wondered why she had taken so much time when choosing her outfit, to go to so much trouble was just silly she said to no one in particular, after all it's just a meeting, nothing special. A voice deep in her subconscious said

"Who are you trying to kid?"

But she closed her mind to it and drove on through the leafy lanes.

The day had been unusually warm for April and the sky was shot with streaks of bright pink with a silvery light that heralded another good day tomorrow. Celia was trying to sort out her thoughts. She had made a real effort with Seb and it seemed to her he was doing the same. They were very polite with each other. Too polite she thought to herself, almost as though both were on their best behaviour, more like strangers than a couple who had been married for three years. Where was the evidence of the intimacy that they had shared? Where was the closeness that comes from knowing the mind and body of the person you love as well as you know your own?

She had tried but found it increasingly difficult to relax and be herself. Mealtimes were particularly stilted and she wished often that it wasn't just the two of them. She was looking forward to both seeing her parents this weekend and the distraction that having them to stay would bring

He had at least stuck to his promise of not drinking, but in truth that seemed to have a counter effect as he seemed to have lost the art of conversation without alcohol to loosen his tongue.

Walking out to Celia's car Gilly smiled warmly at her friend as she lowered herself into the passenger seat. They had spoken on the telephone earlier and Gilly had been reluctant to go with her to meet Mark.

"I'm sure it would be better if you saw him alone, Cee, after all he won't be expecting me to be with you."

"No I really want you to be with me, please, I'll really feel more comfortable."

She knew in her own mind that if she was totally honest, she was using Gilly as a shield against her feelings for Mark. She didn't know how she was going to react when face to face with him and she was hiding behind her friend.
As they drove the short distance to reach the Nag's head, Celia told Gilly about her parent's visit this coming weekend and how much she was looking forward to spending time with them.

"Is it just spending time with them, or is it also not spending time alone with Seb."

Gilly asked. Celia turned her head and looked directly into her eyes.

"You know me too well, don't you? I can never hide anything from you. You're right as usual, Things are not brilliant between us, but he really is trying, honestly. It's probably me!"

"Cee, for God's sake stop knocking yourself. You are always putting yourself down .Remember that speaker we had last month? She told us how important it I to be positive and have faith in yourself, remember her?"

They had both been impressed by Madeline Gray. She had been running a successful training company for twenty years and specialised in the power of positive thinking and self-confidence .She had shown them how many women were often their own worst enemy, constantly putting themselves down and pointing out negative things about themselves and their appearance, making people aware of things that normally wouldn't be noticed. She had talked intelligently and with conviction about mountains that often appear in one's life. She had said that speaking from personal experience; human nature was such that when faced with a mountain, natural reaction was often to run away from it, thinking that it could never be climbed, therefore conquered. She also knew from experience that once you did face your mountains, you felt so much stronger when you got to the other side, as you succeeded in doing something you thought you couldn't do. Also, perhaps more important, even if it wasn't immediately apparent, something positive almost always came out of the negative situation It had made Celia think about her current situation. What good could possibly come out of this?

Gilly reached a hand out and touched her friend warmly on the shoulder, and they both got out of the car and walked toward the doorway of the fourteenth century coaching Inn that was The Nag's Head.

Mark had spent an age looking at himself in the mirror in his room. It wasn't full length so he had to make do with head and shoulders. He had changed from light coloured trousers to dark blue, and donned a paler blue shirt that his mum always said matched his eyes. What a load of nonsense, and exactly what difference did it make whatever he was wearing? He had already decided there was no future for him with Celia that was why he had asked Julie out. The image of Julie moved from his head to his eyes. She was easy on the eye, and he knew there were loads of men who would jump at the chance to take her out. She had agreed easily to the change of day for their forthcoming date, and he was now taking her into Salisbury on Friday evening. He brought his thoughts back to the evening ahead, and tried to deny his excitement at the prospect of seeing Celia again. Snatching the keys to his car he left his room, closing the door quietly behind him.

He was standing at the bar in the Nag's head at 6.45pm. He was always punctual and hated people keeping him waiting, always had. He stood at the bar and realised he was nervous. He was looking at his watch when at exactly 7.00pm there was a blast of cool air as the door opened and Celia walked in. Mark looked up and saw to his disappointment that she was not alone. The woman accompanying her looked vaguely familiar, but he couldn't place exactly where he had seen her before. Looking at Celia he knew he'd been kidding himself by thinking he wasn't attracted to her. He felt his pulse quicken. She looked incredibly beautiful and the colour she was wearing matched her eyes exactly.

He smiled and spoke in a voice that sounded even to him, ridiculously nervous and shaky.

"Hello again, nice to see you, can I get you a drink?"

Celia introduced Gilly as a friend and fellow member of the woman's group and they went to sit at a table near the fire whilst Mark ordered drinks from the bar. The conversation seemed to Celia to be going on around her, almost as if she wasn't part of it. She seemed to be hypnotised by Mark's voice and was mesmerised with the way his lips moved when he spoke, she couldn't take her eyes off his lips. Gilly's voice broke into her thoughts,

"Sorry, Gilly,"

She looked flustered and tried to cover up her inattentiveness when her friend picked up on it and rescued her.

"I was saying that Wednesday April 30th would be a good day for Mark to speak, what do you think?"

Celia took a diary from her black leather hand bag and turning the pages said in a hesitant voice, yes that's fine. They carried on making arrangements and finalising details when Gilly said,

"Please excuse me for a moment, I need to go to the ladies, I'll see you upstairs, Gilly"

And ignoring the wild movements of her friend's eyes and her imploring look, Gilly walked away from the table and out through the door and disappeared from sight.
There was an uncomfortable silence, and then they both spoke at once,

"I really must be going"

They both stopped and Mark said

"After you"

Celia got to her feet and said with a coolness that surprised even her

"I have to get to my meeting they'll be waiting for me, it was nice to see you again and we'll be looking forward to the 30th."

She was on her feet and after the briefest of handshakes; Mark had no choice but to watch her slim figure disappear through the door and toward the stairs that would take her to the meeting room.

Gilly was waiting for her and said

"Gosh, you were quick, I thought I would leave you alone to have a chat, I could almost feel the electricity between you."

"Nonsense, you must have imagined it, he was only interested in the talk and I'm certainly not in the least bit interested in him, I told you that earlier, now let's get this meeting under way".

Gilly wasn't convinced but sensed that the matter was not up for discussion and turned her thoughts to the business in hand.

Later, driving home she thought how cool Mark had seemed. He must be involved with the woman Gilly had seen him with, but who was she to care. She wasn't available and she knew that it was worth making an effort to get her marriage back on track. She had been giving some thought to her not being pregnant. The tests had shown there was no medical reason, so perhaps it was her being so tense all the time. She really must try and relax more. There was a small seed of doubt at the bottom of her thoughts that was saying to her, do you really want to get pregnant feeling this way about Seb? What sort of father would he make? Did she really want her child to be subjected to the bullying that Seb had from his own father and was showing her these days?

Driving back to camp Mark thought how cool Celia had been. She certainly wasn't in the least interested in him, he must have imagined it. He began to look forward to Friday evening.

Chapter 16

Mrs Popple had really done them proud, she had been put out at first when Celia explained that her parents would be arriving on Thursday and not Friday as first planned, but she had soon come round.

The food she served on Thursday evening was superb and Celia knew that she had made a special effort knowing what an expert her Mum was in the kitchen. The main course was welsh lamb shanks, especially for her mum. Celia had had quite a job persuading her to be allowed to make the dessert herself. You know how much I miss cooking and my Dad really loves my Chocolate bread and butter pudding, please don't be mad at me. She had eventually cajoled her housekeeper into letting her loose in the kitchen. Celia knew she didn't have to ask permission in her own house, but it wasn't her way to be pushy and pull rank, so they had worked together, side by side. As Celia had been chopping fresh mint, the sharp blade moving quickly, she had suddenly yelped as the blade caught her finger and drops of bright blood ran quickly into the chopped aromatic herb. She swore softly under her breath and scooped the bloody mess into the bin.

"Lucky we've got plenty in the garden".

She said to Mrs Popple, opening the back door and walking outside to pick more of the aromatic herb.

Later, sitting in the heavy ornate dining room, she wished again for the peace and serenity of her London flat. She had made an effort with the table and there were Anemone's in a small white bowl in the centre of the table, which was laid with all white china and set off by deep blue serviettes and the flowers.

"The table looks lovely, I can see that you had a hand here I recognise your touch"

Her mum said.

"And isn't that lamb and fresh mint I can smell?"

She wrinkled her nose as the wonderful aroma wafted through from the kitchen. Celia smiled and said,

"of course, mum, I know it's your favourite, and yes dad, before you ask, of course I've made you your favourite chocolate bread and butter pudding, you know I wouldn't let you down."

She smiled at both her parents in an effort to relax and ignore the niggling worry deep down that her husband would show her up in front of her parents.

"We're so pleased to see you both, aren't we Seb?"

She turned to her husband who was sitting on her left and opposite her Mum. She tried to see him through their eyes. She knew he had changed a lot since the three short years of their marriage, and knew that the heavy drinking had changed his appearance dramatically. He was now so overweight and his face had the ruddy bloom caused my heavy consumption of alcohol. Where was the slim virile man she had married? She could see her father looking at him and knew that he would be able to see through any veneer that Seb put up. He had been a doctor too long not to recognise the signs. Hugh was deep in his own thoughts. What's going on here, he asked himself. Celia is trying too hard, and if I'm any judge, all is not well. Sebastian has the look of an unhappy man, he's overweight and I'd say he's drinking heavily from the colour of his skin. Hugh hated to see his only daughter this way. She had always seemed quite naïve about men and they'd been surprised when she'd fallen so heavily for Sebastian. He had had his doubts about the man, there was a cruel look in his eyes and for all his status seemed to have a basic insecurity. There was something about the relationship between him and his father. Hugh remembered the wedding and how The Honourable George Stratford had seemed to take pride in putting his son down in front of other people, including his new wife. He had been so different with his other son, Charles. The tragedy of him being killed in the skiing accident two years later had been a tremendous blow for the old man. Hugh had felt sorry for Sebastian but if he was making his beautiful daughter unhappy then he'd have Hugh to answer to. The difficult thing was that Celia would absolutely hate him interfering; no this would have to be handled very carefully.

As Mark and Julie walked toward his car on Friday evening, the heavens opened and they made a run for it. Mark opened the passenger door before moving around the car and getting in to the driver's seat himself. They were both laughing and struggled to remove their wet jackets which was not easy in the confines of the front seat. Mark switched on the ignition and the sound of Bruch's violin filled the car, from a CD that Mark had been playing earlier. He loved violin music and this concerto was one of his favourites. He was reaching out to turn it down when Julie put her hands to her ears and said,

"Oh Mark do we have to have this on, I hate screechy music, it always puts my teeth on edge, let's have something a bit more lively"

And reaching out and she began fiddling with the tuner on the radio until the heavy beat of garage music filled the car.

"That's better" she said and leaned back against the seat shaking her head so that her hair swung from side to side. Mark was aware of the closeness of her. She was wearing a very heavy musky perfume and he found it overpowering. He took a steadying breath and tried to stay positive. Come on give this a chance he thought to himself, relax and enjoy the evening. Julie was talking and he was having difficulty hearing her above the music that was thudding in his head, so he reached out and switched off the radio.

"What's up, don't you like my choice,"

She said

"It's not that, I just want to concentrate on the driving with this rain lashing down."
He leaned into the steering wheel to concentrate on driving in the bad weather.

"So tell me all about yourself Mark, I understand you were in Bosnia that can't have been much fun, I hear there was so much horror enough to give a grown man nightmares"

Mark flinched and almost swerved the car. The tyres screeched loudly on the wet road. He saw through the torrent of rain on his windscreen that the road ahead suddenly became a road in Bosnia, not Wiltshire. He was there and could hear the shouts mingled with gunfire and could see again the bodies lying in the road. His thoughts went back to Celia and the look of fear in her eyes when she had fallen from her horse. What had frightened her? What was going on that he didn't know about? He realised that the woman sitting next to him was still talking and realised with a start that it was Julie, not Celia.

"Oh, come on Mark you know what they say, A trouble shared, and I'm a very good listener Look don't get so uptight, I was only trying to help my dad always says don't keep things bottled up and he should know he was in the Army for years and nearly lost his mind when he was in Korea, almost ended up in an asylum"

"Julie!!"

Mark realised he was shouting, but her voice seemed to be going on and on, he hadn't realised she talked so much.

"Look just change the subject we're supposed to be having fun aren't we, let's get to Salisbury, I think the rain is easing up."

****

Setting off for Salisbury on Friday evening, Celia had such a mixture of emotions whirling around in her head. Seb had insisted on driving despite her Dad offering.

"I won't be drinking so it's really not a problem, It's my car, my idea, and my treat."

He said childishly. He was adamant and wouldn't be moved. They all sat in the car listening to the rain drumming relentlessly on the roof, lost in their own thoughts.

Sebastian was thinking, I'll show them I know how to treat their daughter, the way her Father keeps looking at me you'd think I wasn't good enough.

Celia was tense with shoulders hunched and she had the beginning of a headache. She knew her parents had already picked up on the tension, so she tried to play it down and pretend everything was fine. She was thinking;

please let this evening go well. I know mum and dad think there's something I'm not telling them, so I hope this will change their mind, after all, the lovely Thai restaurant in Salisbury should be a treat for all of us. She leaned back into the seat and forced her shoulders against the cold leather. The rain drummed steadily on the roof and the swishing of the windscreen wipers seemed to match the rhythm of the swishing tension in her head as the pain built up relentlessly. She could smell the heavy overpowering cloying after shave that Sebastian wore and it seemed to make the pounding in her head even worse.

Hugh and Deirdre were both thinking of the conversation they had had last night in bed. They both knew their daughter very well and agreed that she was putting on a brave face probably for their benefit. It was tearing them apart to think of her being unhappy, but saying anything to her was going to be difficult without being accused of interfering.

The conversation in the car seemed stilted to Celia and she hoped against hope that the meal would be fun and the evening a relaxing and healing experience. She took a deep breath and let it out quietly in an effort to relax and stop the pain that now seemed to have settled over her right eye.

Parking in Salisbury on Friday evening wasn't easy and Mark was beginning to wonder what had possessed him to ask Julie out in the first place. She was really beginning to get on his nerves and he wished he had stuck to his original plan of going to see a film, but he had told her now that they would be going for a meal and he knew that as she wouldn't have eaten, it was too late to change his mind although his own appetite was rapidly diminishing. Walking from the car park he was irritated when she linked her arm through his. At least it had stopped raining. The air was clear and cold. Their breath was coming out in steamy clouds as they made their way to the main street which housed most of the restaurants. Julie had seen a Greek tavern and was pulling Mark's arm eagerly toward the door. Greek food wasn't Mark's favourite and this restaurant looked tired and grim. Through the dim widow he could see that there were lots of empty seats, never a good sign.

"No Julie, lets walk a bit further, there's a better choice further along here I think."

"Oh, Mark, I love Greek food and that one looked so quaint, anyway, why haven't you booked somewhere, you know it'll be difficult to get in somewhere on a Friday night without booking, I can't believe you've brought me here without making a reservation"

Mark realised how irritating he found her voice and quickly tried to think of an excuse, he knew he should have booked somewhere but supposed in his heart he was hoping the evening wasn't going to happen. They walked on together. Mark felt his mood worsening as Julie eagerly and noisily kept up her tirade of inane chatter. Out of the corner of his eye he saw across the road a restaurant with a beautiful display of oriental orchids and lilies in the window. He looked up at the name and saw that it was Thai. He loved the exquisite and spicy food of these quiet cultured people and he held his breath as he pulled Julie towards the door and pushed it open. They were immediately greeted by a dark skinned man with hands together and bowed head. He smiled at them and said softly

"Have you got a reservation?"

Mark spoke with bated breath,

"No we haven't could you find us a table for two please?"

He smiled and bowed his head respectfully to the man and was relieved when he said

"Please wait a moment, I'll check for you."

"Wow, what a beautiful place"

Julie said loudly, too loudly he thought, he liked women to be quiet and not show themselves up in public. She was right about the place though. It seemed as though they had walked into a beautiful wooded area. There were oriental trees and flowers growing at the side of still pools reflecting subtle lights, the whole effect was mystical, peaceful and very romantic, Mark thought ironically. The man spoke again.

"You are lucky; we do have one table for two please follow the young lady."

They followed a slim Thai girl beautifully dressed in a long traditional turquoise silk dress that accentuated her tiny frame. Her dark hair was wound into a tight knot at the top of her head and her dark brown eyes were looking demurely down as she led the way over a small bridge to their table next to a sparkling waterfall. Mark had to admit that it was a really beautiful place and wished he was not with Julie and tried to push the image of another slim dark woman that the beautiful Thai girl had reminded him of. He knew he was being unfair to Julie; he must at least give her a chance and make the best of the evening now that they were here.

He looked across the table at her and saw a voluptuous blonde with a low cut black top. She was wearing large gold hoops in her ears and some sort of sparkly necklace that dipped low between her breasts provocatively. He knew most of the guys back at camp envied him and would have swapped places with him like a shot.

She was talking at the top of her voice.

"I'm really not sure about this, have you seen the menu? There's so much to choose, I don't know where to start. I hope it's not too spicy, I hate hot spicy food."

They were interrupted by the wine waiter who was standing at the side of their table. He seemed to have appeared soundlessly and was smiling at them as he handed them both a wine list.

"I won't be able to have any wine as I'm driving, Julie but you go ahead, I'll stick to water."

"Oh, Mark, You choose, I'm hopeless at choosing wine but not too dry for me, and please bring me a rum and coke while we're waiting, a double,"

she said turning to the young man at the side of the table 'it's nice to let my hair down, don't often get the chance. "

"And for you sir, what would you like to drink"

"I'll just have sparkling water; will you bring a bottle please?"

Chapter 16

Sebastian pushed open the door to the restaurant and stood aside to let Celia and her Mum inside. He and Hugh followed on and Sebastian said in a loud voice to the young Thai man at the reception desk.

"The Honourable Sebastian Stratford, we have a reservation for 7.30." Other people nearby looked up and Hugh noticed the look of embarrassment on his daughters face. They were shown to their table and Sebastian said loudly

"We'd like to order some drinks while we're waiting, and please bring the wine list and menu, and a bottle of your best champagne."

The meal, ordered, Celia was beginning to feel a little more relaxed. She was glad Seb had brought them here, and was beginning to enjoy herself. She sipped a glass of champagne and settled back in her chair admiring the sights around her. She felt as though they were in a serene wood with the green of the trees and the quiet reflections in the still pools. You simply wouldn't believe you were in the middle of a busy English City and not in some lush tropical forest. Her mother's voice cut into her thoughts and she brought her mind back to the group around the table.

"Have you been here before?"

"No, we don't often go out to eat, what with Mrs Popple and Arthur's to take care of us, but I must say this is such a lovely restaurant, I'm really looking forward to the food, you know how much I love Thai."

When it arrived, there was such a wonderful aroma and the hot steam rising from the sizzling spicy dishes made them cough as the hot sauce caught in the backs of their throats. There was a large platter of different oriental delights, everything from a wondrous selection of sea food, to hot Thai green coconut curries and stir fry sizzling beef. There were also side dishes of noodles, fragrant aromatic rice and beautifully crafted flowers fashioned exquisitely from carrots and other vegetables. Deirdre Manning said

"Well, Thai people certainly know how to present food magnificently; if it tastes half as good as it looks we should have a fantastic time. What a feast, I hope we can all do it justice!"

Celia noticed Seb pouring himself a glass of champagne from the bottle left in the ice bucket at the side of the table.

"I thought you were driving?"

She spoke softly, putting her hand onto his arm,

"One glass of Champagne won't hurt, besides I'll be eating a lot, can't beat some of this hot stuff,"

He said looking at the beautiful Thai girl walking passed their table with a smirk on his face.

"Don't look so worried, Celia, I'll be fine to drive, you worry too much, relax, that's right isn't it Deirdre, tell this daughter of yours to let herself go for once, she's much too uptight, I'm always telling her to relax and enjoy."

Celia noticed her mum and dad exchange glances and she knew they felt uncomfortable. When had Seb become so arrogant, when had he changed, and why was he behaving this way in front of her parents, he was showing himself up and she took that as a reflection of his feelings for her.

She rose quietly from her seat and said,

"please excuse me I need the ladies."

Her mum also got up and they walked together over the little bridge away from the table. Inside the cloakroom, Deirdre manning asked Celia if she was ok.

"Of course, I'm fine mum relax, isn't it great all being together, I miss having you and dad near, are you enjoying yourself?"

"I'm happy if you're happy love, you know that. You are happy aren't you Celia, that's all your dad and I ever wanted for you, you would tell us if you weren't."

"Oh mum don't fuss, I'm fine, just got a bit of a headache that's all, let's get back, the food will be here soon, I don't know about you but I'm starving."

Walking back, Celia realised she wasn't sure which way they had come. The trees and flowers all seemed to look the same. She knew they had walked over a small bridge but there seemed to be two in front and she stood for a moment confused before turning to the right, striding purposely out with Deirdre close behind. She was just thinking that this was not the way back to their table when she stopped dead and Deirdre bumped into her and almost stumbled. She noticed her daughter was looking at a couple on the table in front, she herself had noticed the woman earlier, their table was near to theirs but almost hidden by the greenery but the woman had a very loud voice and seemed to be a little tipsy. The man looked startled and was getting to his feet. His voice was as quiet as his companion's was loud and he held out his hand in their direction and said softly,

"Hello Celia, what a small world"

"Mark, hello, this is my Mum, Deirdre Manning, Captain Mark Riordan"

He took a step nearer to them and held his hand out to Deirdre,

"So pleased to meet you Mrs Manning" She felt his warm firm grip and saw a tall good looking man with piercing blue eyes and short ash blonde hair,

"Captain Riordan, I'm pleased to meet you too".

Suddenly the quiet was broken by a loud voice and his female companion stumbled to her feet knocking into the table as she did so. There was a clashing of crockery and cutlery as the table rocked and Mark put his hand out to steady it.

"And I'm Julie Stewart, pleased to meet you too."

Celia looked at Julie and thought so this is the woman Gilly had told her about, she took in the long curtain of blonde hair, well developed figure and short skirt. If this was Mark's type no wonder he wasn't interested in her. They seemed very happy together, besides, it really was none of her business, and it had absolutely nothing to do with her. Deirdre Manning's eyes took in the voluptuous figure of the woman before her. She was as loud and showy as her daughter was quiet. It also seemed to her that the tall army captain was not happy with his companion. He looked uncomfortable and ill at ease. She wondered if his discomfort was because of the woman he was with, or perhaps, the woman he wasn't with? Interesting thought!

As they walked back the way they had come, Deirdre noticed the glance Celia gave back over her shoulder as they left the couple at the table. Leading the way they arrived at the table where Sebastian and Hugh were sitting, and she wondered who this Captain Riordan was and why he seemed to have such an effect on her daughter. Now wasn't the time to talk about it, she would leave it until later and try to get Celia on her own. She hadn't seen that look in her daughter's eyes for some time.

Mark realised how much he hated this evening. Julie had had a lot to drink and was getting louder by the minute. Seeing her and Celia together really brought it home to him that he and Julie had absolutely nothing in common and she really wasn't his type He longed for the peace and quiet of his own room and luxury of time to think about having Celia in his arms and in his bed, although he realised that she was far out of his reach and completely unattainable, but that didn't stop his mind and body reacting every time he saw her or thought about her.

Driving through the dark, the atmosphere in Sebastian's car was tense, the quiet broken only by the swishing of tyres on wet roads and the repetitive thud of windscreen wipers. As he rounded a bend in the road the car swerved violently to the left and Celia in the front passenger seat was thrown against him.

"Hey darling can't you wait until we get home?"

Reaching out and wrapping his arm around Celia causing the car to swerve even more. She pushed herself away violently and was glad of the lack of light as she felt the heat travel quickly from her chest to her neck and face. Her Dad's voice from the darkened recess of the back seat only served to increase her feeling of humiliation.

"You should have let me drive Sebastian; I haven't had anything to drink. If you carry on like this you'll get us all killed. Why don't you stop the car and let me take over?"

"Don't be such an old woman Hugh, I'm not drunk, it takes more than two glasses of champers to tip me over the limit."

Celia felt her dad's hand warm against her shoulder and he gave her a conspiratorial squeeze. And she reached up her own hand and covered it letting the warmth and closeness of him reassure her.

The rest of the journey passed quietly and uneventfully. She was relieved to see the lights of the old house, as they pulled into the drive from the gate. Her mum linked arms with her as they walked in through the doorway as Arthurs smiled a greeting.

"There's fresh coffee, in the kitchen, go on through and I'll bring it through to the sitting room"

"Thank you that'll be lovely"

Celia smiled into his face noticing how old and tired he looked.

"Just put it down and then get yourself off to bed. You must be worn out, we can manage."

The four of them sat near to the flickering coal fire, a log fell off and rolled with a crack into the hearth, making them all jump. Celia kicked off her shoes and slowly massaged her toes as she sipped the scalding coffee.

"That's better; I've been dying to do that all evening"

Getting to his feet Sebastian moved to the bureau in the corner and began to pour amber coloured liquid into a heavy cut glass tumbler.

"Whisky Hugh?"

"Not for me thank you it always keeps me awake."

"Deirdre, Celia, anything for you?"

They spoke as one

"No thanks"

Deirdre shot her husband a look and she could see his own worry for their daughter reflected in her eyes. Celia was devastated at the way he was behaving. What about the promise he made to her about not drinking, and it was all so much worse in front of her parents. How was she going to keep her resolution to make this marriage work if he broke his side of the bargain?

Deirdre was very tired and desperately wanted to go to bed, but she also needed the reassurance from her daughter that she was going to be alright. What a ludicrous situation to have to worry about your daughter with her own husband. The memory of the army captain they had seen at the restaurant earlier flashed into her mind. Why had Celia seemed so affected by him? What on earth was happening here, something definitely is not right and she was determined to get to the bottom of it before they left tomorrow for London.

Later as she and Hugh were lying together in the peace of one of the guest bedrooms, she voiced her concerns to him. Talking quietly they agreed to try and talk to Celia before leaving tomorrow morning. It was a long time before they fell asleep, both picturing the worried look on their daughter's face before they had come up to their room.

To Celia's relief Sebastian had gone ahead to bed. She entered their room and was pleased to see that he was already asleep and snoring loudly. She really would have liked to sleep in one of the guest bedrooms but the fact that her parents were nearby was a deterrent. She undressed quietly, carefully hanging her clothes in her wardrobe before going to her bathroom to cleanse her face and brush her teeth. She pulled a brush through her dark hair and found herself thinking of the bright blonde hair of the woman she had seen with Mark at the restaurant earlier. He obviously preferred the blonde voluptuous type. Her hands moved down over her firm breasts to the slim hips, and down lightly caressing the inside of her thighs. She felt her body respond and longed for the tenderness and complete satisfaction from passionate love making. She had had that once with Seb, surely it was possible to have it again, or was she really fooling herself? She felt the bitterness rise like bile into her mouth until she could almost taste it. Why had her life come to this? What had she ever done to deserve this? She felt angry at the impossible situation. There appeared to be no way out. She wanted to lash out and scream and shout, but kept her feelings inside not wanting to wake her sleeping husband.

Before she got into bed, she stood for a moment looking out at the night sky. The rain had finally stopped, and there was a silver crescent of new moon in a starry sky. The clouds were rushing across making the moon dip in and out of sight. Making a huge effort to push all thoughts and worries out of her mind she slipped cautiously into her side of the bed taking care not to touch the sleeping form of her husband, and turning on her side away from him, she reached her hand up and under her pillow and settled down to sleep.

Chapter 17

Julie's voice was grating on Mark's nerves. It hadn't stopped since they got into the car for the journey back to camp. He reached out and switched on the radio and the car was immediately filled with music from a late night local radio station. The husky voice of Van Morrison filled the car. He was singing

"Have I told you lately that I love you?"

Mark's mind immediately conjured up the picture of Celia. He imagined she was in the car next to him and he could almost smell her perfume. He had noticed it earlier in the restaurant. He remembered how beautiful and elegant she looked in a floaty soft green dress made of some silky material that clung to her slim breasts and hips. He felt aroused just thinking about her.

Julie moved closer and put her hand on Mark's thigh. Immediately he was brought back to the present and he moved away from the contact and said, trying to keep his voice light

"Julie, let me concentrate on the road, it's a horrible night and the roads are slippery with all this rain"

The rest of the journey passed quietly as Mark realised with relief that Julie had fallen asleep, her head lolling forward and jerking back violently as she felt it touch her chest. As he pulled the car in through the gate he pressed the button to unwind the car window and spoke to the guard on duty as he showed his pass. They were waved through and as he manoeuvred to park the car Julie stirred beside him and woke up. She seemed disorientated for a moment and then realising where she was said.

"Sorry, Mark must have fallen asleep, but I'm awake now"

She moved nearer to Mark and put her hand onto his crotch. She moved her other hand up to the back of his head and pulling it down put her open mouth to his lips. Mark, taken by surprise, sat still for a moment before removing Julie's hand quietly, but firmly away from his trousers. He felt a flush spread up into his face and was glad of the darkness

"Julie, It's late and we're both tired, come on its time you were in bed"

"Oh Mark, I thought you'd never ask"

She was opening the passenger door and her short skirt had risen up to reveal a large expanse of shapely thigh.

"No Julie, your own bed, I'm all in, and as I said it's late"

As they walked from the car he leaned down to kiss her lightly on the cheek, carefully avoiding her mouth as she skilfully turned her head. He spoke more firmly

"Thanks for a nice evening, I'll see you tomorrow, goodnight."

Walking quickly away, he felt her eyes burning a hole in his back, and breathing a sigh of relief he walked toward his room.

****

The smell of bacon greeted Celia as she walked into the dining room and kissed her father warmly on the cheek.

"Morning, dad, did you sleep well?"

"Yes love, he lied to his daughter"

he and Deirdre had in fact had a very restless night as they both had her happiness on their mind.

"Your mum will be down shortly, is Sebastian joining us for breakfast?"

"No he asked me to apologise and say goodbye, he had an early meeting with his estate manager, that's the trouble with running a large estate, your time is never your own,"

They both turned and smiled at Deirdre as she walked into the dining room.

Breakfast progressed and they were all thinking how relaxed they all were without the presence of Sebastian. Hugh and Deirdre reflected on the heavily ornate dining room. They had talked about how different their daughter's home was now, compared to the small, beautifully tranquil Chiswick flat. She had been so happy there and this place was so vastly different. They never really felt comfortable themselves. The place was dark, gloomy and the presence of servants was alien to them. They knew it had potential to be beautiful with its grandeur and high ceilings, but the décor was so gloomy and directly opposite of their daughter's taste. Hugh reached out a hand affectionately to his daughter and said

"Your Mum and I are a bit worried about you, my dear, it seems as though Sebastian is drinking a lot, are you sure everything is well, you know you can talk to us, don't you"

He noticed the two spots of bright colour on his daughters pale cheeks as she made an attempt to smile, which didn't quite come off.

"I'm sorry about that, he's just got a lot on his mind with the Estate and everything, I promise you I'm fine, please don't worry about me"

"I'm not totally convinced, but if you're sure you're alright, you would tell us wouldn't you?"

"Of course I would, now let's change the subject, what time are you setting off?"

Up in the guest bedroom, Hugh and Deirdre Manning were packing a small overnight bag, Deirdre looked troubled as she put the last item in and pulled the zip closed. Her Husband came up behind her and putting his arms around her waist, nuzzled into her neck and said

"What do you think? Is she hiding something, I'm still not convinced, she never was any good at keeping secrets was she?"

"No but if she won't tell us what's on her mind I don't see what else we can do, we can't force her to open up to us, we only seem to be putting her under even more strain and that's the last thing she needs."

"Yes, you're right, as long as she knows she can talk to us and that we'll always be here for her no matter what".

At the bottom of the stairs Celia looked up and forced a smile as her parents made their way down. She had been looking at the parquet tiled floor and could still picture the horrors Seb had subjected her to a few short weeks ago.

"Arthurs will put you bag in your car, is there anything you've forgotten, well it doesn't matter if you have, you could always stop off on your way home."

It was later the same day and Celia was walking slowly back to the House. Skip was running ahead and she was thinking about the events of the last couple of days. There was a brisk breeze blowing the clouds across a sky heavy with unshed rain, and she felt how it reflected her own feelings. She felt the sharp needle pricks burning the back of her eyes that always signalled tears. Her walk had taken her to Gilly's house; it often seemed that her feet would just take her there without any conscious effort on her part.

Gilly had been engrossed in a major batch of baking and was up to her elbows in flour as she stood next to her small daughter who was standing on a chair, almost completely covered by a large white apron. Celia looked on in envy as Mother and child worked side by side in harmony.

"You both look cosy"

she said as Jake let her into the kitchen. He was playing cowboys and Indians with a school friend and there was a dark feather tucked into a band in his hair The spine stood tall and proud in dark contrast to the small boy's fair shining hair.

"I don't know about cosy, messy certainly, we're almost through, have a seat and then I'll make some coffee."

"It's ok, I'll do it"

Celia said making herself at home

"Great, I'll be ready for a cup by the time we clear this lot up, you know where everything is."

They sat in the warmth of the bright kitchen sipping the coffee and Gilly placed a plate of shortbread biscuits still warm from the oven.

"So, how are your mum and dad, did you have , a good time at the restaurant last night, I hear it's a fantastic place, Ralph keeps promising to take me, perhaps we can all go sometime?"

She noticed the thoughtful look on her friend's face, and waited patiently for her to speak.

"The restaurant is really beautiful and the food is out of this world, we saw Mark with his girlfriend they looked very cosy together"

"Oh, yes, they seemed close when we saw them the other week."

"She's quite a looker isn't she" Celia said,

"Well, if you like that sort, Ralph thought she was quite tarty, and I thought he could have done better than that, personally."

"Did you and Sebastian get an invitation to the officers Ball for May the 31st? I believe it's to celebrate the summer solstice."

"I think I saw an invitation, but I don't think Seb's very keen"

"Oh, Cee, say you'll come, I really don't want to go without you, it'll be fun. We haven't been able to get all dressed up for ages."

"Well, I'm not promising, but I'll talk to him about it, when did you say it was again?"

As Gilly set about cleaning the detritus of baking in her kitchen, she winced as her right hand came into contact with the handle of a pan that was still hot. She put her hand to her mouth to soften the pain cursing herself for being so careless. Her thoughts turned to her friend. She didn't look very happy these days. Perhaps it would be better to give up on trying rescuing her marriage if it was making her this unhappy. The Ball did sound like fun, but she wondered if Ralph would be keen to spend another evening with Sebastian. She also wondered what was happening about the pregnancy issue. Celia hadn't mentioned it for ages, and she didn't want to upset her friend by bringing it up again, however good a friend she was.

The same thought was in Celia's mind as she approached her home and saw her husband's car in the drive. The subject of her not having conceived seemed to have been off the agenda lately. She didn't want to bring it up and evoke another one of his rages, but seeing Gilly with Alice and Jake made her realise how empty her own life was, and how much she longed for a child. Surely it was worth trying to make their marriage work if she could have the son or daughter she had always longed for.

Sebastian was on the telephone in his study. In his hand was a long silver paper knife that he was playing with. The blade glinted in the light from the lamp on his desk. As she put her head around the door, he raised his hand and smiled. She went into the lounge and walked to the side table and began fiddling with a large vase of white lilies, pulling a long stem out and moving it to another position until she stepped back to look with satisfaction on the change she had made, and breathed in the strong familiar scent. At least she could still have her favourite white flowers, even if she couldn't have the pale and beautiful décor she preferred.

She heard his footsteps echoing on the wooden floor of the hallway and turned to face him. Before she had a chance to speak he said

"Celia, I'm sorry about last night, I hope your mum and dad didn't think too badly of me. I promised you I was going to change and I let you down. I've called your Dad on the mobile to say how sorry I am and to apologise for not being here this morning when they left. Please say you'll forgive me,"

Before she had a chance to speak he said,

"I know I've said it before but this time I promise you I mean it. You are the most important thing in my life; I simply can't imagine my life without you. I love you so much, please say you'll give me another chance."

He walked towards her and put his arms out in a gesture of such helplessness that she felt sorry for him and took a step forward into his outstretched arms and rested her head on his chest .

"This has to be the last time Seb, I'm really tired of all this, and can't take much more."

Her thoughts went back to the time only a few short months ago when they had been so close. She felt again the urgency of his mouth on hers and felt the eager anticipation she had felt that day in the meadow next to the lake at the back of the House. The joy they had shared that day had been short lived and she wondered again, where and how everything had gone wrong. Do you promise to make an effort and stop drinking?"

"I promise, you are more important to me than all the whisky in Scotland, and I'm prepared to do anything to keep you."

She stood in the circle of his arms and decided to make a real effort to make things work. Who knows I might get pregnant if I relax more, ad then all our problems will be over, she thought to herself and lifting her face she smiled up at her husband.

Later over dinner the invitation to the officer's May ball came up.

"Do you really want to go Celia, I can't really say it's my thing, but I suppose if you really want to I could make the effort."

Celia felt like telling him to get lost but the idea of a ball and the chance to get all dressed up and an evening with Gilly and Ralph did have some appeal.

"Yes, it would be fun, I think. I can't go on my own Seb, so let's make the effort, shall we?"

Seeing the range of emotions flitting across his wife's face, Sebastian realised he was up against it and making a quick decision said,

"Why don't you go up to London for a few days and buy yourself a new dress. You could stay with your brother, I'm sure he'd love to see you".

Celia thought how much he was trying to make amends for his recent behaviour, and it had been a long time since she had seen her brother Alistair, but he sounded so smug and patronising that she was tempted to turn the offer down. Her longing to see her brother got the better of her and she said with a little difficulty

"Thank you, that's a good idea, I'll call him later to make arrangements".

CHAPTER 18

As Mark pulled into the car park at the Nags' Head, he noticed Celia's BMW was nowhere to be seen and wondered for a heart stopping moment if she wasn't going to be here after all. The evenings had begun to draw out and there were a few primroses, their pale faces seemed to be looking up at him. They always reminded him of his mum and he thought again of the neat garden she took such pride in all those miles away in Yorkshire. Stooping, he entered the narrow old doorway of the Nag's Head feeling the warmth, and realised he was nervous. He couldn't decide if it was from the thought of seeing Celia again, or the prospect of speaking to a roomful of women. Whatever the reason he wished he was anywhere but here. He decided to have a drink to steady his nerves. As usual he was early. The barman recognised him and said in a friendly voice,

"it's on the house; you'll probably need it if you're going to throw yourself on the mercy of a roomful of strange women."

"I hope they're not that strange, I certainly could do with this, thanks".

He lifted the gin and tonic to his lips, the bubbly fizzing sound immediately beginning to relax him and realised how dry his throat was.

"I'd better take some water up with me, I think I'm going to need it"

"Don't worry about that Celia has already taken some up, she asked me to send you straight up when you arrived, it's ok to take your drink up" he added noting the hesitation registering on Mark's face.

He walked up the narrow stairs realising how much smaller people must have been in the fourteenth century. His thoughts went back over the last week. He had cowardly tried to avoid Julie until she had eventually confronted him and accused him of avoiding her.

"I've just been busy"

He started to say then had a change of heart.

"Well to be honest Julie, I don't think it's a good idea to see you again, it's my fault,"

He spoke quickly as she started to protest,

"no really, Julie, it's nothing personal, I'm just not ready for a relationship, but we can still be friends can't we?"

"Look Mark, I know I was out of order the other night, put it down to having too much to drink, I really like you, could we try again, please?"

He thought now of the pleading look in her eyes and felt really bad about her but he couldn't pretend anymore. He knew Celia was definitely off limits but he couldn't substitute her with someone else, and Julie just wasn't his type.

Just as he was thinking about Celia she was there in front of him, standing in the open doorway. Did he imagine it, or did she also look nervous? He thought again how vulnerable she looked. Her eyes a piercing green in her pale face. He was acutely aware of the perfume he had come to recognise as hers. Their eyes met and he tried to imagine what she was thinking, but her face gave little away.

"Mark, thanks for getting here early we're all looking forward to your talk, I'm sure it's going to be very interesting. I hope you're ready, as some of our ladies may give you a hard time; they are very anti the army presence hereabout. I think you are brave to take up my challenge."

Mark couldn't help thinking there was not a lot he wouldn't do for Celia, but kept his thoughts to himself as he smilingly said

"I'm sure I'll cope, lead the way."

As usual when speaking in public, he noticed that his nerves settled down after the first ten minutes or so. He knew his subject very well and was passionate about the Army. He felt the mood change in the room as even the most difficult of the women were won over by his charm and the confidence with which he put the Army's side.

There had been one or two questions at the end which he had handled well, nevertheless he was relieved to sit down at the end of his allotted hour, and he felt his body begin to relax as he sank into the chair and listened to the applause as Celia asked the group to show their appreciation in the usual way. The group was dispersing when she said to Mark

"I've asked John to send up some coffee, you will stay, won't you, I, really like to say thank you for a very informative and entertaining evening. I thought you handled them very well, even old Mrs Finnegan was won over and she can be difficult, thank you Mark."

Left alone with him, Celia was beginning to wonder if she had done the right thing. She had expected Gilly to stay but her friend had declined, feigning baby sitter problems, and she now faced Mark alone and tried to stop her hand shaking as she poured the coffee. To her annoyance, Gilly had also asked Mark if he would mind dropping Celia at home as they had travelled in her car.

"Captain Riordan, will give you a lift, I'm sure he won't mind"

Celia had tried to protest and was determined to have a go at Gilly later but it had been taken out of her hands as Mark had assured them both that it was no trouble and he'd be happy to oblige. The last thing she had expected or wanted was to be left alone with him. The last time they had been alone was that time when she had fallen off her horse and look what had happened then. She felt the heat rising in her face and hastily pushed the feeling of Mark's warm lips on hers out of her mind.

Driving through the dark country lane, Gilly was remembering the look of panic on her friend's face and wondered if she'd done the right thing. The idea had only come to her as she watched Celia with the Army Captain. She would have had to be deaf dumb and blind not to have picked up on the electricity between them. Was it a good idea to make Celia face her feelings? Was she risking their friendship? She put her foot down and drove on through the darkness noticing a sudden beam of light as a silvery crescent of the moon came out from behind a dark cloud.

Half an hour later, Mark's car was following the same route through the same dark lanes. He was acutely aware of the woman sitting next to him.

"Mark, I think it's better if you drop me outside the main driveway of my home, my husband is quite jealous for no reason, and it'll be easier for me."

He answered

"I don't like the idea of you having to walk on your own, are you sure?"

Celia could feel the warmth of his body so close to hers and was watching his hands on the steering wheel. She saw how strong his hands were and what long fingers he had. She thought about his hands on her body, touching her and arousing her, and struggled to put the mental image of their entwined bodies out of her mind.

Mark was finding it took every ounce of his concentration to just keep the car on track in the narrow lanes. His mind was conjuring up pictures of Celia naked and in his arms. His whole body was aching for her. He fought to keep his mind on the driving.

"How did you enjoy the restaurant the other night, do you like Thai food?"

He asked, desperately trying to steer his mind to more mundane things.

"We thought the whole place was fantastic. I really love the way it's like being in a garden, such a great atmosphere, what did you and your girlfriend think?"

As Mark digested the fact that she thought Julie was his girlfriend, he opened his mouth to speak and got a frog in his throat and began to cough violently. Steering the car to the side of the road he switched off the ignition and gasped for air. Celia began thumping him hard on the back and gradually the spluttering stopped and he took a deep breath.

"Sorry about that, don't know what happened,"

Leaning forward he took a bottle of water from the dashboard. He raised it to his lips and swallowed greedily. He realised that her hand was still on his shoulder and was afraid to move in case she took it away.

Sitting very still he said,

"Julie is not my girlfriend, I don't have one, she's just a fellow officer,"

Celia suddenly realised that her hand was still on Mark's shoulder and she moved as if to withdraw it. He caught her hand in both his own and looked into her eyes. They seemed so full of sorrow he brought her hand to his lips and bringing his head down, kissed her fingers gently one by one, all the while gazing into her eyes. Celia felt as though she had been stuck dumb, but her heart was racing and beating so loudly that she thought Mark would probably be able to hear it. She lifted her face to his and suddenly she was in his arms with her mouth opening greedily to explore his. They both felt their passion mount. She realised that she had been pretending that she could really ever feel anything for Seb again and Mark realised that Julie was nothing to him as he felt his body respond to the fragile, beautiful woman in his arms. Celia was aware that the passion she had longed for was there, within her grasp and felt her body respond, wanting Mark suddenly so badly. Breathing heavily he suddenly pulled away with his arms still holding her to his own thudding heart. "Celia I've wanted to do that ever since the first time I saw you, but not like this. I want to make love to you properly, not cooped up on the front seat of a car."

"Oh, Mark, what are we going to do, you know I'm married and he'd kill you and me if he ever found out"

' 'Are you afraid of him, I sensed something that day when you slipped off your horse, if I thought he was hurting you I'd kill him for you."

Celia wanted desperately to unburden herself but wasn't sure how Mark would react. Now was neither the time nor the place.

" I'm going up to London soon to stay with my brother for a few days, would you be able to get away"

"It will depend on the date, call me tomorrow and let me know more details and I'll move heaven and earth to make it possible".

He clung to her and spoke into her hair

"I don't want you to go, but I know you must. Are you sure you'll be alright walking on your own?"

"Just drive a little way along here and I'll only have to walk up to the house".

She said as she took deep breaths in an attempt to calm herself and stop her heart racing.

Looking over her shoulder as she walked the short way from the gate, Celia could just make out Mark's car parked in the shadows. She realised he was waiting to see her safely inside and wished she was still sitting in the warmth and safety of his arms. Sebastian was waiting for her inside and for once seemed to be genuinely interested in the evening's events. She outlined briefly and as dispassionately as possible, how interesting the talk had been.

"I'll be interested to meet this Captain, I'm sure he'll be at this army ball, you'll have to introduce me."

Later in bed, when he reached out his arm to her she felt panic rise and said,

"Seb I'm really tired".

She held her breath as he seemed to accept this and she settled down to sleep luxuriating in the ability to think of Mark's firm muscular body next to her and not her husband's overweight one.

Chapter 19

Sebastian was putting off ringing the specialist for the results of his sperm test. He had insisted that he was not to be contacted, and he was sure that they would respect his decision. He also knew that he must face up to it sooner or later, but at the moment, later suited him fine, much later.

"Hi Cee, it was lovely to hear your voice on the machine earlier, it seems ages since we talked, Enzo was only asking about you this week after we saw mum and dad when they came up for the opera."

It was the following day and Celia was sitting in the comfort of one of the large armchairs in the lounge. There was a fire burning brightly in the hearth and she was luxuriating in deep thoughts of Mark and what it would be like to be making love with him. Her brother didn't mention how concerned his parents had been about Celia. They were sure all was not right and had talked long into the night wondering how best to get to the bottom of things.

"Ali, I was wondering If I can come up and stay with you and Enzo for a few days, I want to do some shopping in town, besides you're right, it is ages since we saw each other, I've really missed our chats."

They talked for a while and made arrangements for the following weekend.

As Celia put the phone down, she thought with affection of her brother. Alistair was two years older than Celia and they had always been close. She had been the first person he had come out to but Celia had had her suspicions for some time, noticing how uncomfortable he was when the subject of girlfriends came up. He had always had a strong feminine side which made him such a nice man in her eyes and she had always found it easy to share things and be able to talk to him about everything. She was very pleased when Seb had suggested a visit and wondered why she hadn't thought about it herself. It would be lovely to be able to talk to him and Enzo.

Her brother's partner was Italian and worked as a house doctor in another London hospital. They had met when they were medical students and been together ever since. She knew that their life wasn't always easy as there were still many narrow minded people who would be quick to attack the intimacy they shared. Celia loved spending time with them, it was like having two brothers and she loved them both dearly.

She was alone, as Sebastian was out around the estate, and she picked up her mobile and dialled Mark's number with hands that wouldn't stop shaking. It was lunchtime and she knew he should be able to speak to her. After a few rings she heard his voice

"Captain Riordan speaking"

And heard her own voice shakily say,

"Hello Mark, it's Celia can you talk?"

There was a lot of background noise and he said,

"Just a moment, I'm in the mess I'll go outside"

Listening to the hub of voices and the clattering of crockery she tried to picture him and remembered how fantastic he looked in his uniform. There was the sound of a door being opened and the background noise was suddenly quieter. She heard a bird singing sweetly and then Mark's voice saying

"Sorry about that, I'm outside now and can talk to you, I've been waiting to hear your voice all day, are you OK?"

"Yes, I'm fine, I'm ringing to tell you I've arranged to be in London this weekend, I'll be catching the train on Friday and my brother will meet me at the other end, can you get away?"

"I'm working on it, I'm hoping to be able to drive up on Saturday if all goes to plan, how can I let you know?"

She gave him her mobile number and her brother's home number and said

"I'll be free on Saturday evening, perhaps we can meet up."

"Try and stop me, I can't wait, I'll ring you tomorrow to confirm, will that be OK?"

"I'll call you Mark, just to be on the safe side, when's the best time?"

As she ended the call she thought about what she had done. There was no going back now, she couldn't deny the excitement she felt at the prospect of seeing Mark away from here and with no one watching them, and she sensed he felt the same. She ran her tongue over her lips and felt a stirring in her body at the thought of the coming weekend. How was she going to be able to wait, it was only Thursday, two whole days away. She would sort out what clothes to take and ask Gilly to come over this afternoon for a chat. She felt she would burst if she didn't tell someone.

The noise of the train only seemed to add to Celia's feeling of excitement. She lay back with her head resting on the cushioned head rest of the seat and feeling guilty, kicked off her shoes and allowed herself the luxury of putting her stockined feet on the seat in front of her. She had never lost her excitement for trains and was pleased she had decided not to drive. The car was just a nuisance in London anyway. The journey seemed to drag, almost as though it was in slow motion. She made an effort to concentrate on the landscape rushing passed the window. The fields and trees flashed by and she looked with curiosity into the occasional glimpse into other people's lives when the train passed through areas that backed onto houses and gardens. A woman was hanging out washing and a large white sheet had blown back into her face. The comical glimpse made Celia smile and realise how different her life was, no mundane laundry tasks for her. She had to admit, there were definite advantages to her life with Seb. In another garden, two or three small children ran around a tiny plot of grass. Their shouts could only be imagined, as the noise of the train drowned out their cries of delight or panic, what exactly was going on was difficult to tell. A bit like watching a film without any sound, she thought. As the train neared London, she drained the last drops from a cold glass of her favourite Chablis and looked forward eagerly to seeing her brother and Enzo again.

Twenty minutes later, alighting from the carriage she scanned the people on the station eagerly looking for her brother's familiar face. She was suddenly engulfed in a bear hug, and she looked up into the dark good looks of her brother's partner. His deep hazel eyes looked kindly into Celia's own and he said.

"There you are at last; I thought you were never going to get here";

"I'm not late am I?"

She said in a muffled voice into the warmth of his shoulder

"No, it's just me being impatient as usual, you know how I can never wait for anything I want"

He smiled broadly at Celia and winked playfully at her as he took the handle of her suitcase and linking his arm through hers steered a path skilfully through the busy platform pulling it behind him.

"Are you thinking of moving in, you seem to have brought a big enough bag for a month, I don't know about a weekend".

"Stop teasing me, I want to have fun and forget all my problems".

He stopped and looked at Celia.

"You shouldn't have any problems my girl, I can see I'm going to have to have words with you, let's get outside and call a cab, you can tell me all about it."

Later, sitting in their flat waiting for her brother to arrive, Enzo explained that he had been delayed at the hospital but would be here soon and that they had planned a celebratory meal out this evening

"What you need my girl is some celebration and tlc and I know two guys who are queuing up to give that to you".

Celia was thinking how great it was to be here, she was beginning to feel very relaxed and the knowledge that she could be completely honest with both of them and not have to pretend or cover up. He had opened a bottle of Chablis, knowing it to be her favourite; it was icy cold and she knew that he must have put it into the Fridge before he left to collect her from the station. As usual, he was very kind and considerate always making Celia feel very special.

Chapter 20

She looked out of the window at the bustling noise and excitement that was London. The inside of their flat was as calm as the outside was busy. It was small, but very light as there was a very large window taking up almost the whole of one wall which was hung with pale creamy voile draped provocatively over a beautiful silvery café pole. The walls were plain, off white with a few bright modern paintings. A soft rug in deep yellow and oranges was on the floor which was pale beech wood. There were two cream leather sofas adorned with stylish yellow and bright orange cushions, and the room was set off with glass tables, large and small. In the centre of the larger table was a beautiful arrangement of creamy, long stemmed yellow roses. The whole effect was a calm restful and beautiful room that Celia was able to relax totally in. The flat was near Kensington High Street Enzo was able to walk to the hospital for his job there every day or evening, depending on his shifts, and she knew they both loved the close knit village atmosphere that was typical of living in Kensington. It made her realise how quiet her own life was and that she had missed the pace of London life more than she realised.

"So my precious, what's on your mind, tell Enzo all about it"

She looked over at him and saw such kindness in his eyes that she immediately felt she could unburden herself, and trust this lovely man. She thought about her brother and his imminent arrival and said

"let's wait until Ali gets here, and then I promise I'll tell you both. It'll be a relief to talk about it or I think I'm going to go mad."

Half an hour later, they were all three seated in the comfortable cream leather sofas, drinking cold Chablis and Celia was beginning to feel almost light headed with a combination of the wine, the comfort and the sheer contentment of being with people that she was able to trust implicitly. She and Ali had flung themselves into each other's arms as soon as he had arrived from the hospital and after a quick shower had asked Celia to tell them what was on her mind.

"Celie, I know you too well not to know that something's wrong so come on tell Ali what's making you so unhappy"

Reverting to the familiar childhood names they had always had for each other, and even that made Celia feel comfortable and relaxed. She hesitated at first but once she began to talk, her word tumbling out in a rush and all her pent up feelings and pain came pouring out. She told them of her frustration and disappointment at not having conceived, of the humiliation of the tests at Harley street and finally with bowed head, the terror of Seb's violent attacks. She raised her eyes and watched their faces as both men sat opposite her with their hands resting on each other's knees. She noticed with a tinge of envy, their closeness and obvious intimacy.

For a long moment, no one spoke and then she was almost suffocated, and felt that all the air was being squeezed out of her as she was enveloped in two pairs of arms.

"You poor girl, you must leave him; you shouldn't have to put up with that from anyone, least of all from your own husband. What I don't understand is why you went for those tests when he hadn't had a sperm test. That should always be the first step, and is relatively simple, didn't you suggest it?"

He stopped, seeing the look on his sister's face and said,

"Stupid of me, you obviously had no choice did you? come on let's talk about this later, we're taking you to our favourite restaurant you look as though you could do with feeding up, there's nothing of you, you're all skin and bone."

As Celia stood under the shower with the needles of hot water washing over her, she felt more relaxed and at peace than she had for some time. She was looking forward to the evening and there was a feeling of excitement at the pit of her stomach at the prospect of seeing Mark tomorrow. They had spoken on Friday morning. She had called him as arranged and she was nervous at the thought of being overheard by Seb who was waiting to drive her to the station. He sounded excited as he gave her the name of the Hotel he was staying in, and asked her to meet him in Covent Garden on Saturday evening. She had wondered if Seb would be able to tell just by looking at her what was in her mind, but she knew that was just her guilt.

Friday evening in Kensington was nothing like Friday evening in Stratford St Peter. As they walked the short distance from the flat to the restaurant, Celia lingered, looking in the windows of the many different shops and café bars. People were jostling shoulder to shoulder on pavements and the busy road. The air was filled with the noise of traffic and the hum of busy London streets. A newsvendor's voice managed to rise above the general hub, his cries of

"Standard, Standard, get yer Evening Standard ere"

Added to the symphony that was a Friday evening in Kensington. Ahead of them just out of sight was the Albert Hall and Kensington Palace that made Celia think sadly of the princess of Wales. The whole effect rubbed off on

Celia and made her feel excited at the prospect of the evening and weekend ahead. Thinking suddenly of Mark, she felt a fluttering in her stomach that she knew it was more than hunger for the meal they were about to enjoy. The restaurant was lively, and busy. They were shown to their table by a dark Italian waiter. Do you two know *everyone* she said as she was introduced to what seemed like dozens of people who stopped at their table?

"This is my beautiful sister Celia Stratford."

Alistair said.

"Thanks for this you two,"

She said with her arm resting affectionately along the back of her brother's chair,

"it's just what the doctors ordered"

They all laughed.

Later, as they walked the short distance back to the flat, they were interrupted by the sound of a mobile phone ringing, and by the time Celia realised it was coming from the depth of her handbag, it had stopped. She pressed the button and saw Mark's name on the screen for missed call and she wanted to weep with frustration. It suddenly rang again and she listened to Mark's voice in a message telling her that he couldn't wait to see her tomorrow.

The comfort of the cream leather sofa was proving to be soporific to Celia and she suddenly realised just how tired she was.

"Hey, come on Celie, you look comfortable there, are you going to fall asleep on us?"

The sound of her brother's voice made her jump and she pulled herself up straight and blinked at him,

"Sorry, Ali, I feel so relaxed here, I feel like I'm going to drop off, oh, thanks"

She said reaching out for the mug of tea that he held out to her.

"Don't worry. I'll put it here for you"

he reached out and placed it on a small glass topped table that was to Celia's right. She looked contentedly around the room noticing the smart comfortable decor.

"You two have absolutely no idea how good it is to be here, it's so peaceful and relaxing"

"What about that grand old house you live in"

Enzo said as he perched on the arm of the sofa she was sitting on,

"That must be a great place to live, Sebastian must be worth a bob or two"

"Money isn't everything, I still miss my flat in Chiswick, and sometimes I wonder why I ever left it."

Her brother exchanged a conspiratorial look with his partner over her head and Enzo walked into the kitchen and they could hear the clatter of china as he started to put things into the dishwasher. Alistair crouched down low in front of his sister and placing his hand on her knees he spoke softly whilst looking into her eyes which he noticed were full of sorrow and unshed tears.

"What is it love, come on you can tell me, and I may be able to help. Is there more than what you were telling us earlier, I can't believe anything could be worse than what you told us he was doing to you, I'll kill him if I ever get my hands on him."

She looked at this handsome, caring brother of hers and thanked God he was part of her life.

"I really don't know what I've ever done to deserve you"

She was stalling for time and weighing up in her mind whether to tell them about Mark or not. She had been honest about how Seb was with her, but she wasn't even sure how she felt about Mark, so how could she explain it to someone else?

Her thoughts were interrupted by the sound of a phone ringing. Enzo picked it up and they all heard him say,

"Certainly, may I ask who's calling?"

He handed the phone to Celia and said,

"Someone called Mark asking for you"

Celia felt her heart racing and knew she was blushing as she took it from him and walked quickly into the empty kitchen.

Alistair and Enzo sat side by side on the sofa and spoke softly to each other.

"So that's what she wasn't telling us, thank goodness she's got something good in her life, did you see how her eyes lit up when you said it was Mark?"

Phone in hand, she walked back into the lounge and they both noticed a change in her. She seemed more relaxed and her face had taken on a glow that wasn't there before.

"So tell all"

Her brother said smiling,

"who's this Mark that has put the colour back into your cheek's, you look like a different person from ten minutes ago"

She hesitated. It wasn't that she didn't trust them, but she was having difficulty with her own feelings of guilt. She knew she hadn't really done anything yet to feel guilty about, yet.......the yet was a burning issue in her heart and mind and the strong feeling of anticipation was overwhelming. As she sank back down onto the sofa, she surprised herself by asking for a drink.

"I'd love another glass of wine, is that OK?"

"For you my sweet, anything."

Enzo was on his feet and walked into the kitchen leaving Celia and Alistair facing each other across the glass table.

"Come on Celie, get it off your chest, I know you want to tell me something, you always have to talk when something's bothering you, and you know you'll feel better when you've told me."

She knew he was right, it wasn't in her nature to be secretive and she started to talk, her words coming out in a rush.

"I've met someone and I fancy him and I already feel guilty although we haven't done anything yet but I'm supposed to be meeting him tomorrow here in London and I don't know whether I'm doing the right thing and...."

She broke off as her brother held his hand up and smilingly said

"Hey wait a minute, stop, you're wearing me out just listening to you."

She took a sip of the wine Enzo had handed her and felt light headed. She began to talk more slowly, explaining to them both her excitement at the prospect of meeting Mark tomorrow, but how guilty she felt at the thought of cheating on her husband.

"It's not that I want to sleep with someone else, it's just that I really fancy the pants off Mark and will always wonder what would have happened if I don't go and meet him, do you think I'm crazy, should I go and meet him or make an excuse and stay here with you two?"

They both smiled at each other

"I thing you already know the answer to that, don't you. You've simply got to put your feelings to the test, otherwise you'll always be wondering what might have been."

She nodded slowly, as a picture of her Nan's face suddenly came into her mind and she recalled the words she had spoken about her own regret a few weeks earlier,

"Yes you're right; after all it may be that nothing will happen."

All three sat there knowing full well that the likelihood of nothing happening between her and Mark was about as likely as Enzo shagging a woman.

"So that's settled then, we'll even escort you if you like, and then leave you to have fun, sounds to me like it's been missing from your life for too long. Now I think it's time we all got some sleep. I don't know about you, but I'm beat, I was on duty at 7.0am this morning, and tomorrow is another day".

Half an hour later, Celia was lying warm and snug in the comfortable bed of the spare room thinking excitedly about tomorrow and the prospect of spending time with Mark alone. She had sent him a text message confirming their meeting tomorrow evening and she could feel a stirring in her body as she pictured his lean, hard body, and imagined being on top of him. Her nipples hardened as she pictured his tongue licking and circling whilst his fingers caressed all areas of her body and she thought with eager anticipation of the feel of Mark hard inside her. Sleep was a long time coming, but eventually she drifted off with a smile on her face.

The tap on her door woke her from sleep. She had been dreaming but exactly what it was about seemed to elude her as soon as she opened her eyes, but she was left with a warm contented feeling and she remembered with excitement that today she was going to see Mark. Alistair walked in with a tray on which he'd set a small china tea pot in pale blue, and a matching cup and saucer.

"Did you sleep well"

as he spoke he leaned over and kissed Celia on the cheek,

"Take your time, there's no hurry, we'll have breakfast when you're ready, we've both got today off and I know you want to go shopping do you want us to tag along or would you be happier going alone?"

"I would welcome your opinion, it's ages since I bought an evening dress, it would be good to have you and Enzo to help, I'm a bit out of touch with London shops."

She remembered telling Gilly once how if you couldn't go shopping with a girlfriend, two gay men would always come a close second as you knew you could always rely on their honest opinion. She realised she was looking forward eagerly to the day and evening stretching out in front of her.

Chapter 21

Arthurs placed the tray of coffee in front of Sebastian and thought how worried he looked. He had something on his mind if he was any judge. He'd known him since he was a little boy and he had a habit of fiddling with his left ear when anything was troubling him. He seemed distracted lately, but at least he didn't seem to be drinking, and that had to be an improvement. As he placed the tray on the bed side table, the telephone rang and he watched as Sebastian snatched it up quickly. The look of eager anticipation was however quickly replaced as he heard him say,

"No Father, I won't be free this morning I'm expecting Harry at 11.00am he's coming over to discuss a problem we've got with one of our tenants, yes I'm sure I can handle it on my own, thank you for the offer but,"

His voice trailed off and Arthurs could hear the loud voice of the Honourable George even from where he was standing some ten feet away.

"Very well if you insist I'll see you about 10.30 then,"

"Well don't just stand there man, get my grey trousers and cream polo shirt and ask Mrs Popple to have coffee and those shortbread biscuits my Father likes ready for 10.45a.m."

****

Mark was late, and he hated being late. Why had Major Jefferson picked today of all days to stop and chat when he had been leaving the mess. He had packed most of his things the night before and it only remained for the last few items to be put into his small overnight bag and he'd be ready for the off. He had eventually managed to get away without he hoped appearing too rude and then he had almost collided with Julie and Caitlin as they came around the corner when he was walking to his car. He put his hand out to steady Julie as she seemed to stumble, and she immediately took the opportunity to hold on to his arm.

"Hey, Mark where are you rushing to in such a hurry, are you going away?"

She said eying the overnight bag clutched in his hand. He felt uncomfortable under her accusing gaze, and heard himself stammer,

"I'm meeting up with some old friend's in London and I'm a bit late, so I've got to go."

She was still holding onto his arm and shaking it free, he walked quickly towards his car. She shouted after him,

"You should have told me you were going away Mark. I could have come with you, just think of the fun we could have had"

He heard their loud raucous laughter as he reached his car and switched on the ignition.

The drive along the M4 was really slow. He wanted to get checked in to his Hotel and have time to relax and sort himself out before meeting Celia this evening. He still couldn't believe it was really going to happen. What if she didn't turn up?
    What if he had imagined the spark between them the other night? What if she didn't fancy him? What if he didn't fancy her? Now you really are being ridiculous he said to himself, calm down, and concentrate on your driving.

Later he drove his car into the underground car park and taking his bag in his hand entered the lift that would take him to the Hotel reception. It was a Modern Hotel with a light and spacious reception area, which he knew well from living in London before moving to Wiltshire. He suddenly thought about Lucy and remembered her office was quite near here and wondered what she was doing now. Probably married to some high flying city type he thought as he approached the check in desk.

He was shown to his room and putting his bag on the floor, walked to the window and looked down into the busy noisy London Street. He realised with a jolt how much he had missed it. The noise the crowds, even the dirt! He turned and looked at the room, liking what he saw. There was a king sized bed covered with a plain white duvet and a sofa and coffee table to one side also in white and pale wood. On the side table nearby was a fridge and a built in shelving area with a basket of fruit and a tray on which stood wine glasses and tumblers together with an ice bucket. Looking at his watch he planned the rest of the day, 3.0 pm. plenty of time. He would go out and take a walk around get a snack and then come back and shower and get ready for the evening. Pushing his way through the crowded pavements outside his Hotel he headed for Covent Garden and felt the exhilaration and atmosphere of the exciting cosmopolitan centre. There was a young girl playing a violin. Her fair hair fell across her face as she bent her head, with closed eyes. The haunting melody of Mendelssohn's violin Concerto vied for attention with loud jazz that was bursting out of another nearby corner. A juggler was throwing silver clubs. They caught the light as they weaved high in the air. How fantastic, Mark thought to himself, where else could you be but London. He was suddenly filled with an overwhelming sense of excitement and anticipation for the evening ahead, as crossing the busy pedestrian area to a flower stall that was ablaze with colour he breathed in the intoxicating perfume of fresh blooms. He pointed to a mass of sweet peas, and held out a ten pound note, smiling and winking broadly at the old woman flower seller.

"Ere you are sweetheart, I hope she liked them."

The old lady said as he walked away in the direction of St Martin's Lane.

****

Arriving at the designer floor of Harrods they all noticed how busy it was which only seemed to add to Celia's excitement. They had already done Bond Street and Harvey Nicks but she hadn't seen what she was looking for the ball, but had bought some really sexy underwear. She told herself it had nothing to do with seeing Mark later, just who was she trying to kid?

It was ages since she had done any major shopping for herself and she now revelled in the luxurious range of wonderful clothes on the rails in front of her. Harrods had always been her favourite, especially this floor, although she had never been able to afford these prices before marrying Seb. Subconsciously, she realised again another advantage of being married to him.

"Right, first priority is an evening dress, that's the main reason I'm here after all."

She picked up two dresses and as if by magic an assistant appeared and took them to the changing area. Enzo had picked up another two and handed them to the sales assistant as she appeared once more by their side. Celia followed her and said over her shoulder,

"Stay near so I can show you without having to parade out here and show off to the whole shop."

She emerged from the dressing room a few minutes later and twirled around in a deep blue dress with only one shoulder.

"It's nice,"

Enzo said

"but I really fancy that silvery one."

"That's the one I like too Celia said, I'll try it on."

She appeared minutes later and they both gasped. The dress was a slim column of silvery grey silk with diamante straps. It was cut on the bias and clung provocatively to Celia's slim hips and dipped low to reveal firm breasts.

"That's the one, you needn't look at anything else, it's absolutely amazing."

"I couldn't agree more Alistair said"

"I must admit, it is quite flattering," she said, "but it's horrendously expensive."

"As if that matters, just ask them to pack it up there's a good girl."

Chapter 22

Bags safely under Enzo's arm they moved through the separates department. Celia had spent an age wondering what to wear this evening and was still undecided. Out of the corner of her eye she suddenly spotted a soft red Karen Millen top. It had long sleeves and was off the shoulder, cut in the typical very slim style of one of her favourite designers. She had brought with her a beautifully cut cream suit which she had considered wearing tonight and this top would look really great with it, she took it eagerly into the changing room.

Half an hour later, they were all sitting in a little café back in Kensington and were amiably chatting over baguettes and cappuccinos. She was filled with a mixture of excitement and apprehension about the evening ahead.

"Perhaps I'll just stay in with you two after all tonight, you wouldn't mind would you?"

"Don't even think about it, a romantic evening is just what you need my girl, you're not going to wriggle out of it that easily. Just lay back and think of England."

Enzo was smiling at her as he spoke and she smiled back and said,

"OK you win."

Leaving the restaurant, they walked companionably back along the length of Kensington High street. The place was busy and noisy and was bustling with excitement. The noise of traffic and people shopping and going about their business combined with street vendors and newspaper sellers gave the whole atmosphere a feeling of expectation which only fuelled Celia's intense feeling of anticipation for the evening ahead. They stopped to buy a large bunch of white lilies from and old man standing by a cart filled with flowers.

"Be careful of the pollen me duck, it can be lethal if you get it on your clothes, best thing is to cut out the stamens, bit of a shame but can save your clothes or even your carpet."

She smiled in agreement at the friendly weather beaten old man as he handed them to her, and they set off in the direction of the flat passing the police station and a garden centre.

"Do you mind if I call Seb, I want to tell him we're all going out together this evening, will you speak to him and cover for me?"

She hated the thought of lying to him but once this deception thing was started, it was necessary to keep it going. Besides she didn't want him calling on her mobile when she was with Mark.

****

Looking at his watch, Sebastian was dying for a drink. It was only 6.30pm but it had been a long day. His Father had been his usual interfering, bombastic self and had dominated the meeting between him and his estate manager, taking the usual delight in making Sebastian look totally incompetent and useless. He knew from past experience that trying to stand up for himself only made matters worse, so he had bitten his tongue. The result of his sperm test still had to be faced and on top of that he was also missing Celia. The place seemed empty and quiet without her and he realised how much he had got used to having her around. He felt the heat in his face as he remembered how badly he had been treating her recently. When he was sober he bitterly regretted his behaviour. It was as though he was two different people. He thought back to the telephone conversation they had had earlier. It sounded as though she was having fun, anyway. He could think of better ways to spend time than with those two poufs. He began to wish he had gone with her to London, they could have stayed in his flat and done the town, although he had to admit it wasn't really her scene. She had never been one for the bright lights and noisy places. It was only 6.30pm and the evening stretched out in front of him endlessly. He wandered aimlessly around the house. Going into the bedroom he shared with Celia he opened the door of her wardrobe and pulling out one of her dresses nuzzled his face into the soft fabric. He breathed in the familiar smell that was his wife, a mixture of her perfume and her own personal scent.

Placing the dress back on the rail, he walked to the window and surveyed the garden. The sun was low in the sky and the rays were catching the lake at the rear of the house. He saw in his mind Celia lying under him, on the grass. He could hear in his head the soft moaning and cries of pleasure she made as they made love. How long since that had happened? He had the grace to feel guilty as he remembered the look of fear on her face these days. Leaving the bedroom, he walked across the wide landing and pushed open the door to the guest room, Celia had been using lately, noticing the light airy décor of white and pale lilac he knew she loved so much, he realised how much she must hate the heavy, dark and ornate style of the old House. He knew she wanted to change things but his father was dead against it, and he didn't want to get on the wrong side of him. The thought of his father made him more depressed and as he made his way back down the wide, dimly lit staircase, he made a decision. He would just have one drink, surely there was no harm in having one, besides, Celia wasn't even here so he wouldn't be able to take it out on her. Making up his mind, he walked quickly to the consul and poured himself a large whisky, noticing absentmindedly that there was only about half a bottle, but as he was only going to have one it didn't really matter.

****

Standing in front of the mirror in her brother's guest room, Celia stared back at the stranger in the mirror. The red suited her well, she decided, although it was not a colour she wore often, and it did compliment the pale cream of her skirt. She pulled the top this way and that until it was sitting comfortably on her pale shoulders. Walking into the lounge she was greeted by a low whistle as Enzo said,

"Beautiful my lady, really beautiful, he's a lucky man."

"I second that"

Alistair said as he appeared in the kitchen doorway handing her a glass of wine.

"I'm not sure I should drink this, I want to keep a cool head" but she raised it to her lips and took a sip enjoying the cold liquid as it slipped smoothly down her throat, and it did seem to steady her nerves.

****

The mirror in the wardrobe reflected a tall slim tanned man in his early thirties. Mark liked the reflection looking back at him and felt confident, if a little nervous. His eyes roamed around the room and took in the bottle of champagne in an ice bucket, and a glass bowl which was filled with sweet peas, the delicate colours standing out against the pale bland decor of the room. Beautiful flowers for a beautiful woman.

Sighing with exasperation and frustration, Sebastian tipped up the empty whisky bottle, as if to squeeze out the last dregs. He shouted for Arthurs before remembering that it was his night off and he'd gone into Salisbury to visit his brother's family until tomorrow. It was 8 .00pm and he'd managed to polish off the last of the whisky which had given him a taste for more. He knew there should be at least another bottle somewhere but he'd noticed that Arthurs had taken to locking it away recently, probably because of Celia's interference. Oh well there was nothing for it but to drive out and get another one. Reaching his car he fell awkwardly into the driving seat and turning the key in the ignition roared off down the drive, the tyres screeching and throwing up gravel as he went. He realised suddenly how dark it was and that he'd forgotten to switch on the headlight's which he now did. The beams picked up a rabbit scuttling across the path and he laughed out loud as it scampered into the undergrowth.

"Missed the fucking thing,"

He said half under his breath,

"Never mind, get it on the way back."

The car roared on down the dark lane and he saw the bright lights of Parsonage farm as he rounded the bend in the road. He pictured Ralph and Gilly all cosy together and thought to himself, they'll have some whisky, I'll drop in and have a drink with them, surely they won't deny a neighbour a glass of whisky. He turned the wheel sharply and almost collided with the gate post as he realised the gate was closed.

Hearing a screech of brakes Gilly peered through the curtains, and was surprised to see Sebastian's Porch in the drive.

"I wonder what he wants?"

She said to Ralph

"You're not expecting him are you?"

"No certainly not, better open the door and let him in before he breaks it down."

He must have put his finger on the door bell and just left it there as the noise was reverberating round the house loudly, much to the delight of the children who had been watching television, but were now both standing and giggling in the hall by the front door. As Gilly opened the door, Sebastian almost fell into the hall. He must have been leaning on the front door, she thought. He walked up to Gilly and putting his arm around her shoulders said

"How the devil are you sweetheart, I thought you were never going to open the fucking door."

Gilly recoiled in horror as she smelt the sourness of his breath and disentangled herself from his arm. Ralph had come into the hall and was standing behind her. She looked at her husband and watched the range of emotions skim across his face from surprise to astonishment and then dark anger as he realised how drunk Sebastian was. She heard him say,

"Take the children into the other room, leave this to me."

Jake had his hand to his mouth and was giggling into it

"He said the F word, he said the F word."

He chanted and Alice looked scared as she looked first at her mother, and then at Sebastian, and back to her mother.

Gilly steered the children back into the room where they had been watching T.V. and pulled the door behind her. Left alone in the hallway with Sebastian, Ralph was very angry. He knew it would however not be wise to show his anger as Sebastian was a nasty drunk so instead he said trying hard to control his voice.

"Come into the kitchen I'll make you a coffee."

"Coffee, I don't want your fucking coffee, I want a proper drink, got any whisky Ralphie old boy?"

"Don't you think you've had enough, you'd be better off with a coffee, I'll put the kettle on."

He reached out and tried to steer Sebastian away from the hallway and into the kitchen, but he shook off Ralph's arm and staggered forward, tripping over a large ball the children had been paying with. He lay sprawled on the floor on his back, grinning inanely up at Ralph. Putting out his hand he pulled at Sebastian in an effort to get him back on his feet. It was a difficult job, as he weighed a ton. With a lot of heavy breathing and a supreme effort he managed to get him back into an upright position where he swayed precariously. With his other hand, he managed to push open the kitchen door open and quickly manoeuvre the dead weight that Sebastian had become inside where he collapsed onto a kitchen chair, the legs screeching against the tiled floor. He slumped low in the seat with his head lolling to one side and a dribble of saliva running down his chin. Ralph sighed and thought to himself, this is going to be a long night!

Chapter 23

As he walked back into a busy Covent Garden bar, Mark realised how much he was looking forward to the evening. The whole place was alive with people who were sitting laughing and talking. There was a buzz about the place which seemed to match his mood. Was it his imagination, or did the whole world seem to be full of couples tonight. Although the place was very busy, there were one or two empty tables and he took a seat at one near to the door and ordered a mineral water from the young waitress who approached him. He wanted to keep a clear head, and besides, he had a bottle of champagne on ice in his room to look forward to later with Celia just thinking about her excited him. He thought to himself how long it had been since he'd slept with a woman, many months, and he missed the shared intimacy you got from a loving relationship. His thoughts went back to his relationship with Lucy. It had started very well, and the sex had been great at first but she seemed to cool off after a while, and then of course his thrashing around in the bed they shared when his nightmares begun, was the final nail in the coffin. He was a passionate man, a typical fire sign, Aries, not that he believed totally in all that stars stuff, but Lucy had talked a lot about it and he had to admit that he seemed to have a lot of the typical qualities of an Aries male. He realised he was nervous about seeing Celia, and felt ridiculous that a grown man should be nervous of meeting a woman who appealed so much to him. He was imagining undressing Celia, slowly peeling off her clothes to reveal her beautiful pale translucent skin. He could almost feel her slim body against him and realised this was not the place to get a hard on. Forcing his mind to concentrate on more mundane things, he sat and sipped his drink all the while keeping his eye fixed on the door. Despite that he missed her walking in as he was distracted by a loud burst of laughter from a group of people on the next table. Suddenly, she was there standing next to him Mark leapt to his feet and smiled as she spoke.

"Hello Mark, I hope I haven't kept you waiting, I'd like you to meet my brother Alistair and his partner Enzo."

She wondered to herself how he would react to her brother being gay. She knew Sebastian had a lot of problems with it, but she somehow expected Mark to be more tolerant ad open minded. He certainly didn't appear to be fazed as he reached out and shook them both warmly by the hand. Celia realised she had been holding her breath and let it out slowly as he turned to her and leaning forward kissed her lightly on the cheek.

"Don't worry, Mark We're not staying."

Alistair said,

"We wanted to make sure this sister of mine got here safely, and now we'll be off."

"Are you sure you won't at least stay for a drink, you're very welcome."

He was still standing and was lifting his hand to summon the waitress.

"Yes, please at least have a drink before you go";

Celia said smiling at them both.

"You've twisted my arm; I'd love a Gin and tonic."

Enzo sat at the table with Alistair next to him.

"Well, just a quick one and then we'll leave you both in peace."

Celia watched them together and realised they all seemed to be getting along fine. If Mark had an issue with Gay men, it certainly didn't show. She began to feel more relaxed and was able to take a good look at Mark whilst he was busy talking. He looked absolutely great, fit, tanned and relaxed. She thought about the rest of the evening and how much she wanted him. She had agreed with her brother that she would call him on his mobile later to let him know if she decided to stay with Mark, or return to the flat.

"You do whatever you want, it's about time you had some fun, so make the most of it, we're happy if you're happy, I'll just make a note of the hotel name and Mark's full name, you know what a worrier I am."

As they watched Alistair and Enzo walk out of the restaurant Celia was reminded how cosmopolitan and exciting London was as she watched Enzo walk with his hand protectively on his partner's shoulder. Left alone she felt a little nervous but Mark was so easy to talk to and he seemed so relaxed that she caught his mood and they chatted companionably as though they had known each other for years instead of a few short months.

"I've booked a table for 8.00pm at a restaurant here in Covent Garden, that has a great reputation, so I hope you won't be disappointed. Are you hungry?"

"Yes, a little, I'm interested to try this place as I've heard about it, and remember one of the guy's I used to cater for telling me how good it was"

Noticing the lift of his eyebrows and the question in his eyes, Celia realised how very little they knew about each other and she began to talk to Mark about her catering business and how happy it had made her. Watching her talk, Mark noticed the sparkle in her eyes as she spoke about her previous life in London and wondered why she had given up something that obviously had given her so much happiness.

"Couldn't you have kept in on after you got married, obviously in the new area, but you seem to have so much enthusiasm and excitement when you talk about it, it seems like such a waste of talent."

"Sebastian wouldn't hear of it, he's quite old fashioned about lots of things, and believes that" ….she stopped as she realised she was going to say about their status and it embarrassed her to talk about it in front of Mark. She had never even told him Sebastian was an Honourable; it seemed so pretentious in the twenty first century, to be talking about Lords and Ladies. Wanting to change the subject, she asked

"What about you Mark, what do you like to do when you're not being a soldier, do you like to cook? How long have you been in the Army, have you travelled much?"

"Sorry, I always talk too much when I'm nervous, you don't have to answer all those questions, and I didn't mean to sound like an interrogator."

She moved her hand up to adjust the edge of her top, suddenly self-conscious of the expanse of bare shoulder. He reached out and took her hand and she felt a jolt of excitement shoot through her as his finger's brushed against the skin of her neck. Her finger's twined around his and they sat still looking into each other's eyes. Celia felt a rush of colour as a blush spread up into her face.

Mark spoke,

"Come on, let's get out of here, I can't wait to get you all to myself."

He placed some notes on the table and putting his warm hand in Celia's cold one, walked out through the doorway of the bar. Hand in hand they came out into Covent Garden. The area was noisy and vibrant with the street vendors shouting and musicians vying to be heard over the general clamour. The evening had begun to turn cold and a chill wind caught Celia's skirt raising it high. She struggled to hold it down, releasing Mark's hand as she felt the heat in her face, as hot as her hands were cold. Mark looked down at her and smiled,

"come on, let's get you into the warm, you look frozen."

The Restaurant was only a short distance and as they walked through the busy London street a woman suddenly stepped from the road and onto the kerb, almost colliding with Mark. She seemed out of breath and spoke hurriedly.

"Excuse me. I'm so sorry I wasn't looking where I was going",

"Typical Lucy in a hurry as usual."

"Mark, what an amazing coincidence, I was only thinking about you the other day and wondering how things were going. My office is just near here, but what are you doing here? I thought you were in darkest Wiltshire, has the army thrown you out or are you still having nightmares?"

Ignoring her last question he said

"Oh yes I'm still in the army, just up for the weekend, still with the same Infantry Regiment."

He suddenly realised he was holding onto Celia's hand and turning to her he said, sorry, Celia, this is Lucy Montague, an old friend of mine, Lucy, Celia Stratford. He looked on as the two women shook hands. Lucy had honey blonde hair that was short and cut in a very trendy spiky style that suited her. She looked successful and contented, and was dressed in a pale blue jacket and trousers. She was very slim and stood a good head taller than Celia. The two women looked at each other each wondering what the other was thinking, when Mark's voice cut into their thoughts,

"Nice to see you Lucy, but we have a table booked so we must be making a move."

Left alone after she had gone, Mark said,

"Now where were we, hungry?"

Celia was thinking about the young woman that had just left. She was very beautiful and seemed to know Mark really well. What was that she had said about nightmares, her thoughts went back to the day when she had slipped from her horse and she remembered how upset Mark had been there was something in his past that was causing him grief. She was also surprised to realise that she felt jealous. What right did she have to such a feeling when she was herself married? Typical illogical woman, she said to herself. She realised Mark was talking to her and she said,

"Yes, let's go and eat."

They were shown to a table in the corner of the room and as they were seated, Celia realised that she'd been lying when she said she was hungry as her appetite seemed to have left her all she felt was the excitement of being with Mark and the prospect of being alone with him. Mark could hardly take his eyes off her. Seeing Lucy had really focussed him on his feelings for Celia. She had such a look of innocence and vulnerability that made him want to crush her in his arms. There was also pain reflected in her eyes and he thought back to the time she had fallen off her horse and the look of sheer terror when he had put out his hand to help her. Something was causing her unhappiness and he wanted to take away her pain and protect her. He realised his appetite for food had left him and only wanted to be alone with her. He wondered how she would react if he told her, oh well there was only one way to find out.

"Celia, looking at you I can't even think about food, let's get out of here."

They stood up as the waiter arrived and Mark said,

"Sorry, something's come up."

Smiling suddenly to himself at what he'd said. And they walked back onto the busy street hand in hand towards the Hotel they were silent both lost in their own thoughts. Celia felt the pressure from Mark's warm hand and his fingers stroked the soft skin inside her wrist as they hurried along towards his Hotel. Going up in the empty lift, he drew her to him and bent is head to kiss her hungrily, his lips warm and firm, opening hers to find her tongue. They clung together hungrily and only sprang apart when the lift doors opened as they arrived at Mark's floor, and a group of people stood waiting to enter the lift.

Arriving at his room, Mark felt frustrated when the key card he inserted in the door lock kept winking and flashing red, indicating that the door was still locked. Eventually after two or three attempts, and what seemed like an age, the green light came on and he pushed the door open with an audible sigh of relief. Celia stopped dead when she saw the sweet peas.

"Oh Mark how beautiful, I love sweet peas, it's very unusual to see them in Hotels"

"Not if you put them there yourself, I just had a feeling you would like them, they seem to remind me of you, they're so delicate and beautiful"

She buried her head in the delicate flowers and was breathing in the wonderful scent as he came up behind her and began speaking softly into her ear with his arms around her waist. She leaned back into him and he moved his hand up and slowly began to circle her breasts with his thumbs. She was acutely aware of the sensation and felt his hardness as she leaned back into him; He turned her slowly and placed his mouth on her throat at the base, pushing aside her hair with his fingers. His tongue traced a path slowly up her pale throat until their mouths met and opened in unison and she felt his tongue exploring her as she opened up to the exquisiteness of the feeling of tongue to tongue. She noticed the sweetness of his breath and that hers was coming in short ragged bursts. She breathed in his aroma, tasted him wanted him. She heard herself moan as the exquisite sensations of pleasure rippled through her body. She felt the moisture between her legs and felt as though her legs would no longer support her. They moved together to the bed and fell onto the white cover. Mark's hand was slowly moving up her thigh, higher and higher until it came into contact with the soft tangle between her legs, pushing aside the silky thong that was at the top of her stockings. Her legs opened up to him and she groaned as…….the sound of a telephone ringing made them both jump

"Ignore it," Mark said into her ear.

"Oh Mark, we can't it might be important."

"Everything that's important to me is right here in this room."

"No really Mark, you must answer it, please"

He reluctantly left Celia and walked over to answer the phone and she frowned as he reached out to her and said,

"It's for you, it's Alistair."

Celia was on her feet and felt her heart racing in her ear from the feelings he had aroused in her and the fear of the unexpected phone call. Taking the phone from his outstretched hand she said

"Alie, it's me Celie, what's wrong?"

"Celie, love I'm afraid it's bad news, it's Nan she's had a stroke, Dad called me ten minutes ago, Enzo and I are on our way to you, we'll all drive to Cardiff together."

She struggled to take in his words and said;

"I'll be in reception waiting, how is Mum, stupid question, see you soon."

Mark was looking at her and in a step was by her side.

"Bad news?"

"Yes Mark, I'm really sorry about this, it's my Nan, she lives in Cardiff and she's had a stroke, Alistair and Enzo are on their way here to drive me there."

"Is there anything I can do?"

She shook her head. "I'm *so* sorry, it's ruined our evening."

"Don't be silly that's the least of your worries, don't worry about me, there'll be other times, I'm more concerned about you, you've gone really pale." He put his arms around her and felt her trembling.

"Oh Mark, I hope we get there in time but if she's had a stroke she may not even know us. We seem to be doomed, don't we? I really do want you Mark, there will be other times won't there you do mean it, don't you?"

"Just try and keep me away, I love you Celia, I've never felt like this before."

Later she realised she could remember little about the journey to Cardiff, it all seemed to pass in a blur. They had stopped at one of the service areas before they got to the bridge. She had been relieved that her brother and Enzo had had the foresight to bring her overnight bag, and mobile phone. She was worried that she hadn't been able to get through to Seb. There was no reply from home which was strange and his mobile rang and rang until it went into voice messaging. In desperation she had called Gilly. She explained in a few words what had happened to her Nan and listened to her friend's sympathetic words which had made the tears start again. When she had told Gilly that she had been unable to contact Seb, she immediately noticed a change in her voice as she had explained the visit they had had from him earlier. Celia had been surprised as she knew there was no love lost between her husband and her friend's family.

"What did he want"

she had asked, and again picked up on hesitation in her friend's voice and manner. "I hardly like to tell you, you've got enough on your plate at the moment but he was worse for wear and was looking for whisky."

"You mean he was drunk?"

Her heart fell as the picture of her husband staggering and cursing swam before her eyes. It was immediately replaced by an image of Mark as she had last seen him, standing on the pavement outside the hotel waving them off. He had looked so handsome and caring even though the disappointment and frustration was still in his eyes. She couldn't help comparing the two images of the two men. She knew now that whatever happened between her and Mark, it was the beginning of the end for her marriage.

Chapter 24

Sebastian was waking. He felt stiff and cold as he realised he was half sitting, half lying in the driving seat of his Porch. He couldn't remember how he came to be here or what had happened for the last few hours. As he struggled to sit up he accidentally put his hand on the horn causing him to jump as the sound echoed around the dark country lanes. How had he got here? His memory was vague but is head was throbbing as he peered out into the darkness and realised he was outside the gates of Parsonage farm. He had a flash of memory as he saw again in his mind the picture of Ralph trying to get him to drink coffee and his violent refusal and his abusive behaviour. He dimly remembered driving to the local shop and getting another bottle of whiskey and he saw the bottle on the floor of the car. There was still a little drop in it. He realised he was sitting on something hard and cold, and reaching down pulled his mobile phone from under his leg. Switching it on he pressed the buttons to pick up his messages and heard Celia's voice. There was something wrong if her voice was anything to go by, although the message was just

"Call me as soon as you get this message".

Now what, he said to himself as he sat in the dark with his head in his hands. Getting through to Celia, he listened to her story, although she was quite difficult to understand through her tears. He had finally spoken to Alistair as he had taken the phone from her hand and quickly and quietly explained the situation.

"How soon can you get here, I think she's going to need your support."

He had explained that they were all still at the hospital, but Johanna didn't seem to know anyone. Now Sebastian was faced with a dilemma. If he tried to drive to Cardiff in this state, he could be stopped and breathalysed, whereas if he didn't leave now they would all guess the reason and he'd promised Celia he wouldn't drink anymore. He looked at his watch and was surprised to realise it was after midnight. He must have been here for hours. No wonder he was cold. He had told them that he was as good as on his way, and making up his mind suddenly, he switched on the engine and headed for home.

The hospital ward was dimly lit and there were sounds of people coughing and murmuring in their sleep. One old lady in a frail voice could be heard calling for a nurse, her voice sounding more and more frail as she repeated the single word. Behind her Celia was aware of the squeak of rubber soles on the tiled floor as a nurse went by. The sound of his rubber soled shoes stopped suddenly, telling Celia he was at the bedside of the old lady who was calling. She heard his voice speaking softly and wondered about the patience it must take to be a nurse. Holding her Nan's limp hand in hers Celia's mind was all over the place. Her Nan's eyes were closed; the pale almost blue eyelids seemed to flicker. Celia wondered what was going on behind the old ladies eyes. What was she thinking? Was she thinking anything? She wanted to talk to her and reassure her that everything was going to be fine, but she knew deep down, this wasn't the case. Her Nan suddenly gave a deep sigh and Celia thought she was going to speak. She leaned forward and put her ear close to the old ladies mouth. Speaking softly, close to her ear she said,

"Nan, Nan, it's me Celia, can you hear me?"

The old lady made no response and Celia felt her mum's hand on her shoulder.

"I don't think she can hear you love."

Celia sat back but continued stroking her Nan's cold hand and willing her to wake up. Her thoughts went back over the events of the last day, so much seemed to have happened that she had difficulty in taking it all in. She looked up and smiled tearfully at her mum who was sitting on the opposite side of the bed. They spoke in whispers.

"She seems to be holding her own, she's such a fighter".

Celia listened to her mum and her thoughts went back to her Nan's words last time she had seen her when they had had lunch in Penarth.

"Follow your heart my dear"

She had said, and Celia wondered what that could mean to her now. She remembered how Mark had made her feel earlier this evening. Looking at the clock on the wall of the dimly lit ward, she realised it was not this evening as it was already 3.0am. Such a lot seemed to have happened in such a short time. The smell of the hospital reminded her of the tests she had undergone recently and an image of Seb in one of his drunken rages came into her head making her shiver.

"Are you alright love, you must be exhausted, why don't you go and get a rest, I'll come and get you if anything happens, I promise."

"I don't want to leave her, what if she regains consciousness; I want to be here for her."

Reluctantly, Celia left her Nan's side and walked to where her Dad was waiting. She felt herself tip toeing as her heels clacked noisily on the tiled floor. Her Dad had managed to get a word with the Consultant in charge of geriatrics when they had arrived earlier and now put his arms around his daughter and said quietly.

"She's a tough old girl, you know love, all we can do now is wait and pray, sit here I'll get you a cup of tea, there's a machine near."

"No dad, you sit down, I'll get you one, you look all in."

She realised her dad looked older and there were deep lines on his face she hadn't noticed before. The realisation made her think how short life is.

"Too short to waste with a man you don't love," a voice inside her head seemed to say.

Sipping the luke warm milky tea Celia thought about the conversation she had had with Seb earlier. Even if Gilly hadn't told her about his drunken visit, she would have known instantly from his voice that he had been drinking. So much for his promise, but who am I to criticize, after all look what I was up to earlier. She hated herself for deceiving Seb. She was usually such an upfront person, and hated lying or being lied to.

Alistair and Enzo had left earlier and found a hotel where they had booked rooms for themselves and Celia and her mum. It was decided that her dad would have to travel back home to Bristol as he had patients to see, but he would get back as soon as he had arranged for a locum to take over. She looked up as her dad came out from the ward and said,

"Your Mum and I think you should go and get some shut eye and then come back in a few hours. You'll be able to sit with your Nan and let your mum get a few hours sleep. Do your best to persuade her love, she'll be no good to anyone if she's completely exhausted. I'll drop you off on my way home."

Celia realised this was the second hotel room she had been in, in the last twenty-four hours. The difference between the two was as wide as cheddar gorge. She tried to stop her mind and heart racing but sleep seemed unattainable. With her head on the pillow Celia tossed and turned and willed herself to sleep. Her mind was still showing her pictures of her Nan, Mark and Sebastian, and she could feel her heart beating loudly in her neck. Although she was absolutely exhausted, sleep just wouldn't come. She must have eventually dropped off however as she was suddenly woken with a start and she realised someone was knocking loudly on her door. Peering through the peephole she opened the door to admit Allie and she knew immediately from seeing his face that her Nan had gone.

Mark was having difficulty getting to sleep. He was so disappointed with the way things had turned out. He knew it was no one's fault and he was sorry for Celia and all her family but that didn't stop him feeling let down. He could still feel her in his arms and the sweetness of her mouth on his. He remembered the feel of the pale silky skin at the top of her legs, and how she had responded to his fingers as they traced a path up, and up until....they had been interrupted by the ringing of the telephone! His body responded now just imagining her by his side. Would there be other times? He had told her there would be but it wasn't so simple. Just the logistics of planning to be alone in the same place at the same time was a hurdle to be overcome. He also knew how much she hated deceiving her husband, and they still hadn't really had a chance to talk. He still didn't know exactly was causing her to be so scared. He looked forward to hearing from her, but knew that it might be a long wait. He tossed and turned in the bed he should have been sharing with Celia and the light from the window picked up the large bunch of sweet peas on the nearby table. With a deep sigh, he turned on his side, and settled down I an effort to sleep, but knew that it was going to be a long night.

****

"Mum, come and sit down you look all in, I've made you a sandwich and some fresh tea."

"Thanks love, but I couldn't eat a thing."

"Deirdre", her Dad's voice cut in,

"you must eat something, you'll make yourself ill and then what will we all do without you."

It was a few days since her Nan had died and Celia was staying with them in Bristol. She hadn't been home since arriving here from the hospital three days ago. Her brother and Enzo had left for London and Celia missed their calm reassurance and comfort. She had sent a brief text message to Mark informing him of her Nan's death and promised to call him soon. She had then called Seb after the sad news and wasn't at all surprised to discover he hadn't even left for Bristol She could hear in his voice that he was still hung over, but he'd had the grace to sound genuinely sorry. She realised he had cared for her Nan, having lost his own Grandparents many years ago. She told him not to come and although he had attempted to argue the point, she had eventually won and assured him she would be fine and that there was a great deal to do and arrangements to be made. The funeral was to take place in Cardiff the following Monday. They were horrified to discover that there would have to be a post-mortem as her Nan had not been ill, prior to her death, but her dad had tried to reassure them that this was just normal practice. Nevertheless it was distressing.

A few days later walking around the room Johanna had occupied they were both in tears as everything seemed to have a reminder of the special person they had lost. There was a humming noise coming from the video recorder and they realised that Johanna's favourite programme was being recorded. She must have pre-set it the day before she had always loved countdown, having been an avid crossword fan all her life and was still solving them right up until the day she died. Deirdre picked up the Times and the crossword was half completed, and by the side of her chair were her shoes, neatly placed side by side as though she had just taken them off. For Celia this was the final straw. To be here in her Nan's room and hear the video recording something that a few short hours ago she must have set up herself was almost too hard to bear. She sat in her Nan's chair and sobbed as though her heart would break. Mother and daughter sat clinging together arms tightly wound around each other until they gradually calmed down.

"I'm so glad we can do this together,"

Her mum said,

"It must be awful to have to cope with all this on your own." Everywhere, there were poignant memories of the old lady and her everyday life.

"Do you think she was happy here, I feel guilty that she was alone when she died, perhaps we should have insisted that she come and live with us."

"Mum, you know she wouldn't do that, you and dad tried often enough, you have absolutely nothing to reproach yourself about."

They had left Johanna's room after a general tidy up, having made arrangements to return to clear all her things.

Back in Bristol Celia was walking across the downs. It was so good to feel the wind in her hair. The sky was overcast and rain hung in the clouds like unshed tears. The weather seemed to match Celia's mood. Tears were very near the surface and she felt as if she had been crying for days. The emotion of her Nan's death had made all her other problems surface and she felt drained. There's nothing quite like death for grounding you. It made her think long and hard about her own mortality. It was good to get out into the wind and fresh air. There were quite a few people about. The downs had always been a favourite place to walk. Celia sat on a bench and gathered her thoughts. In front of her approaching, was a young mum with two small children. A small girl was holding onto the pushchair in which a baby was fast asleep, thumb in mouth and two chubby feet sticking out from underneath a blue blanker she noticed one of his socks was missing and his tiny foot looked pale and vulnerable. The little girl was struggling to keep up and her Mum was looking very harassed as she raised her voice and said not very kindly,

"Come on Kirsty, don't dawdle, try and keep up we've still got a long way to go."

What would life be like with two small children? Very different from her life now. Would she ever find out? She watched the woman and wondered why some parent's took such delight in humiliating their own children. She was reminded of an incident some years ago which had always stuck in her mind. She had been sitting in a small café in Chelsea and on the next table was a couple with a boy aged about six or seven. They were typical of the trendy rich set, common to the area. The small boy had been handed a bottle of coke with a tall straw and in his excitement had accidentally knocked it over. The dark sticky liquid had spread over the shiny table and dripped noisily onto the floor. Celia felt sorry for him as the disappointment shone out of his face. She was even more horrified when his mother raised her voice and yelled out loudly."

"Jeremy, you stupid, clumsy child, now look what you've done."

It had been many years ago, but she had never forgotten the look on the child's face .Some people didn't deserve to have children. She thought again of Seb and how badly he wanted a son. Was it that he really did want a child of his own or was it just because of the pressure from his father to produce an heir? Whatever the reason, she was sure now that she did want to have a child, but not with Seb.

The image of Mark's face suddenly came into her mind and taking her phone from her bag she pushed his number. They hadn't spoken since she had rushed off and left him on the pavement outside the hotel last Saturday evening, and she had promised to call in her text message, but she knew he would understand. She listened as his phone rang and went into voicemail. Disappointed she left a short message asking him to call her as soon as possible and putting her phone back into her bag she got up from the bench and to walk the short distance back to her parent's house.

She suddenly realised how difficult it would be to talk to Mark in front of her parents if he rang when she was with them, and as she was almost bound to be she called back briefly and left another message that she would call him later. She hastily pushed her phone deep into the pocket of her suede jacket and carried on walking.

Chapter 25

Chopping vegetables for a stir fry was very therapeutic and Celia lost herself in the concentration of doing one of the things she loved best. The silvery blade of the knife flashed and dazzled in the light of the sun reflections through the nearby window. She loved being in the kitchen in her parent's house. It was spacious with gleaming white units and pale beech wood work surfaces There was an assortment of fresh herbs in small terracotta pots on the window sill and the smell of fresh basil and coriander was beginning to have an effect on Celia's appetite. The window looked out onto the garden and Celia caught sight of a large magpie, its snowy white tail held high as it flew past the large kitchen window and landed in the branches of the old beech tree that was part of Celia's childhood. The arrival of the bird made her think of the old rhyme. "**One for sorrow, two for joy.**" Well it was certainly one for sorrow today, she reflected. Her Dad came into the kitchen and smiled at her.

"You look a bit better, love. Cooking always did have a cathartic effect on you didn't it?"

She nodded her head in agreement.

"How's mum is she still lying down?"

"Yes, I finally managed to persuade her, she was all in .I remember the terrible feeling of loss when you realise that both your parents have now gone and you are completely on your own."

As he spoke he had moved to the kitchen door and pushing it open stepped out onto the stone patio at the back of the kitchen. There was a sound of someone nearby mowing the grass, and the whine of an electric mower seemed to dominate the air. Celia looked up from her chopping breathing in the smell of new mown grass, and watched her dad, his back seeming to stoop with hunches shoulders reminding her again that he wasn't getting any younger. He spoke again, turning back towards her and speaking through the open doorway.

"Your mum will feel it more too, being an only child, at least I had your uncle Bernard when I lost both mine. You always think of all the things you wish you'd asked when they were still alive. The realisation that it's now too late is very hard to bear. I actually picked up the telephone to ring my mum more than once, after she died. It took me a long time to realise she was really gone and that I could never ask her anything again"

Celia was suddenly faced with the terrible thought that this would happen to her one day, and she really didn't want to think about that. She put down the knife and wiped her hands on a tea towel that hung from her apron. Stepping across the kitchen and through the open door she put her arms around her dad and said,

"I need a hug."

They stood together quietly and heard Deirdre's voice a she walked on soundless feet into the kitchen."

"You two look cosy, what are you cooking, can I help?"

She was shooed away and Celia resumed the preparation of dinner.

It was much later when she finally was alone that she had the opportunity to call Mark. His phone was answered almost as soon as it started to ring. She felt a pang of guilt when she realised how anxious he sounded.

"I'm so pleased to hear your voice. I was so disappointed to have missed you earlier, how are things? Stupid question!"

Talking quietly, Celia brought him up to date with events since leaving him last Saturday.

"I'm so sorry about your Nan, what are your plans now, when is the funeral, when will you be coming home?

Sorry, I seem to be firing questions at you and you probably don't feel like answering any at the moment."

"It's OK Mark, the funeral is on Monday and I'll be coming home shortly after that, I can't come home sooner as I don't have my car here of course as I was driven here from London by Alistair and Enzo." The memory of the journey immediately conjured up a picture of the last time they had been together for both of them. For a moment there was silence as they both were lost in thought. Mark spoke first

"I wish I could be there for you, I realise it's impossible, of course."

"I was just wishing the same thing."

"Well, I'll be thinking of you, you know that, don't you."

"Thanks Mark it'll help, but look I've got to go now, it's not easy to talk here and I need to try and get some sleep."

Putting her phone down Celia was thinking of Mark and the feeling of being with him which was still so strong. She wondered if he felt the same. He certainly sounded as if he did.

Tossing and turning in her bed, sleep was a long time coming. Her mind was racing and she tried to calm herself by taking deep breaths in an effort to relax. She eventually fell into a troubled sleep and was dreaming that she was riding across Salisbury plain on her beloved Amber. Mark was riding by her side and they were laughing. She was aware of the wind in her hair and the exhilaration and freedom she always felt when she was out riding. As they rode on together, suddenly in front of them they heard the noise of gun fire and Mark said,

"We'd better be careful; we must have ridden into a danger area."

The noise of the gun fire got louder and louder and then in front of them a man was standing with a gun outstretched in his hand aiming at Mark. She heard herself scream,

"No"

As she recognised the face of her Husband, but her shout was lost and carried off by the wind, and she woke as the explosion deafened her. For a moment, she couldn't remember where she was. Slowly the sanity came back and she saw her old Teddy staring back at her from the dressing table. She realised that it must have been a loud clap of thunder that had actually woken her, as suddenly the whole room was lit up by a flash of bluish white lightening. Wide awake and trembling from the nightmare she slid out of bed and padded softly to her bedroom window and stood for a moment watching the storm. The trees in the garden were creaking and bending in the gale and there was another flash of lightening that lit up the whole garden. Celia had always loved a storm, although she knew a lot of people were scared by them. She thought nature had never been as magnificent as when there was a good electrical storm. The rain was now coming down in torrents and she could hear rivers of water running down the window .Quietly, she opened her bedroom door. The old house was quiet and still as she made her way on stealthy feet down to the kitchen to make a cup of tea. As she pushed open the kitchen door she jumped as she saw the shadowy figure of her mother sitting in the dark staring out of the window into the garden. The garden was alight with shimmering moonlight and looked almost surreal.

"Mum, you made me jump. Why are you sitting here in the dark?"

"Probably the same reason why you're wandering around the house in the dark at 3.00am, I couldn't sleep, so rather than just lie there I decided to come down here. Doesn't the garden look beautiful in the moonlight even with the storm?"

Celia stood behind her mum her hands resting lightly on her shoulders and she realised with a shock how frail her mum felt under the thin cotton dressing gown. Her parents were getting old.

"I was thinking about your Nan, do you think she was happy, I often caught her with a faraway look in her eyes, but she would never tell me what was going on in her head. She always was one for bottling things up; did she ever say anything to you, love?"

Celia was torn, she wanted to tell her mum what Johanna had told her a few short weeks ago, but it felt as though she was betraying the old lady's confidence.

"I'm sure she was happy, you would have known if it was otherwise, you were always so close."

Deirdre nodded slowly and said,

"We must go and sort out her things, I'm really not looking forward to it, you will come and help me won't you love?"

"Of course I will, it's not a job to be undertaken alone, we can drive over tomorrow if you like."

"Good idea, I'll call the matron first thing. Now let's try and get some sleep. We've got a busy few days in front of us."

Chapter 26

For once in his life, Sebastian wasn't looking forward to seeing his wife. Well that wasn't quite true. On her own would be fine, but in the bosom of her family, that was another matter. He always had the feeling that her family had never liked him and weren't happy about him marrying their beloved Celia. They had spoken on the telephone only a few times and she seemed very cool and distant even allowing for the upset of her Nan. They had agreed that he would drive down on Saturday and Celia had asked him to bring a few things with him. She needed a black suit and shoes and one or two other small items from home. He wasn't looking forward to being under the scrutiny of her whole family, especially her brother and his so called partner. He also had in his mind the recent episode of his turning up drunk on the doorstep of her best friend. He was in no doubt that Celia would have been told all the gory details by now and her low esteem of him would be even worse.

****

Mark tried hard to lose himself in his job in an effort to stop thinking about Celia and how much he was missing her. At last he knew she was sleeping alone at her parents as she had mentioned that her husband wasn't driving to Bristol until the weekend. He had great difficulty coming to terms with her sharing a bed with another man, even though he knew he had absolutely no claim on her. The picture in his mind of her undressing and lying naked in someone else's arms was almost too much to bear. To add to his problems he had run into Julia a couple of times and she seemed very slow to take the hint that he wasn't interested. Perhaps it would be better to see her just once more and be honest with her, really put her straight, otherwise it might drag on forever, and he certainly didn't want that.

The next morning dawn bright and clear after the storm of the previous night and Celia and her Mum set of for Cardiff together soon after breakfast.

As they drove passed the lake the sounds of laughter and children's voices mingled with the chimes of an ice cream van making them realise that life goes on however you may be feeling. Celia and her mum were very quiet thinking of the daunting task that faced them.

"I keep expecting to see her sitting in the window, I still can't believe she's really gone and we'll never see her again."

"I know exactly what you mean,"

Deirdre answered her daughter;

"I will never be able to drive along here again without thinking she's going to be waiting for us."

They both sighed. The sun was shining in defiance of their mood and the lake glinted and shone as the reflections caught the bright rays. Out on the lake, one or two boats were being rowed with families sitting together in the low seats. The sound of children's laughter came up to them from the play area and the whole scene was vibrant, noisy and full of signs that life was going on all around them.

Pulling up at Johanna's old residence, the matron was waiting for them as they walked into the hall dazzlingly bright with the light of the sun. She handed them the key to Johanna's old room and said she would bring a tray of tea through to them shortly.

They spent the next couple of hours engrossed in the task of sorting through clothes and personal items.

"What a sad job this is Mum, it doesn't seem right somehow to be giving these things away."

"I know what you mean, but someone may as well have use of them, I'm sure your Nan would approve."

"I know I'm being silly and irrational, but I keep expecting her to walk in and ask us what we think we're doing, and what have we done with all her clothes?"

As she spoke, Celia was on her hands and knees in front of the wardrobe.

"There's a box of some description here, it's a bit dusty, seems to have been pushed underneath as though she had hidden it."

She sat back on her heels and blew the dust from an old chocolate box. She sneezed violently a couple of times as the dust got up her nose.

"Bless you"

Her mum said looking over her shoulder,

"is there anything inside?"

Lifting the lid of the old box carefully, Celia said,

"Gosh this must have been here for ages the box is very tatty."

She sat and stared at the contents. There was an envelope on which Celia's name was written in Johanna's spidery hand writing. Eagerly she slipped out the contents and held in her hand two smaller envelopes. One was again hand written in the same bright blue ink her Nan always used, and the other one had Johanna's name in a strong hand that she didn't recognise.

"What d'you make of this mum?"

"Well there's only one way to find out, you'll have to open them and take a look."

Celia sat with the two envelopes in her hand. She had such a strong feeling that her Nan was standing right beside her. She even felt she could smell her perfume or was that just her imagination playing tricks. A door slammed making them both jump and the curtains in the open window billowed out into the room, causing the pile of newspaper and magazines to blow onto the floor from the stool they had been placed on earlier. Celia shivered but she wasn't cold. She could feel something hard and metallic in the envelope addressed to her, and making a decision she turned and looking up to Deirdre said,

"Do you mind very much if I save this for later? I have a strong feeling that I want to be alone to really think about Nan, do you mind?"

She asked again. She thought she detected a look of disappointment on her mum's face, but she said,

"if that's what you want to do love, then that's what you must do. I think we're more or less through here anyway aren't we, I can't wait to be out of here now, there are too many memories for me."

Driving away from the home, Celia heard her mum say,

"let's just stop briefly by the lake. I could do with a breath of air after all that and we probably not come here much now your Nan's gone."

She swallowed hard to get rid of the lump that had suddenly come into her throat. They parked the car and walked across the grass. Standing on the side of the water it was so good to feel the breeze on their face's and in their hair.

Looking down Celia saw their reflection in the still waters of the lake. Mother and daughter, so alike and united in the grief they shared for the woman that was ultimately responsible for them both being here They did not mention the box or the mysterious envelopes and Celia was glad her Mum had respected her wish to open them later when she was alone.

It wasn't until much later that she had the opportunity. They had finished dinner and were sitting quietly over a cup of coffee reflecting on the day. Hugh was reading the obituary section of the local Cardiff paper where they had placed the announcement of Johanna's death.

"I wonder how many people will turn up at the crematorium, there are people who knew your Nan that we have simply lost touch with. I hope they see the notice."

The funeral was to take place in two day's time and after the service they had arranged a room at a nearby Hotel where friends and family would be able to meet and pay their respects to the old lady. Celia wasn't looking forward to that, but knew it was expected. It would also give them an opportunity to meet with people that they hadn't seen for some time.

"Isn't it a shame that it takes a funeral to bring families together?"

Deirdre said.

Celia had spoken to Seb when they returned from her Nan's place and he said how much he was looking forward to seeing her the next day.

"It's such an age since I saw you, I've really missed you my dear, you've been away too long."

She thought again of his word's and wished she could summon up some enthusiasm.

"Please watch your drinking in front of my family, especially in view of the circumstances"

"Don't fuss Celia, you know you can rely on me not to let you down, you sound as though you're ashamed of me."

There was a barely discernible change in his tone, which her well-tuned ear picked up on, and she felt with dread the possible scene if he did drink too much in front of all her family.

Chapter 27

At last, alone in her room Celia took out the two envelopes from her Nan's box carefully opened the one addressed to her and a small silver locket fell into her hand. There was also a letter. The sheet's folded carefully in half. It was dated 31st December 1999.She read the words her Nan had written to her with her heart pounding.

My dear Celia,

If you're reading this it will mean that I am no longer with you. Please don't be sad as I've lived a long time and had my share of happiness and my share of sorrow. Happiness in watching my daughter live a happy and fulfilling life and in giving me such a beautiful granddaughter. Sorrow in wondering what might have been.

I'm sure you know that I loved your granddad and we were happy. I think as you get older you tend to notice more about other people and how their lives are. It's probably because we have more time to sit and reflect, and observe. In my recent observations of you, I feel that you are not as happy as you deserve to be. I recognise something in your eyes that I have seen in my own .Because of this observation; I'm going to share something with you that I have always kept secret. Even your own Mother doesn't know.

Many years ago, when she was a small girl I fell in love with another man, and he with me. We were true soul mates, a meeting of mind and spirits that happens rarely, and some people never experience in their whole lifetime.
We wanted desperately to be together but things were very different in those days. Marriage was for life, and walking away from the vows made before god were taken much

more seriously. We were both married to other people and although we desperately wanted to be together, we respected our vows and remained in our marriages. It was the hardest thing I have ever had to do in my life. We said goodbye and never saw each other again.

I was left with only my memories, a letter he wrote me and the small silver locket. Both of these you will find in this envelope.

I'm entrusting these precious thing to you as I know you will understand and take care of them. I also want you to know that if I had my time over again, I would have followed my heart and not spent the rest of my life regretting what might have been. Take note of my words my dear. If you are not happy you must be strong enough to do something about it, or you may live the rest of your life wondering and regretting that they gave up your one true chance of real happiness.

I know you will take care of my memories which are why I am entrusting them to your safe keeping.
Be happy Celia my dear, and remember, follow your heart.

With my love,

Your Nan.

With cheeks wet from the tears running unchecked down her face, Celia took the other envelope and opening began to read.

My darling Johanna,

If I live to be 100 I will never regret meeting you and the exquisite joy our short time together has brought me. I believe that we were meant to be together but I understand the reasons why we never can be, and respect your decision, even though it's tearing me apart.

I want you to know that never before or in the future will I ever love anyone the way I love you. We are true soul mates and have but a single heart.
If ever you need me for any reason at all, you know I will always be here for you. You know how to get in touch with me. I will always be waiting.

Your own true heart,

Edward.

Celia had to go to the box of tissues on her dressing table and soak up the tears that were dripping off the end of her chin before she could go on .Sniffing loudly; she took the small locket in her fingers and noticed it was in two halves. It was difficult to open but eventually, she managed it and walking to her bedside lamp she held it up to the light. She realised she was holding her breath and let it out slowly. In her hand the locket opened to reveal two small photographs, one on either side. The one on the left she realised was her Nan when she was much younger. She was smiling up at the camera and her hair was in a bun with small tendrils of hair curling against her face. She had a thick sprinkling of freckles across her nose and cheeks.

The other photograph was of a young man. He looked to be in his twenties and was dressed in the formal fashion of some sixty or more years ago with a dark tie against a white shirt collar. His hair was short and he had a dark moustache which suited his handsome face.

Closing the locket with a snap she lifted it and put it over her head. Her hand went up to touch it and she felt somewhat comforted from feeling it against her neck.

Chapter 28

Walking into the crowded church at the crematorium, Celia was glad to have Sebastian's arm to hold on to. Having arrived a couple of days before and had been unusually quiet for him. She hadn't mentioned the incident on Saturday evening, or even told him about the conversation she had had with Gilly about his untimely appearance at Parsonage farm the weekend before .The fact that he hadn't mentioned it either, spoke volumes. They followed her mum and dad and she saw her brother and Enzo out of the corner of her eye. The music in the small church brought a lump to her throat, as Ella Fitzgerald's haunting voice was sang

"Every time we say goodbye."

One of her Nan's favourite's. She had promised herself she wasn't going to cry. She thought she would be alright as long as she didn't have to speak.

Listening to the voice of the minister, she was so pleased that they had taken the time to speak to him about their Nan and her life.

As they walked out of the small church, she kept her head down, noticing out of the corner of her eye the throng of people standing at the back, without seats. Her Nan and Granddad had been well loved and had lived here all their lives and so many people had come to pay their respects. She was so touched to see that Ralph and Gilly had made the journey over to give their support. How typical of her dear friend. She noticed that although Gilly was dressed respectfully in black, her bright hair shone like a new penny, belying the feeling of sadness and mourning. Celia caught her eye and nodded to her friend. People were standing in small groups, talking quietly and hugging each other. Dark clothes and sombre faces reflecting sadness and grief that united them all. The minister in his long black and white robes, smiling sadly and shaking hands as he spoke quiet words of condolence to everyone as they filed out of the small church into the grey, rain soaked afternoon. A large black bird swooped down from a nearby tree and settled on the edge of a wooden seat, his yellow eyes watching, as people milled around. Celia noticed out of the corner of her eye the lone figure of an old man, his head bowed and his shoulders hunched. He had the collar of his dark wool coat turned up against the chill of the damp afternoon and was getting into a car, where a driver sat waiting. Before she had a chance to follow, the car pulled away and moved slowly passed the crowds. She looked at his face and thought she saw the glimpse of a smile directed at her, as the car drove slowly passed.

Why did it always rain at funerals, it was as though the heavens had opened pouring out the grief that everyone felt. Celia stood under the large umbrella held by Alistair. Clinging onto his arm she looked up into his face and saw her own sadness reflected in his eyes. There were so many floral tributes. They walked together and looked at the names of all the people who had remembered Johanna. Alistair pointed to a small bunch of hand tied yellow roses. They stood out amongst all the more formal wreaths and arrangements.

"I wonder who these are from;"

He said bending down to pick up the sweet smelling flowers.

"Good thing the card is encased in cellophane otherwise we'd never be able to read it in this awful downpour."

Handing them to Celia, he looked over her shoulder as she read out

"With my love, Edward"

"Who's Edward?"

He said, I don't remember Nan mentioning anyone called Edward, do you Celie? She shook her head thinking that she would probably tell him later about the letter's her Nan had left her. She immediately thought of the old man she had just noticed driving away and thinking with amazement that her Nan's Edward must be still alive. She hadn't recognised him from the old photo, but then she hadn't really been looking for him. She unconsciously put her hand up to where the silver locket nestled in the small hollow at the base of her neck, hidden by her pale grey cashmere sweater, and thought again about the sadness of a lost love and opportunity.

"Have you ever seen so many people, how Nan would have loved to have been here to see them all"

Later gathered at the Hotel, Deirdre and her family were gathered on a table talking quietly about the funeral.

"It all went well didn't it"?

"I told you not to worry love; we gave her a good send off."

Celia sat next to her Dad, comforted by his arm, which was around the back of her chair. She listened to him saying,

"I think we'd better circulate, I can see your Aunty Edna over there all on her own, I'll go and get her a drink."

Looking over her shoulder for Seb she saw him at the bar talking to Enzo, who didn't look very pleased. She had a sudden fear of him having a go at her husband about her confidences the other weekend. She knew Enzo was impetuous and often spoke from his heart without thinking of the consequences. She also knew her husband could be nasty when he'd been drinking.

She brought her thoughts back to the present, knowing that Enzo wouldn't really say anything about her weekend with Mark. Was that only a week ago? She could hardly believe it, seemed more like a month, since she had seen Mark. She was also thinking what might have happened between them if her Nan hadn't suddenly been taken ill. Perhaps it wasn't meant to be, her and Mark. So why had it felt so right? Seb was drinking; she could see him with what had to be a whiskey in his hand. Should she approach him or would he create a scene, here of all places. Before she had time to make a decision she realised that her brother had joined Enzo and they were both leading Seb away from the bar to sit at a nearby table. She also heard her husband's raised voice as he tried to shrug of Enzo's arm but thankfully, he seemed to give in and sit with them.

It was much later when they finally arrived back at the familiar house in Bristol; they were all together as a family, her mum, dad, brother, Enzo and her and Seb. If it wasn't for the sadness of the occasion, she would have enjoyed it. She thought about the impending journey home and was relieved when her parents had persuaded them to leave the drive back to Wiltshire until the next morning.

"You must be worn out; one more night won't hurt."

He had tried to protest, but was outnumbered and had quietly given in. The evening passed quietly and without any problems. She was glad to be finally able to get some sleep. Her brother and Enzo had left for London soon after they'd all got back to her parents' house. They had both hugged her warmly and Allie had whispered in her ear,

"If he hurts you let me know, I'll kill him"

Now, getting ready for bed in the same room as Seb, she had told him how exhausted she was and needed a good night's sleep. Thankfully he'd taken the hint and was soon snoring loudly. She turned on her side facing away from him and slipping her hand under her head, settled down to sleep.

Chapter 29

Mark hadn't heard anything from Celia since that one phone call just before her Nan's funeral. Common sense told him that it was difficult for her to contact him, but since when had common sense had anything to do with affairs of the heart. Every time his phone rang he looked anxiously at the screen, hoping to see her name. So far he had been disappointed. He resisted the urge to call her knowing it might be difficult for her to talk but it was proving to be more and more difficult not to be in contact. He wished he had someone to confide in, but there was only Will and that probably wasn't a good idea. It wasn't that he didn't trust his friend but Celia and her husband were well known around here so he didn't want to take the risk. Then there was the other problem of Julie. She had managed to catch up with him yesterday and he could see from the look in her eyes and her body language that she was still interested. She just didn't seem to want to listen, and finally in desperation he had agreed to meet her this evening. He would take her to a pub in a village the other side of Stonehenge. It was a bit far out but he didn't want to be seen with her at the Nag's Head.

Celia knew she should have been in touch with Mark. They had arrived back early Sunday after driving home from Bristol. The first thing she had done was to take Amber out. She had been so excited to see her mistress and had shaken her head, her beautiful red gold mane rippling like water in the sun. She had called Gilly and they arranged to meet. They rode out together across Salisbury plain and Celia felt the freedom and exhilaration she always got from riding her beloved horse. All the pain and sorrow of the last week gradually fell away as they galloped on across the Wiltshire countryside.

"Gosh, I needed that; it's been far too long."

They had stopped under a large silver birch. The sun was high and was making patterns on the grassy bank where the two horses and riders were.

They had dismounted and were sitting on the grass. Celia lay back and rested her head on her up stretched arms and let out a sigh.

"Penny for them"

Gilly's voice seemed to come from far away as Celia felt her body and mind relax.

"I don't know if they're worth a penny, but it certainly feels great to be here and to feel so relaxed after all the upset of the past few weeks."

For a long moment no one spoke as the friends were comfortable with their silence. There was a bird singing close by, and the rest of the busy world seemed to have receded. After a while Celia raised herself on her elbows and began to speak.

"Oh Gilly, I feel so mixed up at the moment, my head is in pieces."

She was unconsciously playing with the silver locket around her neck when her friend said,

"I haven't noticed you wearing that locket before, is it new?"

Celia lifted it over her head and prising open the two halves with her thumb nail, leaned over and held it out to Gilly, who took it in her own hand and looked intently at the two pictures. Celia began to tell her friend all about her

Nan's box and the two letters she had left for her, She mentioned also the last time she had seen her Nan and what she had confided to her.

"She was obviously trying to tell me something, don't you think?"

"She was telling you to be true to yourself, and to follow your instincts if you're not happy, and you're not are you Cee?"

"Is it that obvious?"

"Well, it is to me, and it also seems it was to your Nan. We both love you and can see that something is making you very unhappy, or should that be someone?"

"You can always see right through me, can't you? It's Seb, I know he's trying to change and there haven't been any more of those savage attacks, and I really mean to try and make it work, I'm just not trying hard enough, that's the problem"

"It always comes back to you doesn't it, Cee why are you always so hard on yourself? Perhaps it's time you stopped trying and realised it's never going to work between the two of you. Would I be prying if I asked what the situation is between you and Mark? You haven't mentioned him for ages"

the silence hung between them and she saw a lone tear slide down Celia's face which she hastily brushed away.

"Oh Gilly I just don't know perhaps I imagined all that as well. I haven't heard anything from him since I got back."

"Were you meant to, surely you must realise how difficult it is for him to call. He probably thinks you might still be in Bristol or with Seb when the phone rings. How were things between you when you last saw him?"

She noticed the pale blush spread up into her friend's face and her green eyes took on a dreamy far away expression.

"O.K. you don't have to tell me, the look in your eyes speaks volumes."

"I think if I carry on seeing Mark, it won't give my marriage a fair chance, besides, it's really difficult to get away, and it's not fair on Mark. He could have any woman he wanted."

"But not *the one* he wants, by the sound of things."

Gilly had leaned over and put both her hands onto Celia's shoulders.

"Think long and hard about what you really want, put yourself first for once. I'm not saying give up on your marriage, if you really want to make a success of it then give it your best shot, but remember, it takes two to make a marriage work, you can't do it on your own and I don't want you to get hurt .Ralph and I were horrified by Seb's behaviour the other night."

"Yes, but it's only when he's been drinking, it changes him into a completely different person, not the man I married or love."

"Do you still love him?"

"Oh Gilly, I'm just so mixed up, I'm not sure of anything anymore. Let's change the subject, I'm getting bored with this and so are you I'm sure, Let's ride."

As they stopped at the Gate of the old house, the subject of the Ball came up.

"I really don't know what to do about it now with my Nan and everything, it hardly seems appropriate to go out dancing and having fun at the moment."

"Well, I am sure that your Nan would have been the first one to tell you to go, she always wanted what was best for you, and after all it's not for another couple of weeks, so think about it, there's a good girl. Ralph and I would really like you to be there, it just wouldn't be the same without you."

They sat astride their respective horses and Gilly smiled into Celia's worried face.

"I'll talk to you tomorrow; think over what I said about you and Seb. If you really want it to work, give it all your effort, but only if you're sure it's what you really want, any way I'm off. Come on Jasper, let's get home."

Digging in her heels and with a shout to her horse, she was gone and Celia watched as horse and rider trotted off down the lane, wishing, not for the first time that she could go with her to the peaceful homely atmosphere of Parsonage farm, rather than to her own big unwelcoming house.

Sitting in his study, Sebastian was reflecting on the events of the last few days. He had been pleased to see his wife but could have done without all her family. They always seemed to be so protective of her, as if she needed to be protected from me, after all I am her husband, as if I'd hurt her. He thought about the times recently when he'd lost it. But that was different, he reasoned with himself. If I stay sober I'll be o.k. and I fully intend to stay sober so what's the problem. He had tried more than once recently to imagine his life without her by his side, and it just wasn't something he could envisage. Life without Celia would be unbearable. He must make her understand how much he needed and wanted her. His life simply wouldn't be worth living if he lost her. He made up his mind to make a super human effort to keep her by his side, and if that meant staying off the whiskey, then so be it. That's exactly what he would do. He saw her now out of the window of his study. She had dismounted from her horse and was talking to the young groom who came up from the village to help out. How beautiful she looked, and so sexy in that get up. He wanted her so badly and imagined being able to make love to her in all that riding gear. He could just see them rolling around in the hay together. He felt himself get hard just thinking about it. He heard Arthurs approaching and tried to think about something else. Taking a deep breath he called come in to the light tap on the study door, and looked up to see his butler walking in with a tray of coffee he had requested earlier. He heard Celia walking in through the hallway and called out to her to join him. She poked her head around the door and said,

"I need a shower, I'm all sweaty from my ride, I'll see you later."

And she was gone. He sat there alone looking at the door, his mind on the thoughts of her naked and beautiful in the room above. He got up from his chair and walked purposefully up the stairs to their room. He could hear her humming softly to herself and recognised Puccini. Not his first choice, but he knew she loved it He heard the sound of the shower being turned on as he entered the room they had shared for the last three years and caught his breath as he saw her. She was completely naked and was in the process of twisting her hair up and catching it in a band of blue ribbon her breasts were pointing upwards and the dark nipples stood firm and erect against her pale skin. He walked to her side and noticed the look in her eyes. He realised with horror that she was afraid of him. She had backed away and picked up a silk dressing gown that had been lying on the bed.

"You startled me; I didn't hear you come in"

Reaching out he made as if to touch her but she backed away again and facing him spoke quickly, as if she wanted to say something before she had a chance to change her mind.

"Look Seb, I really am trying but you'll have to be patient with me. The way you've been lately has affected me a lot more than you realise and you're going to have to wait. I'm not ready yet."

Noticing the look in his eyes she said,

"Please don't look like that, I just need a little more time. Please be patient."

He spoke quietly

"If you need me to wait, then I'll wait. I can't imagine my life without you my darling, without you I have nothing to live for"

He took a small step nearer to where she stood and cautiously put out one hand and rested it lightly on Celia's shoulder which was now covered in the thin silk robe. He should back away but as she stood in front of him like a statue, he gently put his arms around her. He could feel her heart beating wildly and he had the grace to feel guilty as he realised the reason for her distress.

"Please Seb; I need a shower, I'll see you later, please!"

He caught the look in her eyes and taking a step backwards left her.

"I'll see you at dinner, take your time my darling, don't worry, I'll leave you in peace."

Chapter 30

Mark was already beginning to regret his invitation to Julie. They had left the camp and were driving through the lanes. The evening had started well with the sun going down in a red glow but a breeze had sprung up and leaves were swirling around the car as they approached the village of Mendlesham. He began to realise that she had misinterpreted his motives. She was chattering in her usual loud manner which was getting on his nerves, and she had manoeuvred her body until her thigh was as near to his as possible. Mark could feel her body heat and felt nothing except revulsion and an ache inside, which made him realise how much he was missing Celia. He had been in turmoil of indecision as she still hadn't called him and he wondered if he dare risk calling her.

"Mark, I'm talking to you, where are you, you seem to be miles away."

"Sorry, what were you saying?"

"I asked where you were taking me, are we nearly there?"

Before he had a chance to speak, she continued,

"I'm so pleased you asked me out again tonight, I had such a great time when we went to that Chinese place in Salisbury, it was really great wasn't it, are we going to eat tonight, I'm starved, and not just of food, if you know what I mean."

He felt her hand on his thigh and his thoughts strayed again to Celia, and he wondered where she was and what she was doing. Distractedly, he moved Julie's hand away from where it was resting on his leg, and taking his eyes from the road for a second said,

"Look Julie, can we just be friends?"

He immediately noticed her manner change.

"What d'you mean friends are you Gay or something?"

"It's nothing like that Julie, of course I'm not Gay, it's just that,"

….he broke off realising that whatever he said next would be difficult for her to accept. If he said he didn't fancy her it would be hurtful, but how could he explain there was someone else without incriminating Celia, besides he still didn't know where he stood, having heard nothing.

"Well if you're not Gay I don't see what the problem is, we're both available and fancy free aren't we?"

When Mark did not answer straight away, she looked at him more closely and said suddenly wide eyed,

"There is someone isn't there, have you been two timing me, how dare you Mark."

Her colour had risen and she had fury in her eyes as Mark struggled to deny her accusations. It was futile and she slid her body away from his toward the far side of the front seat and raising her voice even louder she said

"Just turn the car around Mark, I just want to go back to camp, NOW!"

She was shouting loudly and with a resigned sigh he slowed and reversed into the gateway of a field and began to drive back the way they had come. Common sense told him that she was beyond reasoning. He drove in silence until they arrived back at the camp where she immediately got out of the car and slamming the door, walked quickly away towards the female officer's quarters, her blonde hair rising in a cloud around her head as it was caught and buffeted by the wind. Mark sat for a long time after she had disappeared and wondered if he dare ring Celia.

Celia was putting the phone down as Seb came into the room. He smiled at her almost shyly.

"Mum and Dad said to say Hi".

That wasn't exactly what they had said. She recalled her Dad's words now as she faced her husband.

"How are things between you and Seb has there been any more talk of you not getting pregnant? Are you sure you're not keeping something from me sweetheart"

She was sure her Dad didn't truly believe her when she said everything was ok, but she really was trying and felt that Seb was too. Her dad had always been understanding and seemed to be on Celia's wave length, but her mum tended to be a bit on the judgemental side and Celia often thought she needed her approval, which wasn't always forthcoming. Now, thinking of her relationship with her own mother, a picture of Gilly baking in her warm kitchen, with her small daughter standing on a chair, covered in flour came into her mind and she tried to imagine herself with a child. How would it feel to have Mark's child, would it have his fair good looks? She was immediately angry with herself for thinking of Mark. She had tried not to think of how being with him in London had made her feel, pushing her true feelings under the surface. She heard again, his voice when he had called her the other day. He had sounded so anxious and said he was missing her and when could they meet? He had sounded so devastated when she said she wasn't going to see him again. She almost gave in then and had had to steel herself against the torrent of words that had tumbled from his mouth, willing herself not to respond to his pleading.

"Celia, please don't do this to us?"

He had said, and she'd heard his anger and frustration. For a split second, felt her resolve begin to weaken and making a huge effort said,

"It's no good Mark, I have to really work at saving my marriage"

"If you have to work so hard at something, surely it's not right in the first place?"

He had answered and if she was honest with herself, he probably had a point, but her mind was made up.

She knew that if she and Seb were going to have any chance at all, she had to give her marriage her whole attention and not have any distractions. Seb was also trying to make it work and he had been very patient with her. When they were in bed he had made no move to touch her and for that at least she was grateful, although she found her resolve was at its weakest when they were lying side by side. Her mind kept recalling Mark's lean firm body and she could almost feel his hands on her, touching and exciting her, but she had made up her mind and was determined to stand by her decision.

The subject of her not being pregnant seemed to have been forgotten, and as she didn't want to rock the boat she hadn't brought it up either. It had been a couple of weeks since they had returned from Bristol and she had tried to get back to normal. She had thrown all her energy into keeping her mind and body full of ordinary mundane things in an effort to drive all thoughts of Mark, and what might have been from her head. She and Gilly spent a lot of time together riding, and she walked often in the beautiful countryside that she had come to love so much. She realised just how lucky she was to have so much freedom and luxury in her life, and had to admit, there was a great deal to be said, for being Seb's wife.

She had mentioned the forthcoming Ball to her parents and voiced her reluctance to go in view of her sadness at her Nan's death, but they had both told her she must. It was what her Nan would have wanted. She knew deep in her heart they were right and the picture had come into her head of her Nan and Edward. She wondered not for the first time, what her Nan would say about her choosing Seb over Mark, but she had made up her mind and wasn't going to change it now.

****

She and Gilly had been shopping in Salisbury and Celia had found shoes to go with the beautiful dress she had bought in London. The busy market town was teeming with people. It was a beautiful warm, early summer day. There were stalls set out, as a Farmers Market was taking place, and many farms from nearby were represented. Gilly knew a lot of the stallholders which kept delaying them, as they called out to her as they tried to make their way through the wooden tables and bright awnings. Many of the local farmers knew Sebastian. Most of them had known him since he had been a small boy, and had listened to stories about his family since they themselves had been children. There was a lot of local resentment. Why should the toffs have it so easy when they had a constant struggle to make ends meet? The older people had sons of Sebastian's age, who had given up the struggle of trying to make a decent living from the land and moved away to other jobs in London, or even abroad, which itself caused resentment. There had been some initial prejudging of Celia, but she had won at least some of them around. The ladies group on Wednesday's had given a lot of the local women a chance to get to know her, and they in turn had talked their men folk around. Despite this, Celia felt many eyes on her as they mingled with the crowds on this beautiful June day.

They had finally stopped at a small coffee shop and sat at one of the outside tables and ordered lattés and double chocolate muffins.

"Should we be eating these?"

Celia said with crumbs of chocolate falling from her mouth,

"I'll never get into my dress at this rate."

"Nonsense, there's nothing of you, not like me."

Her friend had replied.

"Still, Ralph seems to like me the way I am, says there's plenty to hold onto."

Gilly was easing her foot out of her shoe, as she spoke.

"That's better; I've wanted to do that for the last twenty minutes"

She said as reaching under the table, she rubbed her aching toes.

When she had first seen her friend in all the finery for the ball, she had gasped with admiration.

"My God Cee, I always knew you were beautiful but in that dress you are absolutely stunning. You take my breath away, goodness what effect you will have on all those red blooded males, they won't stand a chance. I'm going to look so dowdy next to you."

"Nonsense, you are always beautiful."

She had hugged her friend reassuringly. The morning had been very pleasant, and they were both feeling tired but exhilarated thinking of the forthcoming Ball that was to be held the following Saturday. It was June and the country side was full of rich summer beauty. The trees were heavy with blossom the hedgerows were bursting with hawthorn and the birds were in full song. How glorious the countryside is, how I could ever imagine I had loved living in London in the summer. It even smells so much fresher here.

As Celia dropped her friend off at home she recalled the telephone conversation she had had with her Brother a few days ago. She had been sitting in the large, heavily ornate sitting room in the castle, which even on such a golden day managed to be dark and gloomy. She pictured her brother and Enzo in their light modern and beautiful flat and wished they lived nearer; she could have done with one of Enzo's bear hugs.

Alistair had been horrified when she told him she would not be seeing Mark again.

"Don't try and fool me Celie, remember, Enzo and I saw you and Mark together and I'll never believe you don't feel anything for him, I saw it with my own eyes. How has he reacted to this latest bomb shell, don't tell me he's happy about it."

Celia had struggled with that seeing again the heartbreak etched on Mark's face, and remembering the despair in his voice when she had told him she wouldn't be seeing him again. He had pleaded with her to change her mind, and she had found it hard to stay strong. Now driving the short distance from Parsonage farm to her own home with the sun dazzling in her eyes, her brother's words came back to her,

"Think about Nan's letter, she wanted you to be happy, and not to spend your life regretting, as she did, are you really sure about this? Enzo and I love you and we can't bear to think of you being unhappy. Why stay with a man who treats you so badly, life is too short you know, we only get one chance at life so make the most of every opportunity."

As she pulled her car around into the drive way of her home she could hear him again in her mind.

"Enzo and I noticed that Seb was drinking at the funeral, how has he been since then? "If I find out he's been hurting you I won't be responsible for my actions, Celie, you know how much I hate bullies, god knows, Enzo and I have had our fair share of bullies and I can't bear to think of you being subjected to Seb when he's being nasty."

Despite herself, she had smiled weakly at that, as her brother was one of the least aggressive men she knew. She had tried to convince herself and Alistair that she was doing the right thing, and that Seb wasn't drinking, but she didn't sound convincing even to herself.

Chapter 31

As Sebastian pulled up outside the consultant's practice, he cursed under his breath as he realised there was nowhere to park. The idea of simply turning around and going home came invitingly into his head, but he dismissed it realising he might as well get this over with now that he was here. He manoeuvred his silver Porch into a three point turn and drove off toward a sign for a car park he had noticed on his way in. As he approached the door with Professor Junuszevski"s name in gold lettering he realised he was nervous. What the hell am I going to do if he tells me I can never father a child? The thought was too awful to contemplate. He had told himself all along that he couldn't possibly be infertile. Just look at the rest of his family, they had all been prolific when it came to producing children. No it couldn't be his fault. Why then had Celia's results shown that she was perfectly healthy and normal. A niggle of doubt kept nagging away inside his head like a hammer on a stone. It seemed to reverberate inside his skull as though it was trying to get out. He realised with a jolt there was the sound of a woman's voice coming from the intercom system in the door.

"Hello, hello, may I help you, is anyone there?"

The tone sounded impatient and bending low, he quickly spoke his name, mouth against the grill, and was rewarded with a loud buzzing noise that told him he could now go inside. The same bossy woman was seated at the desk he remembered from a few weeks ago. She looked up and smiled as Sebastian walked in.

"Good afternoon please take a seat, the professor is expecting you."

"Exactly what she said last time."

Sebastian mumbled under his breath, you'd think she'd get sick and tired of smiling that false smile and saying the same thing over and over again. He was suddenly back at school and sitting outside the Head's study. How he had hated school. He'd always seemed to be trying to live up to his brother Charles. He was three years above Sebastian and excelling at everything, he was a hard act to follow. Old Caruthers, the head had taken great delight in throwing up his brother's achievement at every opportunity. He was a bully and reminded Sebastian of his Father. He was sure they both must have got together and gang up on him. Why did he always seem to be surrounded by bullies? Even the boy's in the dorm had picked on him. He'd been very lonely when he'd first started, and missed his Mother. He was only seven. Some of the other boys had heard him "snivelling into his pillow" the first week he was there and had never let him forget it. They had pinched his pyjama trousers night after night and he had been subjected to the utter humiliation of chasing after Travers who held the stripy bottoms high whilst chanting

"cry baby cry baby"

to the delight of the rest of his gang. The picture of himself running through the dorm, hands held protectively in front of his "private parts" as his mother used to call his penis and testicles was still as fresh as the day it happened. So now here I am still missing my pyjama bottoms and exposing myself, figuratively speaking, anyway he thought ironically.

Sitting in the high backed chair facing the Doctor, he tried to take a deep breath to still his racing mind. Professor Januschevski was looking down at a file in his hand. He looked up at Sebastian and said in his accented voice,

"I'm afraid it's not good news."

Sebastian's heart seemed to stop and he felt that the professor's voice was coming from the bottom of a long dark tunnel. Forcing himself to concentrate he looked him full in the eye and waited.

"The tests we have undertaken have proved conclusively that you are not able to Father a child."

Sebastian's voice seemed to come out in a thin strangled version of his normal one, he tried to swallow. His throat felt tight and dry and he asked if he could have a drink. The consultant spoke softly into the intercom on his desk and almost immediately a woman in a white uniform appeared carrying a glass of water. He drank greedily, immediately feeling the cool liquid relieve the tension in his throat, and then said in a barely audible whisper.

"Could there have been any mistake?"

He looked into the face of the man opposite and saw compassion. When he spoke he did so in a quiet and modulated voice.

"The tests are conclusive, there can be no mistake."

"Are you?" Sebastian started to speak, but was cut short as the consultant said,

"Yes, I'm sure, as I said there can be no mistake, without going into too much technical jargon, there are a number of reasons they are all connected with your spermatozoa."

"Please explain"

Sebastian asked in a voice that shook. The professor went on,

"Firstly, you have a very low sperm count and your spermatozoa are malformed, there is also a problem with sperm mobility. This means that in simple terms they are not able to travel fast or far enough to fertilise the eggs produced by your wife."

Sebastian took a long drink from the glass that was still in his hand that he realised was shaking. He was having difficulty taking in the words. In his mind he pictured his father and the sneering look on his face when he found out. If he ever finds out, I'm certainly not going to give him the satisfaction, he said to himself.

"How can you tell all this, is that a stupid question?"

"No not at all, we simply examine your sample under a microscope, and as to the sperm count we see how many there are and then average it up."

The two men sat facing each other. For a long moment no one spoke.

"Have you and your wife ever considered adoption?"

The pompous Sebastian was back

"Adoption! me, in my position, of course not. Surely there must be a cure, I don't care what it costs, and money is no object."

"If only it were that simple, I'm afraid there is no cure at this present time, this of course may change in the future as there is always research being undertaken. For now though you may want to consider IVF treatment by Donor for your wife or as I said adoption is another option."
"Thank you, no, adoption is quite out of the question, so is

IVF, I wouldn't even consider it, no it's definitely NOT an option."

As he spoke he rose to his feet and began walking toward the door. Almost as an afterthought he said over his shoulder as he left,

"Sorry, I have to get out of here,"

And walking quickly out of the room he hurried down the stairs. Professor Januschevski sat looking after the disappearing figure. He had seen many people in all his years as a consultant and human reaction had long since ceased to surprise or affect him, but he couldn't help feeling a little bit sorry for this man who appeared to the outside world to have everything, and yet the one thing he truly craved eluded his grasp.

****

Gilly drove to The House with mixed feelings. As much as she loved having Celia for a friend, it was sometimes hard to be near someone with so much natural charm and beauty, and often made Gilly feel even more matronly and frumpy. She felt so old next to her friend, when in reality; there were only a few years between them.

"I'm still not sure about this dress Cee; it looks so ordinary next to yours. I wish I could lose a couple of stone before tomorrow night."

Gilly and Celia were in the main bedroom at Stratford House. Celia was dressed only in a cream silk slip and Gilly was standing on tiptoes, her feet bear, looking into a full length mirror whilst smoothing down an ankle length black dress which was pulling across her large motherly bosom. Celia held out a pair of black strappy shoes that were decorated with glittery silver sequins.

"You'll feel better with high heels on, and I think you should borrow my Diamond cross, it'll really be the finishing touch."

"I couldn't possibly wear that, besides Sebastian gave it to you didn't he. I'm sure he wouldn't be very pleased to see me wearing it."

The very fact that her friend was offering to lend her the cross gave Gilly a huge insight into her feelings for her husband, and his gift.

"Anyway, thanks for the offer but it are not a necklace I need but a complete makeover."

Celia looked at her friend and said suddenly,

"What a great idea. I'll give you a facial and you already said you're having your hair done in the morning didn't you? Besides you're much too hard on yourself, take a good look in that mirror you are standing in front of and tell me what you see. I don't want to hear any negative stuff, aren't you the one who's always accusing me of putting myself down?"

Below them, Sebastian was walking in through the front door. He shouted for Arthurs and walked quickly into his study where he began to pace up and down, with a hand raised to his forehead. He closed his eyes and took a deep sigh as he crumpled the piece of paper in his hand and threw it towards the waste paper bin. It fell onto the carpet and Arthurs appearing in the doorway made as if to pick it up. Sebastian leaped across the room and snatched it from the floor pushing it deep into his pocket. Arthurs noticed that Sebastian was fiddling with his ear. Never a good sign, what's going on here, something's up, he thought to himself.

In the bedroom above, Celia was looking in the full length mirror in her bedroom at her friend's reflection staring back at her. She saw a beautiful woman with the glow that comes from a happy and contented life.

"So Gilly, what do you see?"

Gilly said

"I see an overweight plain mumsy farmers wife who's deluding herself that she could look anything like reasonable beside a stunning beauty like you."

With a gentle smile on her face, Celia stepped forward and hugged her friend affectionately.

"Oh Gilly, now who's being the negative one, you truly are beautiful, take those blinkers off your eyes and really see yourself."

Gilly's face broke into a wide grin and suddenly they were both choking with hysterical laughter that bubbled up and out of their mouths. They fell onto the bed and lay there in a tangled heap laughing until the tears ran down both their faces. Pushing herself up to a sitting position Celia said

"You really can't beat a good girly afternoon can you, much as I like men, I certainly couldn't do without my good female friends."

Gilly opened her mouth to reply when suddenly the bedroom door was flung open with a loud crash and Sebastian stood framed in the doorway.

The atmosphere in the room changed immediately. It was as though the temperature suddenly plummeted and Celia got to her feet wrapping her arms protectively around her scantily clad body. She opened her mouth to speak but before she got even a single word out her husband's voice cut in slicing through the now chilly atmosphere.

"What the hell's going on here, can't a man have any peace and quiet in his own bedroom anymore?"

Celia realised in an instant, just how much she hated this man. How had she ever thought that she loved him? He was a bully, just like his father and she felt humiliated by his behaviour, especially in front of her friend, who was looking on with a horrified expression on her face. Pulling herself together with an effort, she turned and faced Sebastian and said in a firm, cold voice,

"Please leave us, and remember this is just as much MY bedroom as yours."

As Sebastian opened his mouth to protest he caught the look on Celia's face and closed his mouth again, and turning on his heel walked out. As the door slammed loudly Celia felt herself calm down and taking a great gulp of air realised that she was shaking. The two women clung together and hugged, taking comfort from each other.

"Oh Gilly, I'm so sorry about that, come on let's get on with your facial"

Seeing the look on her friend's face she continued,

"Please Gilly; I need to feel normal again otherwise I think I'll go mad. I'm not going to let him get to me, or change my mind about this ball tomorrow night; I'm going to need your support to get me through it. I'll get Arthurs to bring us a tray of tea and chocolate biscuits, that will make us feel better, and then we can get down to some serious beautifying."

The rest of the afternoon passed peacefully, and there were no more interruptions

****

A few miles away, in the officers mess plans were underfoot for the Ball tomorrow evening. Will and Mark were overseeing arrangements and it was proving to be a very demanding task.

"So have you decided who you're going to take to this shindig tomorrow night Mark?"

"No, I think I'll go on my own, I don't need to go with anyone do I?"

"Well it's up to you of course but you may stick out like the proverbial sore thumb, if you don't mind that."

Mark had been thinking of not going. He was missing Celia so much he couldn't concentrate on anything for more than a few minutes at a time. The image of her beautiful face and body kept appearing in his sub conscious waking or sleeping she had permeated his very soul and he wasn't even sure that he wanted to assuage her. Try as he might the scent and feel of her in his arms the last time he had seen her in London kept invading his senses. Why oh why did her Nan have to be taken ill that night of all nights. What a selfish cold fish that made him feel for even thinking it. He was also bothered by the last confrontation with Julie. She had looked at him with such hatred that night when she had accused him of being gay, or of having a mystery woman. He knew he had hurt her, a woman scorned, and all that. He had tried to keep out of her way ever since, but that was proving to be easier said than done, as they were fellow officers in the same regiment. A few times he had noticed people stop talking when he appeared, or was he just being paranoid.

He struggled to bring his thoughts back to the job in hand and he and Will carried on organising events for the forthcoming Ball. This was to be a very important event for the army and the Colonel was anxious for them all to make a good impression and to repair some of the fences and build up the trust the Army presence in the area seemed to have shaken. He knew all too well that farming today was harder than ever, with many family farms being forced to close down. The fact that many of the young men in the area had had to move away to earn a living was a bone of contention and the army presence only served to inflame local tempers.

There were to be top table's made up of local dignitaries and each table to be hosted by an officer. The Colonel had spoken to Mark directly a few days ago. He was an upright tall man who had been in the army for most of his adult life. He had a large grey moustache that always seemed to quiver when he was speaking Mark knew that he was well respected and liked but everyone also knew not to get on the wrong side of him. They had been standing at the top of the room, near where the regiment band was to be playing for the forthcoming ball.

"I understand you spoke recently at some local women's group meeting at the local hostelry, is that right Mark?"

Seeing Mark's nod of ascent he continued,

"And I believe that Celia Stratford organised that, am I right again?"

Mark suddenly realised what was coming and tried to think of a way out.

"So Mark, as you already seem to be well in there, you'll be ideal to host the top table with me and my wife. I hear

Lady Stratford is quite a looker, but he's the jealous type so you'll need to be careful, by the way, who are you taking?"

They had moved from the top of the room, and Mark was following the Colonel's upright figure as he walked slowly around, pulling at tables and straightening the framed photographs of past regiments that adorned the walls. Mark was at a loss to know what to say

"Well I thought of going alone."

He said lamely and immediately realised the Colonel was not happy with that by the look on his face. He put his hand on Mark's shoulder and said

"We can't have that can we, don't want The Honourable Sebastian Stratford to think you're after his wife"?

He laughed as though he had cracked a really funny joke and Mark felt in a panic just picturing the evening of the ball. How was he going to get out of this? He was now truly stuck in a situation that was rapidly getting further and further out of his control. His mind raced as he tried in vain to think of a way out and listened with sinking heart as the Colonel carried on speaking.

"A good looking chap like you shouldn't have a problem with the ladies, I'm sure you will be able to find someone to partner you, and as I say, we can't upset the local aristocracy, so see what you can do Mark, I'm relying on you not to let me down."

With that he walked briskly and upright out through the door, and was gone. Mark now remembering the conversation of a few days ago was wishing he was anywhere but here organising this damn Ball.

Chapter 32

The atmosphere in the dining room at Stratford Castle was icy. Ever since Gilly had left to drive the short distance home Celia had been dreading confronting her husband. She still felt upset every time she thought of his outburst earlier and the humiliation he had subjected her to in front of Gilly, so much for his promises. She had told her friend that she was alright and that they would still be able to have a good time at the Ball tomorrow evening but later alone, she hadn't felt nearly as sure. They were seated opposite each other at the dining table. She thought, not for the first time, how incongruous the huge table was for just two of them now for once she was glad of its size as she was able to distance herself from a husband she felt such contempt for. Her mind was racing. She thought about just leaving but didn't want to let Gilly down about tomorrow night. She looked around at the drab dark, overly ornate dining room and realised she had come to hate everything about her home and her life. She thought with longing of the tranquillity and simplicity of her small flat in Chiswick, and her heart felt light as she realised what she was going to do. Why stay in a place she hated with a man she had come to hate and who seemed to have little respect for her. He was now seated opposite her and she realised with a start that he also looked very unhappy. She was reluctant to ask him what was wrong, as she knew from bitter experience that it was often better to leave well alone. She often wondered if he was suffering from some form of depression, but she also knew that if that was the case, he would be the last person to admit it, or seek help medically. She decided she would go to this ball, then confront Seb and tell him she wasn't prepared to live this way, and would be leaving.

As they both sat opposite each other with a huge chasm between them the door was suddenly opened and Sebastian's father burst in. Celia hated the way he often did this. She knew he would have waived Arthurs aside. No courtesy of a knock or announcement or even a phone call. He just presumed it was convenient and that they would be pleased to see him. She thought about her own father and how he would never be so rude or presumptuous. He came up to Celia and pushing his face up close to hers made as if to kiss her. She could see his lips glistening with saliva and succeeded in turning her head to one side at the last minute, thus deflecting his kiss which ended up on the side of her cheek. She caught the look on his face as he smiled into her eyes managing to put his hand on her knee under the table and give it a squeeze.

"So, what's happening here, you two look sour enough to turn the milk."

Celia watched the hatred in her husband's eyes as he stared at the old man who was responsible for so much of his misery, and despite herself, felt sorry for him.

"I've come to talk about this Ball thing tomorrow evening; I hope you've got something deliciously sexy to wear Celia."

He spoke to her as he went to the drinks cabinet and began pouring whiskey into a cut glass tumbler. She watched the stream of gold liquid splash into the glass and he raised it immediately to his lips and took a long drink then walked back to the dining table. He pulled out a chair and began tearing at a bread roll he took from a basket on the white linen table cloth. As he did so, his arm caught a jug of water and sent it crashing. The water dripped noisily onto the wood floor and ran quickly into the brown rug where it was immediately absorbed into a soggy mess. Without moving or flinching, he raised his voice and shouted for

Arthurs. Celia was immediately on her feet and was walking to the door when it was opened and the butler stood there. He took one look at the situation and retreated to the kitchen to appear a moment later with a mop and bucket which he quickly put to good use. Celia began to say sorry to the old butler that she had come to care for but was interrupted by her father in law's loud voice.

"Well get on with it man, accidents happen you know. Sit down girl and finish your meal."

Celia sank down in her place and pushed the food around on her plate, aimlessly. All traces of appetite having disappeared.

" So how are you getting to this event tomorrow evening, shall I arrange for my chauffer to pick you up so you can have a drink?"

"I won't be drinking, so no need, I can drive."

Sebastian didn't sound convincing even to himself, and the way he was feeling now he felt as though he could drink for England. Just watching his father down the whiskey made him long for the release from the pain that whiskey always gave him. His thoughts went back to the piece of paper he had held in his hand yesterday. He would die rather than let his father find out that he was infertile as well as everything else he had let him down on.

"Nonsense Sebastian, you don't want to spend the whole evening not drinking, there's no fun in that. You don't mind do you Celia? I'm sure it'll be boring as hell so we'll need a stiff drink to get through the evening. I won't take no for an answer, we'll be here at 7.45pm. Make sure you're ready, you know how I hate to be kept waiting."

As he spoke he was on his feet and with a raised hand walked out through the door and was gone. She noticed with relief that he made no attempt to kiss her this time. Perhaps he had at last taken the hint. It was very quiet. For a long moment no one spoke, and then they both began speaking at the same time.

"Sorry, what were you going to say?"

Celia said. Sebastian replied

"I think I'll go for a walk, I need to clear my head before bed, see you later."

Celia was so surprised she said nothing. Sebastian wasn't one for walks He usually went everywhere in his Porche. Something was up with him, and whatever it was he was obviously very unhappy about it.

****

Mark and Will were both exhausted. There had been a lot to organise, but they were more or less done an on schedule and they now stood together at the bar in the officer's mess.

"It's been a long day, I needed this, cheers!"

Will was raising a pint of lager to his lips and looking over the top of his glass smiled at his friend and fellow officer.

"Yes, me too, I'm shagged out, but I think we've got everything done, let's put it this way, if the old man doesn't like it, he can piss off. If we're not ready now we never will be. He's so uptight about this bloody ball, he wants to make a good impression, he knows a lot of people in this area resent the army's presence and this is a P.R. exercise and good opportunity to set the record straight."

Mark had told Will about the conversation with the Colonel about his lack of partner and Will now brought it up again.

"So what have you done about asking someone to partner you?"

Noting the reaction from Mark he went on, "what the hell Mark, you have done something about it, haven't you?"

He noticed his friend had the grace to look sheepish, "I don't know who to ask, there's really only Julie and I seem to be in her bad books at the moment, I think I've upset her in some way."

He studied Will's face to see his reaction.

"I'll be honest with you Mark; I've heard that she's telling people that you're shagging a mystery woman. How much truth is there in that?"

He noticed a faint colour spread up into Mark's face and thought to himself, there must be some truth in the rumours flying around the camp, although he had never seen Mark with anyone and he never seemed to go anywhere so how was it possible. Mark said,

"There's no truth in it; it's just something she got into her head as I told her I wasn't interested in a relationship with her. She even accused me of being Gay at one stage, fuck me; can you imagine anything less likely?"

"'Now that really is stupid, Mark. You know what they say about a woman scorned. Why don't you try one more time to convince her? It would solve your problem with tomorrow night that is of course if she's not already promised to someone else, she's a very popular girl, is our Julie."

As they were speaking there was a burst of laughter from the door and Julie and Caitlin walked in together. Will put up his hand and called them over.

"Hi you two, come and have a drink, what would you like, I'm in the chair.''

They came and stood next to the two men. Julie was the first to speak.

"So how are the arrangements going for tomorrow night, is everything ready?"

Her eyes were on Mark the whole time she was talking, a fact not missed by Will. Seizing the opportunity he said

"So Julie, who are you going with?"

Julie had been hoping against hope that Mark was going to ask her to partner him. She had been approached by two other officers but had turned them both down. She told herself she was mad, and that Mark had made it clear that he wasn't interested in her, but she still went on hoping. She now realised the way things were going she was in with a chance. She ought to turn him down but she also knew she wouldn't if he asked.

"Well, that would be telling, wouldn't it, I'm spoiled for choice."

Will saw the look on Mark's face and decided to step in and help.

"I think Mark has got something he wants to say to you, come on Caitlin, let's sit here I've bought you a drink."

They moved away to a nearby table and Mark found himself face to face with Julie. He took a large gulp of his lager as his throat suddenly felt very dry and saw Julie looking up expectantly at him. He could see she wasn't going to make this easy for him.

"So Julie, are you going to the ball?"

"Well Mark I really don't know, I guess it depends on who's asking me."

"Well I am of course."

"Well there's no of course about it Mark; I seem to remember you telling me you only want us to be friends, am I right?"

"Well friends can go to a ball together can't they? I'd really like you to come with me, please say you will."

He realised he was nervous. He had no idea what he'd do if she turned him down. Whatever the outcome, he was dreading tomorrow evening. The thought of being close to Celia and seeing her with her husband was enough to make him miss the event completely. Why oh why had the Colonel been so insistent about him being on the top table. He tried to think of a way out and realised there wasn't one. He was well and truly trapped! He realised Julie was talking.

"Well I guess I'll say yes then, being friends is better than nothing, but don't expect me not try and make you change your mind."

Chapter 33

The morning of the Ball dawned bright and clear. Celia woke and blinked her eyes thinking about the day ahead. She realised Seb was not in bed next to her. The bedside clock told her it was 7.45am and she had no idea where he was. He hadn't said anything last night about going anywhere early, but come to think of it he hadn't said much about anything, he had been frighteningly quiet, most unlike his usual self. She was sure something was on his mind, but also knew she hadn't changed hers about leaving. Putting her feet to the floor she stood up and stretched lazily. Her reflection was looking back at her in the full length mirror in the built in wardrobe, and she saw the inner conflict etched on her face. She wished she had not agreed to go to this ball tonight and suddenly had the idea to pack a case and just go. Just as quickly she realised she would be letting a lot of people down and really had no choice but to stay with the plan of telling Seb tomorrow that she was going to leave him. She felt such a mixture of emotions and on impulse reached out for the telephone and punched in her brother's number. She listened to the ringing of the phone until it clicked into voice mail, and she left a short message. Her mind went back to the last time she stayed with him and Enzo and she wished suddenly that she was waking up in their spare room. Her mind was instantly filled with the image of Mark, and the last time they had been together. She could smell the clean fresh maleness of him and taste his lips and tongue as they had kissed in his Hotel room. Her body began to respond and she put her hands up to her breasts and slowly began to circle her now erect nipples. She was aware of the sensation between her legs and almost cried out Mark's name. Her legs were moving apart as she sank down onto the bed and began moving her hands upwards toward the inside of her soft pale thighs. She heard a low moan escape from her lips that were parted to reveal the tip of her small pink tongue when suddenly the creaking of the old floorboard on the landing alerted her to the fact that someone was outside the door.

Seb had arrived back from his walk. The beauty of the lake at the rear of the castle was lost on him, as he walked, head down inside his head and his thoughts. He went over and over in his mind, the meeting with professor Januszewski and what he had told him about never being able to father a child. Perhaps he had been mistaken. Was it worth another try? Should he seek advice elsewhere? Common sense told him, he'd be wasting his time, but the thoughts of never being able to produce a son and heir and the added humiliation of facing his father was just too much to bear. He came through the main hallway, shading his eyes at the sudden darkness after the glare of bright sunlight. The frustration he felt seemed to fill his head until he thought it would explode! He took the stairs at a run, which summed up the way he felt, full of anger and frustration, and he strode quickly across the landing towards the room he shared with Celia, noticing as he did so, the creaking of the old floorboards on the landing.

Celia saw out of the corner of her eye, the bedroom door slowly opening, but before she had a chance to react, Seb walked into the bedroom and stood looking down at her. Celia made a move as if to get to her feet, but Seb was too quick for her. He pushed her back onto the bed and placed his hands onto her pale thighs as he lowered himself onto her. She opened her mouth to protest but his own mouth covered hers bruising her lips and forcing them apart. His breath was coming in short heavy bursts and as she began to struggle, it was suddenly all over as quickly as it had begun. She lie there for a moment looking up at him and realised that his erection had disappeared. The expression on his face was not the usual arrogant mocking Seb. She saw a mixture of humiliation and sadness, as without a word he adjusted his clothing and turning, walked out of the room. For a moment Celia continued to lie where he had left her, then she suddenly got to her feet and walked slowly into the shower. She thought how incredible it was that no one had uttered a single word in the brief struggle that had just taken place. As the scalding water gradually washed away her feeling of horror she wondered again just what was wrong with him. Something had changed over the last few days, but what? The evening ahead now filled her with even more apprehension. Whenever she thought back to the events of that fateful day, she wondered how different her life would have been if she had done what she really wanted to and left that morning, and not gone to the ball.

Walking through the house and out into the garden, Sebastian was full of pent up anger. He knew he had behaved badly to Celia, *again* and he hated himself. That probably made two of them he thought. He knew she must despise him and who could blame her. He had seen the look of fear on her face and that combined with the feeling of helplessness and failure that was eating away at him led to his inability to maintain an erection. When he had walked in on her and seen her exposed in all her sexual beauty, he had been unable to control himself. What a miserable failure, I can't even get that right. The result of his sperm test was still burning in his head. He had hidden the paper inside his wallet. He had been initially surprised that she obviously wanted sex, but not apparently with him. Who could blame her, he was muttering to himself as he strode round the garden for the second time that day. He sat down heavily on the wooden seat near the lake and felt his head pounding. He reached up and fiddled absentmindedly with his left ear and realised his cheeks were wet. All around him, signs of early summer were everywhere The Castle had beautiful gardens, well-tended by a small team of men from the village. The rhododendrons were a mass of pinks and purples and a song thrush perched on the old willow was singing its heart out. The long green leaves of the old tree dipped languorously into the water, and a mallard and her chicks sailed quickly by, ripples of water fanning out behind them. On any other occasion he would appreciate the beauty, but today, all was lost on him.

"I've also got this bloody ball to go to tonight."

The evening ahead was going to be a real pain and he wished fervently that he could be miles away, anywhere rather than have to sit and participate in polite conversation with a load of pretentious army types with whom he had absolutely nothing in common. Added to that was the thought of seeing his beautiful wife being eyed up by some handsome officers. He knew she would look absolutely stunning, she always did, and that dress she had purchased in London was amazing, and was guaranteed to have men tripping over themselves to dance with her. Dancing was another thing he could add to his long list of failures

"What the fuck am I doing here, now I can't even get it up to shag my own wife."

He said out loud, but the only answer was the sweet song of the thrush trilling away oblivious to his pain and self-loathing.

****

Mark was getting dressed in the small room that he had slept in since arriving in Salisbury. He paced between the bed and the small vanity unit in bare feet vigorously brushing his teeth. He spat into the sink and rinsed his mouth with warm water. Pulling open a drawer he took out a pair of socks and sitting on the edge of the narrow bed, pulled them onto his feet. He was dreading the evening ahead. He'd rather have been on duty than have to spend the evening at the ball, and the prospect of being so close to Celia and not be able to do anything about it, combined with the fact that he was going to be stuck with Julie, filled him with dread. He hated the Colonel for interfering. Minutes later, buttoning himself into his dress uniform, he bent his knees and examined himself in the small mirror on the wall of his room. The face looking back at him seemed outwardly calm and belied the feelings, and turmoil swirling around inside his head. With a raised hand to smooth his short ash blonde hair, he turned and walked out of the room, pulling the door behind him with a heavy heart.

As Celia stood under the blissfully hot needles of water, the telephone rang in the bedroom. Struggling to dry the worst of the moisture dripping off her hair and body she reached the phone just as it stopped ringing.

"Damn"

She said out loud

"Why does that always happen."

She quickly dialled 1471 and recognised her brother's number. Taking only a moment to wrap the towel more securely around her body she pushed the number 3 to be connected.

"Hi Allie, it's me."

She said as her brother's soft voice came down the line.

"Celie, lovely to hear your voice, you called earlier, how are things?"

She was tempted to pour everything out to the understanding ear of her brother. She held back as she imagined his persuasive voice telling her to leave now if that was what she really wanted. She had made a commitment to herself to see tonight out and she wasn't about to go back on it. With this thought in the forefront of her mind she answered her brother.

"I'm fine"

She said thinking it didn't sound convincing even to her.

"We're going to the army Ball this evening, remember, the dress I chose with Enzo's help?"

"How could I forget, you're going to look absolutely amazing. Will Mark be there?"

He heard the deep sigh that escaped from his sister's lips and pictured her as he had seen her with Mark in Covent Garden. It had been so obvious to him and Enzo how much they felt for each other.

"Look Celie, tell me to mind my own business but are you sure you're doing the right thing, remember Nan's letter?"

She blinked hard to stop the tears that were threatening to spill onto her pale cheeks, and taking a deep breath said,

"Allie, don't worry about me, everything is under control, you'll see, it will all work out for the best."

"I'm not convinced, just remember we're both here if you need us, anytime, and I mean anytime"

She felt reassured by her brother's kind and caring voice and assuring him she would be in touch, she clicked off the phone.

It was some hours later and she was leaning forward peering into the magnifying mirror she always used to apply her makeup. The eyes looking back at her were accentuated by the silvery grey eye shadow and dark mascara that she had applied with a steady hand that belied the inner turmoil she was feeling. Her cheeks had been highlighted with the faintest blush of colour and she had to admit that she looked a lot better than she felt. She shook her hair that was loose and brushed her pale shoulders. She always preferred to wear it loose loving the sensuous feel on bare skin. All that remained was to step into the dress that was hanging in the walk in wardrobe in front of her. She had already fastened in white gold and diamond earrings Seb had bought for her on their honeymoon in Barbados. They hung long and low, almost to her chin and reflected the slim column of the silver shimmer of silk that was her dress. Suddenly she was back in the Caribbean and the perfect honeymoon they had had there. She heard again the pulsing beat of reggae and felt the heat of the sun as they strolled hand in hand into the warm sea that sparkled like the diamonds in her ears. She recalled the passion they had shared on the King sized bed with the faint whirr of the overhead fan and the gently sound of waves hitting the shore. They had been so happy and so much in love. She brought her thoughts back to the present, and wondered, was as that only three short years ago, when had it all gone so badly wrong?

The final touch was the pale silver leather shoes that she and Gilly had purchased in Salisbury. Standing now in front of the full length mirror, she knew she had never looked more beautiful, or felt more unhappy. Sebastian was already downstairs, waiting for her. He had been very distant and off hand with her ever since their earlier encounter and she was glad to be alone but couldn't help feeling that all was not as it should be with her husband.

Something was definitely bothering him, but she had no idea what.

As Celia walked down the wide staircase that was a focal point of the traditional old hall, she saw Sebastian waiting. The look on his face was hard to read. Making an effort, she smiled but he noticed it did not reach her eyes. Walking forward he reached out his hand to his wife and took her own cold one in his. He thought he felt her flinch, but could have imagined it.

"You look absolutely amazing my dear, you'll be the belle of the ball."

During the short drive to the army camp where the ball was to take place, the atmosphere in the limousine was tense. Sebastian's father was his usual vociferous self which served only to highlight the quiet and tense mood of Sebastian and Celia. All three were seated in the back of the luxurious vehicle and Celia was acutely aware of her father in law's leg pressed along the length of her own. It was difficult to move away as they were all in such close proximity so instead she slipped her hand down to the side of her own leg and pulled it as close to her body as possible. Sebastian who was seated on her other side seemed to be totally in a world of his own and not aware of her discomfort. She was relieved when after a short drive they were soon pulling in to the camp where a stream of cars were driving slowly through the gates and stopping to show the invitation and have their names checked off against a list being held by the guard on duty. When they were through they were directed to the entrance of a large hall where they alighted, and Celia watched as the chauffer drove away, wishing she was anywhere but where she was. Sebastian took her arm and together they walked in through the entrance. Standing in the entrance hall, Celia struggled with all the feelings whirling around inside her head. Her heart was beating fast from a mixture of dread at what lay ahead, and excitement at the prospect of seeing Mark again.

As they were ushered into the spacious and imposing hall they were met by the colonel and his wife who were greeting everyone. Nearby a waiter held a tray of crystal champagne flutes and Colonel Winston took two and handed them to Celia and Sebastian with a smile. Celia noticed the look on Seb's face and thought for a minute he was going to refuse, but he took the proffered glass and murmured his thanks whilst looking directly into Celia's eyes as if to say, well what else can I do? The Colonel was talking to them and Celia realised to her utter dismay that Mark was walking towards them.

"May I introduce Captain Mark Riordan, he's going to look after you and show you to your table, I believe you two have met"

As he spoke he was smiling at Celia and Sebastian and as Mark approached he said, turning his head in Mark's direction,

"Captain Riordan, I'm trusting you to look after our guests of honour."

Celia's mouth had gone dry despite the champagne. As she looked into Marks blue eyes she felt all the feelings of longing that she had been trying desperately to deny, rush to the surface as the tell-tale flush spread up into her face. She realised Mark was extending his hand and she reached out to take it feeling the warmth of his firm fingers against her own slim hand that she was desperately trying to stop from shaking.

Before she had time to say anything she heard Sebastian's loud voice,

"I believe you were a guest speaker at one of my wife's Women's group thingies, good of you to have given up your time to talk to a group of women."

He had stepped forward and grasped Mark's hand in his own and began pumping it up and down. Celia noted the look on Mark's face at the typically thoughtless remarks and wondered what he was thinking. Mark was filled with a mixture of jealousy and rage that Celia was married to this ignorant pig of a man. All the feelings that he felt for Celia over the last weeks came to the fore and gave him such a longing for her that he was sure everyone would be able to see just how he felt. Sebastian was walking towards the doorway that led to the main ballroom leaving Celia standing looking at his back. Mark stepped forward and took Celia's arm and they walked after the retreating figure.

As they went through the door one of the young soldiers who were acting as waiters caught Mark's eye and led Sebastian to the table at the top of the room. Mark and Celia followed in silence Mark desperately wanting to tell her how he felt and Celia feeling all the pent up longing for the warmth and tenderness that she felt for Mark surfacing once more. She thought that everyone there must be able to tell from looking at her what she was thinking, and she was afraid to speak as she was sure her voice would give her away. She was acutely aware of Mark's arm against her own and his body radiating heat into her own body so close to him. As they approached the top table Celia noticed the men all standing and was relieved to see the familiar faces of Gilly and Ralph amongst the group. There were five couples in all, the Colonel and his wife, Mark and his partner and one other couple that Celia did not recognise. To her relief she noted that Sebastian's father was not amongst the group. As they were all seated she began to look at her surroundings and noticed how beautifully the room had been decorated. There were fresh flowers everywhere and silver and white ribbons intertwined with white roses and lizianthus, set off by the dazzling white table cloths and sparkling crystal glasses. The whole effect was stunning and ethereal and the air was heavy with the scent of the roses. At one end of the room, on a raised dais was the band that was all wearing dress uniform and was playing softly. She recognised a Glen Miller medley, and taking a deep breath tried to relax. Gilly was speaking to her. She leaned forward as Sebastian was seated between them, to catch her friend's words.

"You look amazing Cee; I don't think I've ever seen you look so beautiful".

She wanted to add or sad but realised that Seb and other people were listening. She extended her right hand and squeezed her friend's arm in a gesture that spoke volumes.

"You don't look so bad yourself"

She smiled at her friend, although it felt as though her face was stiff and in danger of cracking. Sitting back she lifted her champagne flute to her lips and tried to relax. Sebastian was seated on her right and Gilly was next to him. Around the small circular table the other couples were grouped and Mark was directly opposite her with the colonel on her immediate left and his wife Veronica on his other side. She realised that the Colonel was speaking to her and asking her about the Woman's group he had heard about from Mark. Colonel Winston always prided himself on researching people he was going to be meeting and was therefore able to talk knowledgably about subjects that were important to them. He directed his next remarks across the table to include Mark whose eyes had not been off Celia since she had sat at the table. Celia was watching her husband and thinking to herself, please don't let him say something embarrassing and show us both up. She was about to answer the remark's directed at her when her worst nightmares were realised as she heard Sebastian's voice booming out. She was aware that everyone on the table had stopped talking and felt the colour spread up into her face as her husband's remarks echoed loudly around the now silent table.

"Just a load of Women with too much time on their hands, so good of you to give up your valuable time to speak to them Captain, probably bored to tears by the whole thing, you should have given him a medal old boy."

This last remark was directed at the Colonel, who flinched at the over familiarity. Everyone seemed to notice except Sebastian who was about to continue when he was interrupted by Mark who said quietly but firmly,

"On the contrary Lord Stratford, I found the group intelligent and eager to listen and learn, and your wife made me extremely welcome and at ease, and was charming."

As he spoke his eyes did not leave Celia's face and he noticed her face soften slightly as his words helped to ease her obvious embarrassment at her husband's crass remarks. There was a deathly silence and then everyone on the table seemed to talk at once and Sebastian was silent.

CHAPTER 34

The evening progressed slowly. It seemed to Celia that everything was in slow motion. She wished with all her heart that it was all over and she realised it would have been better not to have come. Sebastian was drinking heavily and getting louder and more and more embarrassing as time went on. Celia, sitting immediately opposite Mark and his partner, she certainly didn't seem to be Mark's type. She was wearing a scarlet halter neck dress that was cut very low revealing ample breasts. She seemed also to be the only one who was matching Seb in his consumption of alcohol. Mark was uncomfortable if Celia was any judge. The meal was almost over and the young waiters were now pouring coffee and offering liqueurs. The Colonel asked for a brandy and Sebastian said

"Whisky for me and make it a large one, would you."

Julie said

"Could I please have a Baileys with whisky and ice?"

Celia noticed Mark's reaction.

"Are you sure that's what you'd like, wouldn't you rather have a coffee?"

He'd spoken very quietly, almost under his breath.

"Don't be a spoilsport Markie, I only want a little Baileys with whisky, I'm not even a teensy weenie bit drunk. I'm off to the ladies, to powder my nose."

Celia noticed Mark's face as they both watched Julie walk a little unsteadily in the direction of the cloakrooms.

The band was playing a slow waltz and one or two couples were moving around the dance floor, one of the band was standing at the microphone singing softly and Celia recognised the beautiful old tune,

"I only have eyes for you".

As she sat there wishing she was in Mark's arms Sebastian got up and walked away from the table towards the cloakrooms. The Colonel, who was sitting next to Celia turned his head in Mark's direction and said,

"I'm sure Captain Riordan would love to dance with you, my dear."

Celia started to protest but he waived his arm and said,

"Now don't spoil it for me you two."

He had extended his hand and was lifting Celia gently to her feet, and she had no option but to move into Mark's arms as they gently waltzed into the middle of the ballroom.

She realised Mark was singing softly in her ear,

"Are the stars out tonight, I don't know if it's cloudy or bright, I only have eyes for you."

Celia's heart was hammering in her breast and she waited for Mark to speak. She was having difficulty concentrating, remembering the last time she had been in his arms. It seemed like a lifetime ago when they had stood together in the Hotel room in London, but it was only a few short weeks. So much had happened. Mark was also remembering the last time he had held her in his arms, and what might have been. He recognised her perfume and felt his body stir as her hair brushed gently against his chin.

"I always knew you were beautiful, but tonight you take my breath away, I don't want to live the rest of my life without you Celia, Please tell me you still feel the same."

She was acutely aware of his arms around her and the stirring in her own body matched his. Her excitement was heightened by the hardness she felt in his body as they pressed closer together.

"Oh. Mark, I've missed you so much, I don't ever want this to end. I wish we could just stay here like this for the rest of our lives."

Before he had time to answer they both realised the music had stopped and couples were walking back to their tables. Taking her by the elbow he began to lead her back in the direction of their table. They both noticed that Julie and Sebastian had returned. Celia noticed the look in Seb's eyes and recognised that he was really drunk with dread in her heart. Please don't let him show me up here in front of all these people, she thought to herself.

Sebastian realised that the room was spinning. He put out his hand and leaned on the table in front of him. He had noticed the tall good looking army captain dancing with his wife and couldn't help think how good they looked together. Well, he could dance with her, but it was him, Sebastian she would be going home with.

"Look, don't touch."

He realised he must have spoken out loud, as the Colonel's wife said,

"Sorry, what did you say?"

"Nothing"

He mumbled, "just thinking out loud."

The time seemed to drag on with both Celia and Mark watching each other across the table, and hoping no one was noticing. Celia danced with the Colonel and noticed Mark out of the corner of her eye dancing with the Colonel's wife. Celia watched Mark and thought how fantastic he looked in his dress uniform, which showed off his tall slim figure and highlighted his ash blonde hair and tanned complexion. It was the first time she had actually seen him and Seb together and it only accentuated to her, how Seb had let himself go. She knew he hated dancing and out of the corner of her eye saw Julie get to her feet and attempt to get him to dance with her. Sebastian was shaking his head as the Colonel steered her sedately past their table, but the next thing she saw was Julie and Seb swaying somewhat as the music changed to an upbeat old stones number. The Colonel said,

"Please excuse me my dear, I'm getting too old for this, do you mind if we sit this one out"?

Sitting at the table, she was in conversation with Gilly when the band stopped playing and both Mark and the Colonel's wife and Seb and Julie all returned to the table at the same time. There were two bottles of Champagne in the middle of the table each in an ice bucket. Sebastian was reaching out for one, but as his hand clasped the heavy glass bottle, a waiter appeared at his elbow and began to move around the table filling glasses. Both Celia and Mark declined and she watched with dismay as her husband's glass was filled yet again. Leaning near to him she whispered in his ear,

"Don't you think you've had enough?"

To her absolute dismay he replied in a loud voice,

"No I don't think I've had enough, don't fuss woman"

Celia felt her colour rise and noticed the looks of embarrassment and sympathy on people's faces. Mark shot Sebastian a look that was pure hatred and wanted so badly to take hold of Celia's hand and just leave with her. He imagined them walking out and walking and walking until they were miles and miles away. Oh to be alone, just the two of them. Surely she wasn't happy with this ignorant man? Why would she choose Sebastian over him? He was afraid to think what could be. When he had danced with her he knew he hadn't imagined the way her body had responded to his. He had to know what she was thinking and where he stood. He watched her now as Ralph took her arm and led her onto the dance floor. He looked at his watch and realised that it was still only 11.30 pm and that he had to get through another one and a half hours of this. He was just thinking of asking Gilly to dance when Julie said in a very loud voice

"Come on Mark, you've been ignoring me all night."

As she spoke she reached out and dragged him toward the dance floor. Standing close together she pressed her body against his and reaching up, attempted to pull his head down. He pulled away and said

"Please Julie, don't do that, this is not the time or the place."

She looked disappointed

"Oh Markie, don't be such a spoilsport."

"And please don't call me that, you know I hate it."

It seemed to Mark that the dance would never end. One tune seemed to run into another and he desperately wanted to get away. After what seemed to be an age the music slowed and he led Julie back to the table. He had noticed out of the corner of his eye, Celia walking in the direction of the cloakroom with Gilly and excusing himself he walked in the direction they had gone. He hovered near the door to the ladies, trying his best not to look conspicuous until he saw Celia and Gilly emerge. He walked up to them and turning to Gilly said

"Do you mind if I have a word with Celia for a moment?"

Without waiting for an answer he guided Celia away through a small door marked "no entry" and taking her by the hand led her through a dark passageway until they came to a small room which he quickly opened and leading her inside pushed her gently up against the door. They were in a small room which was lit only with the silvery glow of a full moon which shone through a small window. He put his hands on her shoulders and bent his head and kissed her with all the passion he had been trying to deny for all these past weeks. His mouth was on hers and her mouth opened as his tongue moved against hers. She tasted as sweet as violets in rain and he felt himself get hard as her body matched his. Neither of them spoke for a minute as their tongues continued to explore and taste. Lifting his head he placed his hands gently around her shoulders and she leaned into him with her head resting on his chest. He could feel the beating of her heart through the silk of her dress and said,

"I've been wanting to do that all night, my darling"

"Mark, I feel the same but I must get back. If Sebastian misses me we'll both be in real trouble. You've seen the sort of mood he's in; it's too much of a risk he'll kill us if he finds out we've been here together."

He realised again how scared she was and his thoughts went back to the day on Salisbury plain when he he'd first kissed her, and her fear then. Are you afraid of him, I'll kill him if he ever hurts you."

Mark we must get back, send me a text message tomorrow and we'll arrange to meet, I promise."

She reached up and kissed him gently on the mouth and he felt the warm softness of her lips on his own before reluctantly taking her by the hand retraced their steps back down the narrow corridor where they had come. "This door will take you back to the main hall; I'll wait here so as not to arouse suspicion."

With that he opened the door and closed it quickly as Celia disappeared. He stood alone in the dark and waited for the beating of his heart to subside. He felt light headed with happiness as he recalled the way she had returned his kiss and the thoughts of them being able to meet up tomorrow. It seemed an age away, but he could be patient now he knew that she felt the same way as he did. Nothing else mattered anymore if Celia loved him.

CHAPTER 35

Sebastian was having a miserable time. He wished he hadn't come. He knew he had had far too much to drink but the thought of the piece of paper he had been given with the results of his sperm test was driving him insane. In his mind he saw it tucked away inside his wallet. He wished there was someone he could confide in. Just as quickly as the thought came to his head he realised how useless that thought was. There was no on he could confide in and that made him feel ten times worse. Imagine reaching the age of forty one and having no friends close enough to be able to talk to and ask their advice. He could just imagine his father's reaction if he were ever to find out.

The band was playing loudly, too loudly. Sebastian had a headache. He looked at his watch and realised there was still one and a half hours to go before he could get out of here. Gilly was sitting opposite him and he could tell from the look in her eyes just what contempt she held for him. He knew Celia must have confided in her and he had the grace to feel ashamed as a picture of his rough treatment of his wife came into his head. They're all the same these women, they all like it rough, just pretending they don't like it, it's just pretence. I bet she's a real goer; you've only got to look at her to see that. Gilly's voice startled him and he realised Celia and Ralph were approaching the table. The way Celia looked tonight almost took his breath away. The dress might have cost a small fortune but it was worth every penny. Pity he had to share her tonight with all these other men. He could see the way they were all looking at her, particularly that good looking army Captain. Well he could look, but that was all. She was his wife and he couldn't wait to get her alone. His mouth watered as he imagined what he would do to her later. As good as she looked in that dress, he knew she would look even better without it. He got to his feet and held out his arms to her as she approached the table, but she stepped swiftly to the side and asked Gilly to go to the ladies cloakroom with her. Why women always had to go in pairs was beyond him. Watching the slim form of Celia and the way the silk clung to her beautifully rounded bottom only served to increase his desire. He sat down and reached for the champagne. Ralph's voice cut in to his thoughts.

"Don't you think you've had enough"?

Yet another person who seems to have little or no regard for me, Sebastian thought to himself, what have I ever done to make so many people hate and belittle me? Don't they realise who I am.

"Excuse me, and what the fuck has it got to do with you, Ralphie old boy?"

He made as if to sit back down in his seat but misjudged and fell to the floor with a thud. He had reached out for the table in trying to save himself and having only caught the white cloth brought an ice bucket and half full champagne bottle crashing down to the floor. He sat in the mess of ice and spilled champagne just as Celia arrived back at the table. Her cheeks were pink and flushed and he put it down to the spectacle he was making of himself, little realising the true reason for her excited appearance. Before she had time to say anything there was a loud bellow as his Father appeared in front of him and said in a voice that could be heard above the sound of the band.

"What in hell's name is going on here, get up boy and don't disgrace the family name."

Colonel Winston appeared as if by magic and held out a hand to Sebastian and pulled him to his feet.

"Are you alright Sir?"

As he spoke he was beckoning to a young waiter who began quietly and unobtrusively to clear up the mess.

In the middle of all this mayhem Mark appeared back at the table and taking one look at the tableau before him thought that for once he was glad to see Celia's husband making a spectacle as it had managed to deflect any interest in away from himself and Celia. The Honourable George took charge and in his usual bossy way took his son by the arm and led him away from the table. Celia hesitated, not knowing for a moment quite what to do, when Gilly and Ralph came to her rescue and said

"Don't worry Cee; we'll give you a lift home."

"Yes"

Ralph agreed,

"That's a good idea, and we won't take no for an answer."

Celia sank into the seat and watched as Julie dragged a protesting Mark onto the dance floor. Her loud voice could be heard above the noise of the band as she almost shouted.

"Well I don't think much of the cabaret; if that's what the aristocracy behaves thank God I'm only an army officer."

Mark had to steal himself to move away from the table, and Celia. He felt as though his legs were weighed down with lead and every step was an effort. Looking over his shoulder he saw her sitting staring into space with such a sad look on her face that it took all his self-control not to rush back to her side. Julie was wriggling and gyrating to the loud music and he wanted to walk away and take Celia by the hand and simply leave. Common sense told him to stay. He remembered the way she had kissed him and promised to meet up with him the following day so making up his mind to make an effort to pretend he was enjoying himself, he moved slowly to the music, with Julie mouthing against the noise of the band.

"Come on Markie, loosen up, you're not on the parade ground now."

The rest of the evening dragged for Celia, despite the efforts of Gilly, Ralph and the Colonel and his wife, Sebastian's father had thankfully not appeared again, and she supposed he had gone in the car with Sebastian. It was later that his driver sent a message that the car was waiting for her outside to take her home, but she politely declined as she wanted to go with Ralph and Gilly. She did not have another opportunity to talk to Mark as he seemed to be either dancing with Julie or in conversation with the Colonel and another army couple that were on their table. Every time she saw in her mind the picture of Sebastian sitting on the floor with all the debris of ice and champagne around him she felt herself blush and was sure everyone was feeling sorry for her. She hated people feeling sorry for her. She suddenly remembered being at school and in her early teens. She had been very small and slight for her age and still looked a child compared to some of the other girls who had blossomed, with woman's bodies and outward maturity. That, combined with the fact that her Mother was a teacher, gave them plenty to be nasty about. The constant ribbing and generally feeling put down reminded her of how she felt now. It seemed to Celia that all eyes were on her and she wished she was miles away from here and the man she no longer had any feelings of love for. Whoever said that love and hate were very close together was certainly right. With this thought in her head, she knew without any doubt at all that her decision to leave him was the right decision. All that remained now was to tell him and get it all over and done with as soon as possible. The thought of being free to walk away and really be with Mark, lifted her heart and gave her renewed hope.

The early evening summer sunshine had become a torrential downpour and as Celia Ralph and Gilly emerged from the front door of the hall they were met by sheets of driving rain that blew into the doorway. They all, as one moved back into the warmth and shelter of the hall and Ralph said

"you two girls stay here, I'll bring the car round."
As they waited Celia was wondering what she was going to face when she got back home and wished that she could go with Gilly and Ralph. As if on cue Gilly said

"you don't have to go home you know Cee, you know you're welcome to come with us"

For a moment Celia hesitated, tempted to just disappear with her friends and never have to see Seb again, but she knew she would have to face him sooner or later so shaking her head, she said

"Thanks Gilly but I'd better go home, don't worry about me. I'll be fine."

She spoke with a conviction she did not feel.

As they drove along the dark country lanes the atmosphere inside the car was tense. Pulling in through the gates of the home she shared with Seb she knew that she was at the end of the road in more ways than one. She would definitely tell him tomorrow, her mind was made up.
The lights were on in the hall but the rest of the house seemed to be in darkness. As she and Ralph approached

the door, she was relieved when it was opened and the familiar figure of Arthurs was silhouetted against the light. She was so happy to see him and as he held out a hand to help her over the step she grasped and held it for a long moment and felt comforted by his steady familiarity.

"Good evening, I've got some hot chocolate ready, I thought you might need it on such a night."

"Thank you Richard, that sounds lovely."

Turning to Ralph who had walked with her to the door, she asked if he and Gilly would like to come in but he declined as they wanted to get back to the children. The use of the old servant's first name was not lost on either of the two men. Turning she watched as Ralph got back into the waiting car and stood waving to her two friends until the car disappeared through the gates and into the darkness beyond. She followed the old butler into the kitchen, waiving aside his protest that she should go into the drawing room, she perched on the edge of one of the stools in the kitchen kicked off her shoes and putting her head down onto her arms resting on the breakfast bar sobbed quietly. She felt the old man's hand warm and firm on her shoulder and raised a tear stained face to the gentle caring look in his eyes.

"Richard, what would I ever do without you?"

"There, there, I'm sure you'd cope very well, now drink your hot chocolate and wipe your eyes."

As he spoke he handed a tissue and she smiled weakly into his kind face.

"I've decided to leave him Richard, I've really tried these past few weeks to make it work, but I just can't stay any longer. I'm sorry to unburden myself to you, but you've always been such a good friend to me, and I know I can trust you."

"Well my dear, I'm sure you will do the right thing, and I'm happy for you, but I will miss you very much."

Celia was left with a strange mixture of feelings now that she had made up her mind and all this fear and unhappiness would soon be a thing of the past. She realised the old man had become more a friend than a servant, and sipping the hot drink she felt it beginning to thaw her out. She shivered suddenly and said,

"I'll be getting to bed, it's been a long night."

Picking her shoes up in one hand and her evening bag in the other she walked slowly up the winding stair case. She could here Seb's snoring from where she was. Pushing open the door of one of the guest rooms she undressed slowly and began to get ready for bed. She seemed to toss and turn for hours as sleep eluded her although she longed for the release that it would bring. She squinted in the dark and saw the illuminated letters of the clock telling her it was 3.25.am she always seemed to be awake at this time. She must ask her Mum what time she was born, perhaps it was significant. At the thought of her mum she wished fervently that she was in her old familiar bed back home in Bristol.

She must have eventually dropped off because she became aware that there was someone in the room which she realised was now light with a watery greyness creeping in through the chink in the curtains. Struggling to sit up she saw the figure of Seb outlined in the doorway. The whole sight of him made her want to be physically sick. He was naked except for a pyjama jacket that was buttoned up wrongly and only added to the total look of comic horror. His hair stuck up in thin wisps and his eyes were bleary and bloodshot. He was naked from the waist down and his pale legs, covered in dark hair were apart showing his erection.

She sat up quickly and stood by the bed uncertain of what to do next. He started to move toward her with his arms outstretched ready to push her back onto the bed. He caught his foot on the edge of the rug next to the bed and stumbled, landing on the corner of the duvet which slid silently to the floor as though in slow motion. Celia dodged around the heap that was her husband and made for the door, but he was too quick for her and reaching out caught her by her slim ankle. As she resisted he pulled harder and she fell, crashing into the pale wood bedside table. Her hand came down heavily onto the pillow that had fallen to the bedroom floor and a puff of small, downy feathers flew into the air, and sailed gracefully down, and down, until one landed softly on her dark head. Absentmindedly brushing it away, she sat on the floor for a minute feeling the room spinning around her.

Raising a hand to her face she was shocked to feel it sticky with blood. She sat for a moment looking at the bright red drops which were falling onto the pale beech floor, and forming a small sticky puddle. The sight of her seemed to sober Seb up and his erection disappeared rapidly. He put a hand out to help Celia, but pushing it away, vigorously. She pulled herself to a standing position and unsteadily looked into the full length mirror on the front of the wardrobe. There was a gash above her left eye but it had stopped bleeding. Her eye was already beginning to darken into a bluish bruise. He stood unsteadily behind her and as she looked into his face in the mirror, she said in a voice that was surprisingly steady compared to the turmoil she was experiencing inside,

"Don't dare touch me."

Before he had time to answer she walked out of the room and into the adjoining bathroom, locking the door behind her. She sat and waited for her heart to stop racing before taking a clean cloth she held it under the cold tap and pressed it to her throbbing face. Back in the bedroom Sebastian was sitting on the bed, a forlorn figure filled with self-loathing.

Chapter 36

Awakening in his bed in camp, Mark's first thought was for Celia. He felt at peace for the first time since they had been together in London. The feeling of having her in his arms again, her slim body moulding into is, her warm lips opening to let in his exploring tongue made his body respond as he lie in the narrow bed. He turned over and stretched languourously wishing she was lying next to him. Her reaction had given him such hope and he couldn't wait to see her again later today. She had asked him to text her and reaching out his hand he took his mobile phone from his bedside locker and thought of what to send .Resisting all urges to pour out his real feelings he manoeuvred his fingers until the message read

I will be at the old oak on Salisbury plain at 2.30 pm. can't wait to see you, M.

Pressing the send button on his phone he swung his legs over the side of his narrow bed and headed for the shower humming to himself the words of the lovely old song he had been singing in Celia's ear less than twelve hours ago. *"I only have eyes for you."*

As she pulled out a pair of jeans from her wardrobe Celia's mobile phone rang. She picked it up quickly hoping to see Mark's name on the screen but seeing instead Gilly's name she spoke softly into the phone.

"Hi Gilly, yes I'm fine",

she cut across her friend's anxious voice about her welfare. As she spoke she saw her reflection in the dressing table mirror and realised to her dismay that her eye had swollen and was now half closed. There was an area of blue/green bruise which extended down to the top of her cheek bone. The bleeding had stopped and the actual cut was quite small so she was sure it wasn't going to need any medical attention. The main problem was going to be other people's reaction to it. How was she going to explain it? She also needed to speak to Seb and tell him of her decision to leave him. Just thinking about him made her feel physically sick as she replayed last night's scene in her mind. The image conjured up was one of total revulsion. She couldn't ever imagine feeling love and gentleness towards the man her husband had become.

"Well, fuck him, I've had enough"

She realised she'd spoken out loud and Gilly was speaking,

"What was that Cee,"

She made an effort to bring her thoughts back to Gilly's voice in her ear realising she hadn't been listening.

"Sorry, Gilly I was miles away, what did you say?"

"Cee, are you sure you're ok you sound distracted. Was everything ok last night?"

Gilly was reluctant to ask outright on the telephone if Sebastian had been up to his usual tricks, but she didn't like the sound of her friend's voice and was worried. She decided to let it drop until they saw each other.

As Celia came down the wide staircase she was met by Arthurs who was immediately appalled at the state of her face. After the closeness they had shared last evening, she felt she could talk to him, but still held back, reluctant to expose her true feelings for Sebastian. His look spoke volumes, but before he had a chance to say anything, she said

"Don't look so worried, it looks worse than it is."

The look on the old butler's face was not lost on her and she knew that this was the first of many such reactions. Sitting over breakfast she had difficulty swallowing even the smallest crumb as she went over and over in her mind what to do next. Sebastian did not appear at the table and she didn't know whether to be glad or sorry. She decided to talk to him and tell him of her intentions. Now that she had made up her mind and the ghastly events of the previous night were still fresh she wanted to get it over with. She would tell him and then meet up with Mark as arranged via his text and let him know her plans, after all she knew now that Mark was going to be her future.

Wanting to get it over with, she went upstairs to look for her husband to confront him. As she walked into the bedroom they shared, she realised with disappointment that the bed was empty, and he was not in the bathroom either, although the shower was still wet and there was a damp towel on the floor. The bed was unmade and there was still the indentation of his body. All the signs pointed to the fact that he wasn't long gone. Unsure of what to do next she realised he must have gone out and that the confrontation she was anxious to have would have to wait. She decided to drive over to see Gilly and wait until later to speak to Seb. She was filled with such a mixture of emotions. Part of her was dreading telling him, and witnessing his reactions and another part of her wanted to get it all out in the open and get on with the rest of her life.

The short drive to Parsonage farm gave Celia time to think. She knew it was useless to pretend with her friend about what had really happened to her face. The weather seemed to match her mood. There was a strong breeze that blew the leaves and dirt from the side of the road into a whirlwind. The sky was overcast and heavy with unshed rain, and the trees were bending and rustling. A large black bird swooped low in front of her car, and she slammed on her breaks cursing as it soared untouched into a nearby tree. Sitting in her car, the middle of the lane, she took a deep ragged breath in an effort to stop her heart racing before driving shakily, the short distance to Parsonage Farm. Stepping from her car, she shivered although it wasn't cold. Celia felt that at that moment in time she would never be really warm again. Gilly's kitchen was a welcome haven of peace and security. She had been met with the usual enthusiastic welcome that turned to shock and anger when her friend had seen the bruise on her face and her half closed eye. Despite her reassurances that she was not in any pain, Gilly insisted on handing her a pack of frozen peas to hold against the bruise.

"Gilly, I feel ridiculous sitting here with this held to my face."

"Never mind that, it'll help the bruise to come out, and I think you should go and let the doctor take a look at it and get it checked out"

"Really, I'm fine, please don't fuss."

The fact that she was snapping at Gilly told her friend more than any words.

The two women sat at the kitchen table sipping the scalding coffee. The silence broken only by the swinging of the pendulum on the old grandfather clock, and the drumming of rain on the window pane

Celia got up and walked distractedly toward the kitchen sink, her hands placed on the white porcelain, as she leaned in towards the window.

"This weather certainly suits my mood."

She spoke without turning, almost as though she'd forgotten Gilly was there.

Gilly was on her feet, and moving towards the sink, in her hand was the delft blue cup and saucer, now drained of coffee, and she made as if to rinse it under the tap. Celia reached out and took them absentmindedly, from her friend.

"Oh Gilly, I need something to occupy my mind, otherwise I feel like I'm going mad! However am I going to tell him? I'm both relieved and scared at how he's going to react. I just want to get it all out in the open and take my freedom."

The two women both jumped, as a sudden flash of electric blue lightening lit up the room, shortly followed by a tremendous roll of thunder. Celia spoke,

"That's all we need, a storm, well perhaps it'll clear the air, in more ways than one."

As the two women stood huddled together, still standing at the kitchen sink, staring out at the sodden garden, there was a sound from the other side of the room, as the door opened slowly, and the tear stained face of a small girl appeared in the gloom of the hall beyond.

Gilly was across the room in an instant as she remembered guiltily that she had momentarily forgotten Alice was at home and had been playing in her room. She picked up her small daughter and hugged her closer to her neck, her hand smoothing the mop of strawberry blond curls.

"There, there sweetheart, it's only a storm, don't be frightened."

As she spoke, she had moved toward Celia and said softly to the child

"Go to Aunty Celia for a minute and mummy will make you a drink of hot chocolate, which will make you feel better."

She watched as her friend sat at the kitchen table with Alice on her lap, and thought how comfortable they both looked. She realised also, not for the first time, how good her friend was with her small daughter and how she would make a great mother.

Later, looking down at the child on her lap, Celia realised she had fallen asleep. Her thumb was in her mouth and her golden curls were sticking to her damp forehead. Moving slowly and quietly, she place the sleeping form of the child on the comfortable old sofa that was in the corner of the kitchen, and both women stood watching as the child flung out an arm in her sleep.

Gilly had made more coffee, and the two women sat in companionable silence until Celia spoke.

"I've decided to leave him Gilly, I can't stay with a man that I don't love, and I can't live with the fear of what he might do next."

Gilly was quiet, waiting to hear if Mark's name was going to be mentioned. She had seen them dancing together last night and knew that Celia should no longer be able to deny her true feelings. She got up and walked over to the window where heavy rain was hitting the glass. She watched the torrent of water blocking out the view and dripping noisily onto the ledge. Turning to face her friend, she looked at the pale face with its dark bruise and said a silent prayer for the stability and happiness she and Ralph shared.

"So are you really certain you're doing the right thing, it'll be too late once you start the ball rolling, and after all, it'll be a lot to give up."

Celia had risen from her seat and was walking distractedly around the kitchen. She stopped and leaned back with her bottom resting against the large refractory table.

"I know you're right, Gilly, don't think I haven't wondered if I should be leaving, but I've really come to the end of the road, it's not as though I haven't tried these last few months, but the man I fell in love with seems to have disappeared underneath an overweight, bully I don't like, or want to be with or certainly spend the rest of my life with."

Gilly took a step nearer and put her hand onto the other woman's shoulder and gave it a squeeze.

"Don't Gilly, if you're too nice to me, you'll start me off again."

She went on

"I wanted to tell him this morning but I missed him he must have gone out early without telling anyone. There is something on his mind, I'm sure but I really don't know what, and to be perfectly honest I really don't think I care anymore. Does that shock you?"

"My dear girl, I'm surprised it's taken you this long to come to your senses, Ralph and I wanted you to leave him weeks ago after that horrible evening when he came here and was drunk and abusive in front of our children."

As she spoke, her eyes moved to the sofa, and the small form of her sleeping daughter, and still the subject of Mark hung before them in the air.

Gilly poured more coffee into their empty cups as she waited for Celia to go on,

"I've been denying my true feelings for Mark for weeks now, ever since my Nan died. Seeing him last night and also comparing him to Seb, and the way he humiliated himself last night has made me realise just how much I love Mark. I'm so sick and tired of people feeling sorry for me. I'm going to meet Mark this afternoon, in fact"

She said looking at her watch,

"in two and a half hours from now, and I can't wait. But I need to speak to Seb and end it once and for all, and I'm not sure how he's going to react. Don't worry; I've no intention of bringing Mark's name into this,"

She added hastily catching the look on Gilly's face.

"Talking of time, I really must be going; I want to get this over and done with."

Standing on the doorstep the two women hugged and Gilly said,

"you know where we are if you need us, anytime, and I mean anytime. Take care Cee and please let me know how you get on, I'll be thinking about you."

Back in the comfort of her warm kitchen, Gilly sighed deeply as she bent over the sleeping form of her small daughter and realised again how lucky she was.

Celia felt strangely light headed and peaceful as she pulled her car into the gates of her home. The fact that she would not be doing this for much longer lifted her spirits. Seb's car was parked in the drive way and she noticed it was at a funny angle, as though it had been parked in a hurry. The gravel on one side was deeply ridged and the car was also heavily spattered with mud. On entering the hall she looked across to the open doorway of the study and saw him sitting at his desk. There was a glass of light honey coloured liquid in his hand and as she watched he lifted it to his lips and swallowed. Walking towards him she picked up on the unmistakable smell of whisky.

He had got to his feet when he heard her in the hall and stretched out his arms as if to welcome her. She realised incredulously that he still thought that she would respond to his advances. The very thought repulsed her. Surely he couldn't be drunk already?"

"Oh Cee, look at your poor face, I'm sorry, you know I didn't mean to hurt you."

As he spoke he took a step nearer and to her.

Backing away she started to open her mouth when he interrupted her.

"I know you don't want me anymore but please Cee don't look at me like that, you know how much I love you."

"But *I* don't love *you* anymore Seb. I've really tried to make things work between us, but you haven't even tried to meet me half way and now it's too late. I'm leaving you. I want a divorce, end of story."

To her horror he started to cry, great loud sobs wracking his body and his face contorted with sorrow. The sight repulsed her even more and she sat down in one of the arm chairs in his study and waited for the sobs to subside. For a minute or two she thought he wasn't going to stop but suddenly with a shuddering breath he raised his wet face to hers and spoke.

"I know I don't deserve you but I really do love you, Please don't leave me, If you do, I don't want to go on living so I might as well drive my car into a brick wall."

"You know you don't mean that. I've tried Seb, I really have, but you've changed so much and you're still drinking heavily. You are like two different people, the sober one and the drunken one. Sadly the one I prefer and fell in love with is not much in evidence anymore, and I don't love the person you've become, so I've made my decision and I'm definitely leaving."

"Please Cee, don't leave me, I promise I'll change, I'll stop drinking, anything, but don't leave me."

She began to leave the room and he fell back into his chair. The sound of his sobs filled her ears as she closed the door quietly behind her.

CHAPTER 37

Celia's heart was hammering in her chest. She felt breathless as if she'd been running up hill. She glanced at her watch and seeing that it was only 1.30 pm and too early to meet Mark she decided to get out of the house anyway, she couldn't stay here. The sound of her husband's pleading whining voice and the sight of him only served to make her realise she was doing the right thing. She ran quickly upstairs to grab a jacket and was on her way down to the front door to collect her hand bag when the door of the study was flung open and Sebastian made a lunge towards her.

"Don't leave me Cee, I'll do anything, but don't leave me."

Shaking him off she made for the door with him hanging onto her arm. She made a grab for her hand bag that she had left on the Hall table, but he beat her to it and held it away in triumph. She remembered with relief that she had left the keys in her car parked on the drive and she ran out, slamming the front door behind her. With a screech of tyres she swung the BMW out through the open gates and drove too quickly into the leafy lane. The rain that had been threatening all day started to fall at last. One or two large drops fell onto her windscreen and they soon became a torrent of water that streamed down the glass making it difficult to see where she was going. She drove for a few minutes and then pulled over to the side of the road in the hope that it would ease off.

Looking at his watch, Mark realised it was only ten minutes since the last time he had looked. There was still another hour before he had arranged to meet Celia. He wished he had said earlier, but it was too late now. He thought about calling her on her mobile but dismissed it almost at the same time realising how risky that would be. He decided he would go early and just wait. You never know, she might also just be early. He drove toward Salisbury plain as the rain started to fall.

Sebastian was slumped in the leather chair in his study. He lifted the glass of whiskey to his lips and took a long swallow. He knew he was drunk, he also knew he wasn't drunk enough to stop the pain of Celia's words. The worse thing was he knew that what she said was right. A lot of it was his fault, but then she didn't know the real reason for his drinking. He felt the humiliation of the result of his sperm test again, and heard the professor's words as though it was yesterday. He had still told no one, and the pain was becoming more and more difficult to bear. He saw again in his mind his beautiful wife and her obvious revulsion for him when he had tried to get her to touch him today. His thoughts were suddenly interrupted by the sound of a mobile phone. He realised it was coming from her handbag that was now on the desk in front of him .Reaching into the depths of the tan leather bag he pulled out Celia's mobile phone . He saw from the name on the screen that it was her Brother's number and pressing the button he spoke. Alasdair was surprised to hear his brother in law's voice, and noted with disgust that he sounded drunk, again!

"Sebastian, hi, is Celia there?"

"No, she's not she's left me, she's gone!"

Alasdair was shocked at the words and the sound of Sebastian's voice.

"What do you mean, she's gone. Where has she gone, when will she be back?"

"How the fuck should I know, I'm only her husband, she's not likely to tell me."

"Why hasn't she taken her mobile?"

Alasdair was worried. Something was very wrong here. He realised he wasn't going to get much sense out of Sebastian and saying goodbye he quickly ended the call. Staring at the now quiet phone, Sebastian thought about the man at the other end with disgust. He had no time for Gay men. He realised he still had Celia's phone in his hand and began pressing buttons and looking through her address book. There were lots of names he recognised as being her friend's from that Women's group. He carried on pressing buttons and a name suddenly jumped out at him.

"Mark"

was displayed on the screen. Mark who? He wanted to know. He couldn't think of anyone called Mark except that good looking young Army Captain at the ball last night He pictured him and Celia dancing together and felt the heat of his jealousy rise up like bile in his throat. He carried on pressing buttons and began to scroll through text messages. He stopped when he came to the one Celia had received this morning from Mark as realisation began to dawn. So she was leaving him because of his drinking, was she? Funny how she had forgotten to mention Captain Mark in the equation. He looked at his watch and realised it was now ten past two and unless he was very much mistaken, she had gone to meet up with her *boyfriend*. Well, they were in for a little surprise, oh yes a beautiful little surprise! Rising unsteadily to his feet he walked out to his car taking the key's from his pocket as he ducked into the Porche out of the pouring rain.

Celia had driven on through the rain that seemed to be easing a little, but it still drummed on the roof and washed back and fore with the windscreen wipers swishing noisily. She wanted to see Mark so badly and the events of the last couple of hours went round and round in her head. She knew she was going to be early. The large old oak was shrouded in wetness making it seem almost like a mirage. Celia had half expected Mark's Land Rover to be already here waiting for her but was disappointed to see that there was no sign of any vehicle in the misty greenness She pulled her car to the small lay-by near the old tree and turning off the ignition, leaned forward to examine her reflection in the mirror in the sun visor. She was not pleased with the face looking back at her. She looked pale and drawn and there was a dark smudge under her remaining good eye. The bruise on the left one had darkened to almost navy blue. She wished she had her bag, She felt almost naked without it. She couldn't even touch up her face with makeup and try to disguise the injury, and she felt the gap of her mobile phone from its usual bracket in the car. With a sigh she settled back in the seat to wait for Mark, wondering what Sebastian was doing. With any luck he'd be sleeping it off, probably fallen asleep in his chair in the study. She realised that he soon wouldn't be her problem and she couldn't wait to start a new life that didn't involve being terrified.

When Enzo arrived back at the flat in Kensington, Alasdair was sitting on the cream sofa with a very thoughtful look on his face. His brow was wrinkled.

"Hey, what's up? You look as if you've got the weight of the whole world on your shoulders. It can't be that bad surely."

As he spoke he sat down beside him and put his arm around his shoulders. They smiled into each other's eyes with the good feeling that comes from sharing and knowing your partner really well.

"It's Celie, I'm worried about her."

He quickly summarised the earlier events when he had spoken to Sebastian.

"It's just not like her to go anywhere without her mobile phone, and I really didn't like the sound of Sebastian. He'd obviously been drinking and it was only 1.30pm."

"Why don't you phone your mum and dad see if they know anything."

"I thought of that but I don't want to worry them, besides I think they would have let me know if anything had happened. Sebastian definitely said she'd left him."

"Well if you ask me, that's the best news we've heard in ages, if it's true."

Enzo had wandered into the adjoining kitchen and was directing his voice over his right shoulder as he was pouring boiling water into a china teapot. He placed it with two matching cups onto a tray which he carried back into the sitting room and placed it on the low glass table next to a large vase of white roses. As he did so a few petals fell onto the table top and he scooped them up and placed them on the tray.

"Do you think I ought to drive down and make sure she's ok?"

"No, let's wait until later this evening and try her again, I'm sure she'll be in touch if she needs us."

The two men sat in companionable silence sipping their tea, both lost in their own thoughts and both picturing Celia and hoping she was not in any trouble. After a few minutes, Alasdair suddenly sprung up from the sofa and put his cup and saucer down with a loud clatter.

"I know who I can call, Gilly. If anyone knows what's happening, it'll be Gilly I'm sure I've got her number somewhere"

He left the room and returned almost immediately.

"Got it! I knew I had it somewhere."

Enzo listened as to the one side of the telephone conversation that Alasdair was having with Gilly, and tried to imagine what was being said. He didn't have to wait long.

Alasdair's face was grave as he briefly recounted what Gilly had told him. They were both appalled and concerned to hear that Celia had a black eye. Gilly had spoken with hesitation and explained to Alasdair that she felt as though she was betraying her fiend's confidence. With some gentle probing from Celia's brother, she had also told him of their conversation earlier and of Celia's intention to tell both Sebastian and Mark of her plans for her future.

"Do you know where she was planning to meet Mark?"

He asked, but drew a blank as Gilly admitted she did not know.

"If I had to make a guess, I'd say it'd be somewhere out on Salisbury Plain, but exactly where...?"

Her voice tailed off.

"Thanks for that Gilly, try not to worry, I know that's easier said than done."

They both agreed to let the other one know if they heard anything from Celia and hung up the phone. Enzo stepped near and gave his partner an affectionate hug.

"Do you want to drive to Wiltshire? I can hold the fort here."

"Thanks, I really feel that I should go, I'd hate to think of her being in trouble and not have anyone to turn to. That bastard has hurt her and I want to make him pay."

"I share your sentiment but don't go looking for trouble; it's Celia who needs your attention. Come on let's get a bag packed, the sooner you're on your way the sooner we can get to the bottom of all this."

****

Driving toward the old oak where he had arranged to meet Celia, Mark struggled to see through the rain washing down his windscreen. The wipers hissed loudly back and forward but seemed to have little impact on the torrent of water that was causing so much difficulty with visibility. He slowed the land rover whilst saying a silent thank you for four wheel drive. He ran his tongue over his lips that were dry with tension and leaned forward in the driving seat to concentrate on the road ahead.

Celia was watching for his arrival. Peering through the rain she let out a loud sigh of relief as his land rover came into view. She realised suddenly that she had been holding her breath and felt the lifting of tension from her body. As he drew alongside she watched eagerly as the door was flung open and Mark rushed from his vehicle and quickly got into the passenger side of her car. There was a loud noise as the wind and rain entered with him and she felt the wetness of his face as it mingled with her own tears of relief. His wet hair was cold against her neck as they clung together. They both started to speak at the same time and pulling apart she saw the look of horror on Mark's face as he saw the dark bruise of her eye against the pale of her face.

"What the hell has he done to you, I'll kill him."

"'No Mark, it's not as bad as it looks, I'm fine now that you're here, just give me a hug."

They clung together and sat quietly with only the sound of their hearts merging with the drumming of the rain on the roof of Celia's BMW. Raising her face to his Mark put his lips to the bruise under her eye and spoke softly.

"My poor darling, I'm so happy to see you, I can't believe you're really here, I've dreamed of this moment for so long, have you really left him?"

As he spoke he was looking into Celia's eyes that seemed to be dark green with unshed tears. He saw her love for him reflected in them and breathed a deep sigh of contentment as she said.

"Yes Mark, I've told him it's over and that I don't love him anymore, I'm all yours if you'll have me."

Oh my darling, you know the answer to that and he pulled her to him and their lips met and explored each other with the sure knowledge that at last they could really be together.

"So where do we go from here?"

Mark spoke as they sat arms around each other with the world outside a watery backdrop.

"Well I'm not really sure, I have nothing with me, not even my hand bag and I don't think I can go back at the moment, he was very angry and had been drinking so I need to wait until the time is right. I haven't even got my mobile phone. I thought I might call my brother and see if I can go and stay with him until the dust settles, or perhaps Gilly and Ralph as then I can at least get some of my things."

As they sat together they both suddenly became aware of the sound of a car above the deluge of rain. Celia saw to her horror a silver Porche appearing dimly through the greyness that was the wet landscape. They both sat as though turned to stone as the car approached. It was swerving erratically and was heading for Celia's side. As it got nearer it seemed to skid on the wet path and with a screech of brakes it slewed wildly and with a sickening crash hit the driver's side of Celia's BMW.

Chapter 38

Driving down the M4 Alistair was finding the going very difficult. He was worried about his sister and the weather was giving him a hard time. Driving conditions were very bad and he strained to see out of the windscreen that was awash with a torrent of water that poured from the heavens. Gilly had told him about the conversation she had had with Celia earlier today and when he had pressed her for more information about her meeting with Mark scheduled for 2.30pm. He looked at his watch. It was 3.00pm and he had been driving for an hour having left almost immediately after speaking to Sebastian and he recalled now with fear in his heart the slurred speech and drunken tones of his brother in law. He had given Gilly his mobile number and asked her to let him know of any developments. What to do when he arrived in Wiltshire hat was the question whirling round and around in his head. Mark and Celia would be long gone from their meeting place and he didn't relish the thoughts of confronting a drunken Sebastian. He knew his brother in law had no great love for him and "his sort" as he put it, at the best of times. Would Celia return home? He wished not for the first time since leaving London that she had her mobile phone with her. It was so difficult without knowing where or how she was. His thoughts were interrupted by the ringing of his own phone and his mind leaped eagerly to his sister but he saw with disappointment that it was not her name on the screen. Instead it was Gilly's voice and he knew instinctively that it was bad news.

Sitting in the ambulance, wrapped in a blanket Mark let the tears run unashamedly down his cheeks. His thoughts went back over the events of the last hour and he saw again the car coming at them out of the rain and heard the sickening crash of metal on metal, the noise had seemed to go on forever, and then suddenly it was eerily quiet. Celia was slumped lifelessly across the front seat and there was a trickle of blood above her right temple her right arm hanging by her side at a strange angle. Nearby Sebastian's Porche was upside down with all the windows smashed and of Sebastian there was no sign .The rain had eventually stopped, he realised as he got out of the car and reaching his Land Rover, quickly reached in for his mobile phone and dialled 999 and then Gilly's number thinking stupidly how pleased he was that it was still in his phone from the talk he had given at the Ladies group. That had all seemed like another lifetime. Whilst waiting for the police and ambulance to arrive he had cradled Celia's lifeless body and sobbed like a baby.

The waiting room at the hospital was bleak and cheerless and Gilly sat lost in her own thoughts. She saw Celia in her mind, dressed in the beautiful silver silk dress she had worn to the ball and tried to picture her now. She started as Alistair's voice interrupted her thoughts. He reached out as she stood up to greet her and they hugged.

"I'm so pleased to see you,"

She spoke into his shoulder as the tears flowed unchecked down her face.

"They won't tell me anything as I'm not a relative. I only know what poor Mark has told me and he's in a terrible state."

"Where is he?"

As he spoke a Doctor appeared and Alistair introduced himself and was immediately taken through a door to the ward. He said over his shoulder to Gilly,

"I'll be back soon, try not to worry."

Left alone again Gilly wished Ralph was with her but he had stayed with the children. Her thoughts went back to the phone call she had received from Mark earlier. He had been almost incoherent with grief and Gilly had had to tell him twice to slow down as she couldn't understand. Finally she had managed to ascertain that there had been an accident and that somehow Sebastian was involved. Mark was obviously in shock and she had told him she would come at once and meet him at the hospital. That was when she had phoned and broken the news to Alistair. Time dragged on and Gilly thought she would die if someone didn't come and tell her something soon. The only person she had spoken to was Mark and he had only had time for a few words before she was asked to leave him so that he could be checked over. He seemed to have escaped with hardly a scratch but they said they had to make sure he had no internal injuries. There was the noise of a door opening and she looked up expecting to see Alistair but instead saw the shocked faces of Celia's parents. They had just arrived from Bristol and she realised how old they both looked. The pain etched on their faces white with fear and apprehension. She watched as the receptionist spoke into the telephone on her desk and the white coated figure of a doctor appeared with Alistair close on her heels. Gilly got to her feet and said

"Please tell me what's happening, I can't bear all this waiting, how is Celia?"

Alistair was holding the arm of his Mother and spoke in a voice that shook with emotion.

"She's going to be alright. She has a broken arm and concussion and of course, is suffering from shock, but there's nothing really serious."

Gilly sank into the chair and with her head in her hands sobbed uncontrollably. She realised Deirdre was by her side and they clung together supporting each other. Hugh Manning spoke,

"Thank God, I don't know what we'd have done if anything had happened to her."

Alistair was speaking again.

"Im afraid the news of Sebastian is not so good. He was trapped under his car and both his legs are crushed. They fear he will never walk again."

Celia was dreaming. She was in a field and all around there were poppies. The scarlet petals were bright against the pale gold of the corn. The sky above was blue above her and there were white clouds that seemed to be rushing along across a bright sun. She realised the sun was very bright. Too bright and it was making her head hurt. The red of the poppies seemed suddenly to turn to the red of blood and she felt herself panic. She tried to put her hand up to shade the light and realised she couldn't move it. The fear of not being able to move woke her up as she realised the bright light was not the sun, but a torch someone was shining into her eyes. She tried to speak but her throat was dry and no words came out. She heard a familiar voice and realised suddenly her Dad was talking to her.

"Shush sweetheart, don't try to sit up, you're o.k. There's been an accident but you're going to be fine."

She suddenly had a flash of recall and remembered seeing Seb's car coming at them out of the rain. She heard again the tearing sound of metal on metal as his car had smashed into hers. What had she been doing? Where was she going? Her mind struggled to piece together all the pictures that seemed to be floating disjointedly around inside her head. Suddenly she remembered she had been with Mark and she said urgently

"Dad is Mark ok. Please tell me the truth."

She realised she was holding her breath and said again,

"Mark, is he……."

Her Dad's voice cut in and she felt the warmth of his hand reassuringly over hers.

"He's fine love, hardly a scratch."

"You are telling me the truth Dad, please don't lie to me, I couldn't bear it."

Reassuring her Hugh Manning thought how telling it was that his daughter's first thought was for Mark. She hadn't even mentioned her husband.

"You just rest now, my girl and try not to worry about anything. I'll try and get Mark in to see you when they've finished with him, and don't worry"

He said as the frown on her face gave away her feelings of anxiety,

"I promise you he really is fine, but he has one or two minor abrasions that need attention; I'll go and check him out myself if it'll make you feel better. I know your Mum and Gilly are also both waiting, d'you feel up to seeing them?"

She nodded her head and lie back on her pillows watching the tall figure of her dad disappear through the door of the side ward. She watched him through the glass partition and tried to manoeuvre her position in the bed to catch her own reflection, which proved to be far too difficult a task. Putting her hand up she moved her fingers slowly over her face trying to imagine what she looked like. The cheek beneath her left eye was very tender and she suddenly remembered the fall in her bedroom when Seb had lunged at her. She shivered involuntarily and thought how long ago all that seemed. Was it really only two days ago? She felt a pang of guilt as she realised she hadn't once mentioned him or asked her Dad about how he was. The thought suddenly came to her that he might be dead. No, surely she would feel it, anyway her Dad would have said, wouldn't he? How would she feel if he was dead? She would be free to be with Mark. The though made her feel guilty and the tears started to fall, just as Gilly and her Mum came into view.

Hugh Manning was standing in a small curtained cubicle next to Mark, who was lying on a bed with a young nurse dressing a cut above his right eye. They had already introduced themselves and Hugh sensed the other man's discomfort.

"I'm so sorry we had to meet like this, has Celia mentioned me?"

Telling a white lie, Hugh said that she had, but in fact it had been his son who had brought him up to date. Alistair had been sketchy about the situation between Celia and this Army Captain and Hugh had had the feeling that there was a lot his son wasn't telling him. This however was not the time or place. It would keep until later.

The nurse spoke to Mark in a soft Irish accent and told him he was free to go.

"Dr Manning, I really need to see Celia, will you arrange it?"

Hugh had spoken to one of the Doctors who it turned out had been an old friend of his from medical school and soon they left the cubicle. Walking together to the lift that was to take them to the ward where Celia was, Mark asked in a hesitant voice what the news on Sebastian was.

"It's not good, we are still running a few tests but I'm afraid he'll never walk again."

Try as he might, Mark could not summon up any pity for the man who had dominated Celia's life and caused her so much pain and suffering. He was dismayed to realise that all he felt was worried that this news might affect Celia's decision for them to finally be together. His thoughts went back to the moments before Sebastian's car had come looming out of the rain and into them. He remembered the feeling of elation when Celia told him she really was leaving her husband, and now a few short hours later, everything had changed. Thank God she hadn't been badly hurt. Waiting for the ambulance had been a nightmare. He had convinced himself that she was dead, but feeling for a pulse had been relieved to hear the faint beat in her pale neck.

As he walked towards the small side ward, his heart now leaped as he saw her lying in the bed. Her beautiful hair now a dark matted and tangled mess against the white of the pillow. Her face was almost the same colour except for the large dark shadow of bruise that covered her right cheek. Seeing his approach Gilly and Deirdre got to their feet. Leaning forward, Deirdre kissed her daughter on the cheek and said,

"I'll leave you two together, and then I suggest you try and get some rest."

Turning to Mark she said,

"You won't keep her too long will you?"

Left alone at last Mark and Celia clung together and Celia again felt the hot tears course down her cheeks.

"Shush my darling, don't cry, everything's going to be alright now. I'm not hurt and the doctor says you'll be up and about in a couple of days."

"Oh Mark, hold me, I really need a hug. I thought they were lying when they said you were o.k. I'm so happy to see you."

They clung together until Mark felt her body relax and lifting her chin he kissed her gently on her pale lips. After a moment she spoke in a voice that he had too lean low to understand,

"Is there any news of Seb? I was going to ask my Dad, have you heard anything, is he"……..?

The word stuck in her throat and Mark said quietly,

"He's alive, that's all you have to worry about now, and I really think you should try to get some rest."

"I love you Mark", she said her eyes never leaving his face

"I love you too, my darling, now get some rest, I'll be here when you wake up."

Looking at his son the honourable George Stratford felt a stab of guilt. He had never really loved Sebastian as much as he had loved Charles. He knew also that he had never been fair in his treatment of Sebastian. God, he must have done something very bad in his life to have one son killed and now this with his only remaining son. Sebastian was unconscious and there was a drip in his arm. The raised blanket covering his legs formed a cage and he knew that although his son had been given something for the pain, he was still suffering. His face was pale and only a small plaster on his temple gave any indication that he had been in an accident. The doctor had spoken to him and told him about Sebastian's legs

"Are you sure he'll never walk again, isn't it too soon to tell?"

"I'm afraid there's no possibility of a mistake, your son is paralysed from the waist down."

She wanted to say more about the disgust she felt for a man who had so obviously been drinking heavily when he was brought in, but looking at this old man who was his father he thought he looked as if he was suffering enough. Besides, the police were waiting outside to ask Sebastian a few questions when he regained consciousness. Sebastian's father tried to sort out the jumble in is mind. What had been going on? The police had said the accident had happened on Salisbury plain. What the hell were they both doing on Salisbury plain in all that weather and in two separate cars, and where did that army captain fit into all this? He was tired and suddenly felt very old. There was a tap on the door and the figure of Arthurs appeared at the side of the bed. He stood up and spoke to the old man who had been part of his family's life for so long.

"Thank you for coming, will you stay with him whilst I go and get a cup of coffee? I need a break, please call me if there's any change."

The old Butler was amazed to hear the civil and kindly way his employer had spoken to him, it was so out of character he must be in shock. He watched as he walked out of the room and noticed the figure looked old and very tired.

CHAPTER 39

Three weeks later.

Mark and Celia were driving along the country lane. The sun was trying to peep out from an overcast sky and bands of bright sunlight kept appearing and disappearing as they drove through the leafy lanes. They were both quiet. Celia's face, which now only bore a faint discolouration was the only outward signs of the accident. Mark knew that the internal scars to her mind would take a lot longer to heal. Pulling in through the gates of Parsonage farm, Mark put his hand on her knee and gave her an affectionate squeeze. Smiling at him she said,

"Thanks for taking me Mark; you know I have to go and see him don't you, after all he is still my Husband."

"its o.k. my darling, I understand. How long will he be in there for?"

They had been to a private hospital ten miles away that Sebastian's father had arranged. Sebastian had regained consciousness three days after the accident and had taken the news of the damage to his legs badly, as you might expect. He seemed to have forgotten the events leading up to the crash, and Celia had been told by the doctor that he was suffering from retrograde amnesia, and it was likely that he may never remember what happened or even the preceding few hours. That had been a major blow to Celia as she realised that this meant he probably couldn't remember that she had told him she was going to leave him. Besides how could she go now when he was going to be so dependent on her? She had lain awake night after night turning it all over in her mind, and wondering how she was to tell Mark about her decision to stay with her husband. Looking at his profile now, her heart turned over with wanting him. They really were doomed. She had decided to stay with Ralph and Gilly, not wanting to go back home. She refused her Mum and Dad's offer as she wanted to be near Seb. She knew they were worried about her but had reassured them she was fine and Gilly had been fantastic. As Mark pulled up in front of the old farmhouse they sat for a moment before opening the car door.

"So, that's arranged then, tomorrow night, it's a date, yes?"

"Mark, I'm not sure it's right to be out celebrating the way things are with Seb,"

"Come on Celia. Please, for me, after all this is the first birthday that I've known you and I really want to spoil you. I'm taking you somewhere really special. It's all arranged, besides you need to lighten up a bit with everything that's happened. It will do you good."

Part of her thought about what she had to tell him, but another part of her wanted so desperately to just be with Mark that she nodded her head and smiled

"Ok you win, what time will you pick me up''?

They agreed on the arrangements for the following evening and after declining her invitation to come in, he leaned over and kissed her urgently. He felt her respond and once again felt the frustration of their situation. They seemed doomed not to be together and he wanted her so badly, and knew she felt the same.

As Mark drove away he pushed in a cd and listened as the mellow tones of Anita Baker washed over him. She was singing one of his favourites which began with the line "with all my heart I love you baby" and it seemed to intensify his deep longing for Celia. His mind went back over the last few weeks. He couldn't help it, he asked himself again, why oh why did this have to happen. If only Sebastian hadn't got drunk. If only they had gone away together that morning. Stupid to say if only but he couldn't help himself. His thoughts turned to the following evening. He wondered how Celia would react to his plans. He hoped it would all work out and he wasn't expecting too much.

Back at Parsonage farm, Celia and Gilly were sitting in the conservatory at the back of the old farmhouse. The doors were open and the sun was setting on the horizon. The sky was streaked with silver and deep pink and Celia let out a deep sigh as they sipped their cups of coffee companionably.

"Penny for them?"

Gilly said, or is that a stupid question?"

"Oh, Gilly, I don't even know where to begin. So much has happened over the last few weeks, if only we could put the clocks back."

Sensing her friend's melancholia and wishing to lighten her mood, Gilly said, as she leaned forward in her chair,

"So tell me about tomorrow evening, where is Mark taking you?"

"Well, that's a good question, he's being very secretive and won't tell me much at all, except that I'm to get all dressed up and relax and leave everything to him."

"Sounds great to me"

Her friend responded,

"As much as I love Ralph, romance is not one of his strong points. Are you looking forward to it?"

"Yes and no. I have something to tell him which is going to tear him apart, and me for that matter, but it has to be done, I've made up my mind"

The next day, as Celia ended the call to the hospital, she sighed deeply and tried to imagine the rest of her life without Mark. Worse than that was the fact that she was to spend the rest of her life with Seb. She didn't love him but also really didn't see how she could walk away and leave him now. He needed her so much. She knew everyone would probably try to talk her out of it, but he mind was made up. It was going to be so hard telling Mark.

The nurse in the side ward of the private hospital where Sebastian was took a deep breath and told herself to count to ten. She had been nursing for twenty years and knew that patients often took their fears and frustrations out on the nurse who was looking after them, but this man really was impossible. Nothing she ever did for him was right. She tried to imagine what it must be like for him to lose the use of both legs. She shivered involuntarily as she looked down at her own sturdy legs encased in black tights and sensible lace up shoes. How would you come to terms with the future?

Don't be so silly Siobhan my girl, at least he's alive, and from what she'd heard when he'd been brought in, he was lucky. She knew this particular patient had so far not even wanted to discuss his future with the physiotherapist and had earned himself a reputation with all the hospital staff for being rude and difficult.

****

Driving through the leafy country lanes Mark was filled with such a mixture of emotions. The car was filled with the sweet scent of the flowers he had for Celia and he glanced at his reflection in his rear view mirror and wondered for about the thousandth time how the evening was going to be. The face gazing back at him in the mirror looked calm, belying the tumble of emotions he knew to be bubbling underneath. As he swung the car into the driveway of Parsonage farm Ralph and Gilly's two dogs rushed up to the car stood waiting for him to open the door. As he stepped out with one hand ruffling the warm soft fur of Barnaby's neck he realised that Ralph was standing at the open doorway. The two men exchanged smiles as Mark walked toward the farmhouse.

"Hello Mark, you've got your arms full there haven't you?"

The two men smiled at each other as together they walked into the hallway and through to the conservatory where the evening sun bathed everything in pale gold. Gilly was seated in one of the cream woven chairs reading a book. He leaned forward and kissed her lightly on the cheek and looked around for Celia.

"Don't worry, she'll be down in a minute, she's making herself even more beautiful for you, would you like a drink?"

"Thanks, but no thanks; I'd better keep a clear head as I'm driving."

He was about to lower himself into an armchair when Celia appeared in the doorway. Mark thought again how every time he saw her, it took his breath away. He actually felt excited like a schoolboy on his first date. They smiled at each other and he held out his arms which were full of

Sweet peas. The beautiful vibrant colours and the wonderful scent seemed to fill the room.

"Oh, Mark my favourites and such a lot! The really are beautiful, thank you."

As she spoke she had stepped forward and reached up to kiss him lightly on the cheek. He took the opportunity of her closeness to whisper softly in her ear

"Love you"

"I'll just go and put these in water."

Mark watched the slim figure and took in the cloud of jet hair falling in loose curls onto her pale shoulders which were bare. The skirt was a deeper shade of creamy gold and swirled around Celia's pale slim legs.

They were soon in the car and waving to Ralph and Gilly framed in the doorway, drove into the lane and headed away towards Salisbury.

"Where are we going?"

Celia said.

"It's a surprise, wait and see, be patient my darling."

On the drive Celia told him about the phone calls she had had that day from her parents and brother and Enzo who had all wanted to wish her happy birthday. Sebastian's name hung unspoken between them

"I can't believe I'm thirty three Mark, I'm getting old."

"What nonsense, you're in your prime."

He placed his hand over hers as he spoke and squeezed it gently. They drove on in companiable silence for about half an hour and Celia realised she did not recognise where they were going and was relieved they were nowhere that was familiar to her or where she was known. After driving for another ten minutes or so they drove down a narrow road and came to stop outside a small country Inn that was tucked away behind a small wood. The sign told her it was called

"The Hawthorn Bush"

Mark said

"Well, here we are, what d 'you think?"

"It looks lovely Mark, however did you find it?"

"Oh, I have my ways and means, let's park the car, I hope you're hungry."

CHAPTER 40

Bill and Margaret had been running the Inn for twelve years and seen many couples dining in their restaurant. They knew their menu had a reputation in these parts and took pride in the wonderful food served up by Gino, their Italian Chef. This couple seemed to be totally wrapped up in each other and yet there was something Bill couldn't put his finger on. There was sadness about the beautiful young woman that seemed to wrap itself around her like a cloak. He noticed the way they seemed so engrossed in each other and saw young Jenny the waitress walk away as they admitted they hadn't yet looked at the menu. He remembered Margaret telling him about the man making the booking by telephone. He had booked a double room and said that they were to keep it quiet, as it was a surprise. He noticed she was wearing a thin band on her wedding finger that she twisted nervously, and yet they seemed perfectly relaxed with each other, and the booking was made only in his name, not Mr and Mrs.! Well, you never could tell with folk, anywhere it was really none of his business was it. They certainly were a beautiful couple, the two heads so close together, one so dark and the other so fair.

As Mark and Celia discussed the menu, the subject of wine came up. Mark leaned forward and placed his hand gently over Celia's as he said softly,

"I'd like to order Champagne, but there's something I need to ask you first. I've made a booking for a room here for us tonight, but it's your decision my love, I don't want you to feel I'm pressuring you. If you'd rather I took you back to the farmhouse that's o.k. with me."

Looking at his anxious face, Celia realised just how much she loved him. She also knew how much she wanted to spend this night with him, especially as she knew it would probably be the last chance they would have to be together this way.

"I'd love to spend the night here with you Mark, we've waited so long for this and you've been so patient."

Mark raised his hand and beckoned the young waitress over

"We'd like a bottle of champagne please, and we're ready to order."

They both made an attempt to eat, pushing the food around on their plates, but they only had eyes for each other and finally, Mark said,

"please excuse me; I'll go and sort out the key."

"I'll pop to the ladies while you're doing that Mark."

As he watched her walk away, Mark caught his breath and he felt himself begin to getting roused in anticipation of finally being able to show Celia exactly how he felt about her.

The room was lit only by a small table lamp which cast shadows over the pale carpet. The window looked out onto a small wood and the sun was dipping out of reach against a purple sky. Celia felt almost shy, as she stood looking up at Mark. His eyes were dark blue against the shadow of his face and he reached out his hand and slowly traced the outline of her face with his finger. It moved slowly and sensuously down over her chin and travelled down touching the hollow in her throat and down moving out with splayed fingers to circle her breast. Her nipples rose in response to his touch. Celia moaned quietly as she felt her whole body coming alive. She could feel the moisture between her legs and the heat rose up and spread until her whole body felt as though it was on fire. She was wearing a pale silky blouse that was off the shoulder and with his other hand; Mark pushed it down until her pale breasts were exposed. He took a step and covered one of her breasts with his mouth as his hand found the heat and wetness between her legs. As his tongue and fingers continued to caress and slip inside her she gasped as her body spasmed and she let out a long shuddering sigh as she reached a climax. Oh Mark, I wanted you so much."

"Wait, my darling, I've only just begun."

As he spoke he was pushing her skirt down over her slim hips and then quickly stood to remove his own clothes. Celia moved until she was astride him on the bed. She shook her head and the cloud of dark hair brushed her shoulders. Reaching up her hands she put them into the dark shining mass and writhed in ecstasy and pleasure. She leaned forward until her lips met Mark's and her tongue explored the inside of his mouth, finding his and feeling the wet softness. They both moaned as their passion mounted and they both climaxed and fell back totally exhausted and very happy Celia could hardly believe that it had been so good. After all the brutal treatment by Seb, she had thought that she wouldn't be able to respond. The last hour with Mark had made he feel alive and content and also made her realise just what she had been missing. She knew then, it was going to be so difficult to stand by her decision, but she really couldn't see any other way out.

Waking the next morning, Mark put out a hand and feeling the emptiness beside him, sat quickly upright and looked for Celia. She was standing looking out of the window, with her back to him and the sun behind her, he felt as though his life was finally complete. Pushing back the duvet, he walked on silent feet and put his arms around her to encircle and cover her breasts. She leaned back into him and gave herself up to the warmth and pleasure of his firm body. She was immediately aware that he wanted her again and it was an hour before they were ready to think of breakfast.

"I don't know about you my love, but I'm absolutely ravenous, all this exercise has given me an appetite, let's see if we are not too late for room service."

CHAPTER 41

"I don't understand why I can't remember anything before the accident, the last lucid thought I have is the day before, then nothing until I woke up here."

Sebastian was talking to the Doctor who was standing beside his bed in the private Hospital his Father had organised.

"It's quite common in road accidents, I often think it's nature's way of shielding you from the pain."

"Good god, don't you think I'm in enough pain, how am I going to cope with not being able to walk again, I'd rather be dead."

The Doctor looked down at the man in the bed. Try as she might, she couldn't feel any sympathy for him. She knew the police were going to prosecute for drinking and driving and that the tests had proved he had been way over the limit. He could have been killed, and the people in the other car too. If she was any judge, he was a heavy drinker, she recognised all the signs.

"As, I explained, you could say that retrograde amnesia is nature's way."

"Do you think it'll ever come back to me?"

"It's doubtful. What you should be concentrating on is responding to the physiotherapist and cooperating."

As she left his room, she walked quickly to her next patient and was glad to be away from Sebastian. She hated negative people who only ever felt sorry for themselves and didn't even seem to try. Left alone Sebastian wallowed in self-pity and tried to conjure up in his mind what had led up to the accident. He remembered some sort of row with Celia but it was all a blur and try as he might he couldn't even remember what it had been about. How had he come to be on Salisbury plain? Why was he there? There was a movement at the door and Celia walked in. She looked pale and as though she'd been crying. Well she certainly had something to cry about being stuck with me, a cripple. She approached his bed and leaning down put her lips briefly to his. He noticed that she reacted as though his lips were red hot and she'd been burned. He could also see the look of revulsion on her face and he was filled with self-loathing and disgust.

Reaching out his hand he took her cold one in his and stroked the pale skin inside her wrist with his finger. She made a conscious effort not to pull her hand away and forced her face to stay impassive and not reveal her revulsion for the man in the bed.

"The Doctor says I should be able to come home before the end of the month. They are going to fit me up with a wheel chair, Father's organised one from a leading company in London. I'm told it's state of the art. If I have to be stuck in a contraption for the rest of my life, might as well make sure it's the best, eh my darling?"

Celia sat and wondered how soon she could leave without making it too obvious that she'd rather be anywhere than here with Sebastian. He seemed to tire very easily and it was not long before she was able to leave. Leaning over she kissed him lightly on the cheek and walked quickly away from the side ward out into the bright summer's evening. The day had been unbearably hot and there was a distant rumble of thunder. As she walked to her car, the first few drops of rain began to fall as she let the tears flow freely down her cheeks. She was crying soundlessly as she turned the key in the ignition and the car roared into life. She could still see Mark's face when she had left him this morning.

"But, why Celia, you know how much I love you, and don't try and tell me you don't feel the same because I won't believe you. I can't understand why you are prepared to throw away our happiness for the sake of someone you don't love, and who's been so awful to you. Please tell me you'll change your mind, I can't bear to think of the rest of my life without you."

"Please Mark, don't make it even more difficult for me. My mind's made up, I love you and always will but I can't leave him not now the way he is, I could never live with myself ,If you love me, let me go."

She let the tears run unchecked down her cheeks as she drove through the storm to Parsonage farm and her future without Mark.

CHAPTER 42

TWO YEARS LATER April 2003

Sitting in the warm kitchen of their farmhouse, Gilly was watching the news on television. A group of Iraqi's were toppling a statue of Sadam Hussein and there was a lot of cheering and celebration. Gilly tried to imagine what it must be like to live under such a cruel regime, but it was difficult, sitting in the comfort of her home surroundings. Her thoughts went to the phone call they had had from Mark when the war that no one seemed to want, had begun. He was leaving for Iraq. He had kept in touch with Gilly and Ralph ever since the terrible day when Celia had told him she had decided to say with Sebastian. Gilly knew it made him feel closer to her and was happy to keep in touch and let him know how her friend was getting on. She picked up the phone to call Celia. She and Ralph were worried about her. In the two years since the accident, she had lost weight and looked pale and drawn. She was constantly at the beck and call of her husband, a selfish man in a wheel chair. There was a live in nurse, but often Sebastian insisted that it should be his wife who tended to his more intimate needs. Listening now to the flat voice of her friend Gilly couldn't help wondering how different Celia's life would have been if she had left with Mark.

"Have you seen the news today? The war's over."

"Yes, I watched the lunchtime news and was hoping Mark was ok."

Gilly was surprised as Celia rarely mentioned Mark.

"I don't suppose you've heard from him."

She asked Gilly

"No, communication is really difficult, but I have a feeling he's fine."

"I was calling to ask you over for coffee tomorrow, please say you'll come, we haven't seen you all the week."

Celia started to refuse, but Gilly said in a firm voice,

"come on Cee, this time I'm not taking no for an answer, I'm expecting you tomorrow about elevenish."

****

Mark was tired desperately tired. Totally exhausted and weary, inside and out. The heat and dust seemed to permeate his whole body and soul. The sound of gunfire and random explosions filled his ears and his mind, whether waking or sleeping. He thought achingly of the peace and quiet of Wiltshire and he longed for the feel of soft English rain on his face. All his demons had returned as soon as he had arrived in Iraq. The nightmares from Bosnia recurred and rolled into the original nightmare of war once more ensuring that sleep was not even a blessed release from his pain. War was everywhere, inside his head, invading his ears, eyes and even his taste. He wanted to be able to spit it out. It was never that easy. He watched as a solitary bird flew out of a skeletal tree and wondered at the incongruous strength of nature. It was his last conscious thought before the earth and air around him exploded with a deafening roar.

****

At 10.45 am the next morning, Gilly was in her kitchen boiling the kettle to warm the cafetiere for coffee. The wind blew hard against the old farmhouse windows and she could see the trees in the yard bending and swaying in the gale. Her thoughts were interrupted by the ringing of the phone. She reached out her hand and took the handset from the wall. Putting it to her she heard Celia's voice mixed with loud wracking sobs.

May 2003

In a country churchyard Celia raised her face to the soft rain of a Wiltshire shower. She knelt in the spongy wetness of the turf and placed a small posy of spring flowers on the grave in front of her. The dampness sent a chill through her slim body as it clung to her knees and she shivered, as shaking her head, drops of clear spring rain dripped inside her upturned collar. She pushed herself to her feet and began walking briskly toward the gate and the warmth of her waiting car. She felt the sharp taste of salt on her tongue and realised she was crying. She suddenly realised that for the first time in years, she felt free. As free as the solitary bird that swooped down from the green wetness of the overhanging branch of a nearby oak tree.

It was a week later that Celia standing on the tarmac watched the plane high up in the sky, glinting silver in the early summer sun. The drone of the aircraft became a deafening roar in her ears and it fought against the thudding of her heartbeats. The plane touched down and taxied along the runway where it came to a halt about thirty yards in front of her.

Out of the corner of her eye, Celia noticed two blackbirds sitting together on the roof of the airport building, as she walked slowly and calmly toward Mark and raised her eyes to meet his.

THE END

Printed in Great Britain
by Amazon